A DANGEROUS MAN

A DANGEROUS MAN

CHARLIE HUSTON

BALLANTINE BOOKS

New York

A Ballantine Books Trade Paperback Original

Copyright © 2006 by Charles Huston

Published in the United States by Ballantine Books,
an imprint of The Random House Publishing Group,
a division of Random House, Inc., New York.

BALLANTINE and colophon are registered trademarks
of Random House, Inc.

Library of Congress Cataloging-in-Publication Data

Huston, Charlie.
A dangerous man / Charlie Huston.
p.   cm.
ISBN 0-345-48133-X (trade pbk.)
1. Russian American criminals—Fiction.
2. Murder for hire—Fiction. I. Title.

PS3608.U855D36 2006
813'.6—dc22   2005048173

Printed in the United States of America

www.ballantinebooks.com

9 8 7 6 5 4 3 2 1

Book design by Jo Anne Metsch

sweet Virginia
at last

PART ONE

MONDAY, JUNE 20, 2005

PRESEASON

FIND THE GUY in the Laughing Jackalope just like they said I would.

I take a seat at the bar, order a seltzer and ask for a roll of quarters. I let the seltzer sit and start slowly dribbling the quarters into the video poker game built into the surface of the bar. I stare at the cards as they blip across the screen. I play a quarter a hand, flying in the face of the most basic rule of video poker that says you always bet the max. Quarter bets pay a bare fraction of the max bets. Hit a big hand on a quarter bet and you're gonna feel like an asshole.

I hit a straight flush with a quarter once, paid 1,200 to 1. Sure enough, I felt like an asshole. Well that's happened before and it'll happen again.

The machine blips me a pair of jacks along with a nine, a ten, and a king. I pass on the even money the pair promises, throw one of the jacks and go for the inside straight. Deuce. I drop another quarter in the slot.

There's only a handful of people in here. The guy; the bartender; a couple sitting on stools, feeding nickels to one of the slots; an old-timer nodding a bit at the bar; and the evening cocktail waitress straightening the tables and getting things set for the crowd that will come in when the shifts change across the street.

I keep my face in the game, sneaking peeks at the guy, keeping my hand next to my face, hoping no one notices the palm-size patch of white scar tissue around my right eye. I'd just as soon no one remembers that scar if the cops come around later. But really, I only have to worry about that if a body turns up.

I'M ON MY third roll of quarters and little has changed. The couple's shifted from the slot machine to the jukebox, so now "Crazy on You" complements the blips of the poker games and the recorded come-on of the slots. The guy still hasn't moved.

He's been sitting at the far end of the bar, sliding C-notes into his own video poker game and going through them about as fast as I've been going through my quarters. Every fifteen minutes or so he throws back another shot of chilled Jäger and bangs the glass on the bar, indicating the bartender should get his ass over there and give him a refill.

Back in the day, when I had to do that job, when my biggest worry was getting the drunks out the door before the sun came up, I'd never have put up with that shit. Someone banged a glass on my bar or snapped their fingers or something like that and they'd be sitting dry a long fucking time before I remembered they were there. This bartender is different, he's working the day shift at the Laughing Jakalope for Christ sake, glasses banged on the bar are the last fucking thing he's gonna raise a sweat over.

The bartender pulls the frosted green bottle of Jägermeister out of the cooler, fills the guy's shot glass and puts the bottle back. The guy doesn't even look at him, just keeps peering into the game screen, his credits rolling up and down as he scores on two pair here, three of a kind there; searching for a full house or a straight flush or even a royal.

There's a blast of sunshine as someone opens the tinted front door and two drunk couples come stumbling in. They're college kids, the boys in shorts and tank tops, their faces sunburnt except where their eyes have been raccooned white by their sunglasses, the girls in shorts and tube tops, skin tanned cancer brown, harsh bikini lines climbing up out of their stretchy tops and creeping around their necks. All of them are double-fisting plastic cups full of something bright blue and frozen.

The bartender looks down from the TV hanging above the bar. He's been watching one of those behind-the-scenes shows; this one cracking the lid open on a reality show that teamed up stars from older shows that have already been behind-the-scened. He sees the cups the kids are carrying and shakes his head.

—Uh-uh, not in here, can't bring outside booze in here.

One of the guys, his tank says DON'T DRUNK WITH ME, I'M FUCK!, looks at the drinks in his hands and back at the bartender, trying to connect the dots.

—What the fuck, man? We been carrying drinksh in and out of cashinosh all fucking day.

The other guy, his shirt says I'M WITH ASSHOLE and has an arrow pointing up at his own face, hoots.

—Been drinking all fuckin' day! All fuckin' day! Gonna drink all fuckin' night! All fuckin' night!

The bartender nods.

—Sure, just not those drinks in here.

Everyone's watching now; the guy, the old-timer, the slot couple, the cocktail waitress. Asshole takes a couple quick sloppy steps toward the bar.

—The fuck, dude? Gonna drink!

Drunk Fuck grabs the tail of his shirt and yanks him back.

—Dude, no, sheck it out.

He drapes an arm over his buddy's shoulder, spilling a little blue slush down Asshole's arm, and whispers in his ear. Asshole listens for a second and then busts up.

—Yeah, yeah, dude, tha'sh it!

He straightens up and bows to the bartender.

—Yesh, shir, we will be pleased to do ash you wish. Fuckin' A.

He gestures toward the door and Drunk Fuck leads the way. Asshole pushes the door open and they turn into dark silhouettes against the fierce late afternoon sun. Asshole points out the door.

—After yoush.

Drunk Fuck bows.

—Shank yoush.

He takes one step outside and chugs the contents of his cups and throws both empties into the parking lot. He steps back in and holds the door as Asshole steps out and repeats the performance. The girls are laughing and snorting, hanging on to each other to keep from falling down and struggling to keep their tits from popping out of their tops. Asshole steps back in. He wags a finger at them.

—Ladiesh! No fucking drinksh from outshide! Pleash!

He points at the door. One of the girls straightens up, tries to curtsy, almost falls, and weaves out to the sidewalk. She upends one of her cups and gets half of it in her mouth while the other half slops down her chin and neck and into her cleavage. She explodes laughing and the slush that went in her mouth sprays onto the ground. She stuffs a hand inside her top and tries to dig out the blue daiquiri. Asshole wiggles his fingers.

—Allow me.

He tries to jam his fingers between her tits and she slaps his hand, still coughing and choking. Drunk Fuck tries to get into the act and they jostle the girl around, plucking at her top. The other girl steps outside.

—Hey! Hey, assholes! Check this out!

She tilts her head back, holds both cups over her face, opens her mouth wide, and starts to pour. Frozen blueberry daiquiri fills her mouth and overflows down her face. The guys watch, one with his arms wrapped around the waist of the choking girl and one with his hand halfway down her top. The two-cup girl lets about half of each daiquiri pour over her face, then just dumps the remainder over her chest and belly. Asshole and Drunk Fuck abandon Choking Girl and pounce on Two Cups. Asshole kneels in front of her and sucks blue ice from her pierced navel while Drunk Fuck picks up a straw from the pavement, sticks it between her tits and starts to suck on it. Two Cups giggles and screams.

By now the door has swung shut and we are all watching the action as a shadow play taking place beyond the tinted glass front of the Jackalope. Still, we hear it pretty clearly when Choking Girl coughs, gags and begins to vomit blue onto the sidewalk and her friends' sandaled feet. By then the bartender has come out from behind the bar, crossed to the door and locked it. He walks to the kitchen door and sticks his head inside.

—Jesus!

A Mexican kid in greasy dishwasher whites comes out. The bartender points at the scene outside.

—Clean that shit up.

Jesus stares at the carnage taking place beyond the window and nods.

—*Sí*.

The bartender walks back to the bar, picks up the remote and turns up the volume on his show; the slot couple punches in another song and "Saturday in the Park" starts playing; the old-timer shakes his head and mutters something about *Goddamn fucking college kids;* the cocktail waitress goes back to cleaning out the votives that she'll be setting on the tables soon; the guy knocks back another Jäger and bangs it on the bar. I take a last look out the window just in time to see Two Cups start puking, too. The boys watch, laughing and high-fiving each other.

Then the guy gets up and goes to the bathroom.

Jesus is standing by the glass with a mop bucket, waiting for the kids to leave so he can do his shitty job. I follow the guy into the bathroom so I can do mine.

HE'S PISSING LOUDLY into one of the urinals. I edge past him into a stall, close the door and pull the handful of tiny coke-filled glassine bags out of my pocket. The urinal flushes and I pinch one of the bags open and drop it along with several others onto the floor, most of them scattering out under the stall partition.
—Shit! Oh, shit!

I slam my shoulder loudly against the stall as I get down on my knees and start scrabbling under the partition for the dropped bags. I peek out and see that the guy has moved to the sink and is washing his hands and ignoring me. I scoop up the bags and flick the open one with my middle finger. It skitters across the tiles, leaving a thin trail of white powder, and comes to rest at his feet.
—Fuck! Oh, fuck!

I stand up, jerk on the locked stall door a couple times, bang it open and stumble out. The guy is just straightening, the open, now almost empty, bag pinched between his thumb and forefinger. I shuffle toward him, the rest of the bags peeking from my fist.

—Um, that's mine.

He stands there, a couple inches shorter than me, balding, flashy tasteless clothes, pinkie ring, a bulky upper body that's settling into his midsection but still powerful around the shoulders. The same build my body is starting to develop. He looks from the bag to me.

—Yours?

—Yeah. So, you know.

I put out my hand.

He points at the bag.

—This?

He points at me.

—Is yours?

I shrug.

—Yeah.

He shakes his head.

—Well.

He reaches for his back pocket.

—Looks like this might be your lucky day.

He pulls out a wallet, shows it to me, and lets it fall open, revealing the LVMPD badge within.

—Except it ain't.

—You actually staying here?

I squint up at the sign for the Happi Inn Motel as we cross the parking lot it shares with the Jackalope.

—Yeah.

—Place sucks.

I don't say anything as it kind of goes without saying that a place called the Happi Inn Motel sucks. Besides, I'm busy. I'm wondering if this is it. Did they finally get sick of me fucking up? Have they set me up?

Is this the guy who's going to kill me?

I get out my room key and the guy puts a hand on my shoulder.

—Wait up, hoss. You got anyone in there? A partner, maybe?

I look at the pavement and shake my head.

—Naw, just me.

—Uh-huh. Well, you go ahead and unlock that door, but don't open it.

I turn the key, the lock clicks open and I step back from the door. He puts one hand on the knob, tucks the other one up under the tail of his silvery jacket and rests it on the butt of his piece. He looks at me again.

—Last chance. Anyone in there, now's the time to tell me. I see someone I'm gonna go bang bang.

I shake my head again.

He nods.

—OK.

He pushes the door open, makes sure it lies flat against the wall so he knows there's no one behind it, then nods me in. I step in and he follows me, closing and locking the door behind us. He goes to fasten the chain, but it's broken, so he puts his hand on his gun again and looks the room over, peeking under the bed, looking in the closet, and sticking his head in the bathroom. Then he claps his hands and points at me.

—OK, hoss, let's see it. On the table there.

I stick my hand in my pocket, dig out the twenty or so gram bags of coke and dump them on the table. He presses his lips together and shakes his head.

—Not good, hoss, not good. That's a very felony-looking pile there.

He fingers the bags.

—You got enough weight here to cause you some problems right out the chute. But all packaged up like that? Shit, that looks like intent to distribute to me. What do you think?

I look at the floor and shrug.

—Uh-huh. You got any more? Better tell me now. I gotta take this room apart I'm gonna be irritated.

I nod.

—Yeah.

—You got more?

—Yeah.

—How much?

—A half.

—Half ounce?

—Kilo.

He blows Jäger-scented air out his nostrils, pulls a Kool from his breast pocket and lights it.

—That is some serious weight. You got it here?

—Yeah.

—In this room?

—Yeah.

—Uh-huh.

He blows a cloud of smoke.

—Where?

I tilt my head at the bathroom.

—Toilet tank.

He smiles.

—I tell ya what. You got a half kilo in the shitter there, and this might turn out to be your lucky day after all.

He puts a finger under my chin and tilts my head up so he can look into my eyes.

—You get me, hoss?

Great. Better and better. A dirty cop. And I have such a good track record with dirty cops.

—Yeah. I get you.

He drops his finger from my chin.

—But you fuck with me, hoss?

He slaps me lightly on the cheek.

—And I'm gonna school you. Get me?

—Yeah. I get you.

He gestures for me to lead the way to the bathroom.

—So why the sad face? Let's get happy.

I slouch past him to the open door of the bathroom. He stands close behind me, blowing smoke over my shoulder.

—You go ahead and take the lid off, but don't you go reaching in there or anything. Just take that lid off and step to the side.

I nod, lift the lid from the tank and step to the side. He points at the lid.

—Set that on the floor there.

I set the heavy lid on the floor.

—There ya go. Ain't no one wants to get whacked with one of those mothers. Now step on back.

I take a step back toward the shower. He shakes a finger at me, winks and looks into the tank. He glances at me, looks in the tank again, and crooks a finger.

—Come here for a sec, hoss. Got something to show you.

I step over for a sec, knowing what I'm gonna see, and look into the tank that's empty except for the standard hardware. I start to open my mouth and he grabs me by the back of the neck and slams my face into the mirror. I'm lucky today, it doesn't break.

—What the fuck, hoss? You messin' with me? You fuckin' with the law?

He presses my face harder into the mirror. My luck may be wearing out.

—This a setup?

He sticks his cigarette in his mouth and uses his free hand to pat me down.

—You wearin' a wire? You fuckin' IAD or somethin'?

My mouth is smashed against the speckled mirror.

—Nu-hugh.

He plucks the cigarette from his lips and thrusts it at my right eye. The scar is dead and feels nothing, but there's a sudden flash of heat on my eyelid as I close it. He holds the cigarette close to my closed right eye, and from my still open left eye, pressed to the mirror, I see a dark blur reflected behind him. He touches the cigarette to my eyebrow and I smell burnt hair.

—So where's the fuckin' half key, shithead? You tell me the deal or I'm gonna burn a hole right through your fuckin' eyelid.

There's a ringing ceramic clunk as the toilet tank lid comes down on his head and he's driven to his knees. I pull away from the mirror.

—He has a gun.

But Branko is already pulling the cop's gun from its holster and stuffing it into the back pocket of his dark blue Dickies. The cop is still on his knees, eyes glazed and one hand holding the back of his head, blood oozing from between his fingers. Branko points at me.

—Water.

I grab one of the plastic cups from the sink, not bothering to tear away its wrapper, and fill it. I hand Branko the cup.

—He's a cop.

Branko takes the cup.

—Yes. He is a cop.

He throws the water in the cop's face, drops the cup, and slaps his cheeks a few times.

—Wake up. You are awake, yes? I did not hit you so hard. Wake up.

The cop pulls back, but Branko grabs a fistful of hair and slaps him harder. The cop winces.

—You guys are fucked. You have any idea? You know who? So fuckin' fucked.

Branko yanks the cop's hair, pulling his head up.

—Hey! You know who I am, yes? You see me now? You recognize me, yes? You know who I am in here for? Yes?

The cop's face goes a shade paler. Branko nods.

—Yes, you know. So now, you tell me, who is the fucked one in this toilet?

Branko lets go of the cop and reaches into the pocket of his Windbreaker.

The cop looks at me.

—Hey, wait now. I. Hoss, this is a mistake. Tell your friend here.

Branko's hand comes out of his pocket holding a racquetball.

He grabs the cop's face, forces his mouth open and shoves the ball inside.

—You shut up now and take it like a man.

He pulls a roll of duct tape from his other pocket, tears off a strip and seals it over the ball. He stands up and looks at me.

—You are OK?

I finger my singed eyebrow.

—Yeah, I'm fine.

—Where is the coke?

—It's on the table in there.

He glances over his shoulder into the room.

—Good. OK.

He points at the big man kneeling on the bathroom floor.

—His fingers.

I open my mouth. Branko shakes his head, cutting me off.

—His fingers. I will get the coke.

He steps out of the bathroom, but calls back through the open door.

—And do not forget his thumbs.

I look at the cop, his hands held out in front of him, his face red and tear-streaked as he pleads through the rubber ball. I try to grab his wrists, but he wrenches them away, so I kick him in the stomach. Air explodes out his nose and he folds.

There are reasons why people do the things they do. You have to have a reason, otherwise you couldn't do them.

I have a reason.

A good one.

And at times like these I remind myself of what it is.

I kick him in the stomach one more time and grab his wrists

and lay his fingers across the lip of the open toilet seat and slam the lid so hard the seat cracks and I have to get the blood-splotched tank lid off the floor to finish the job.

And the whole time I say the same thing to myself over and over.

This is for you Mom and Dad. This is for you.

Then Branko comes in, nods once at my handiwork and tells me to go wait in the car while he cleans up.

THIS IS HOW you lose your life.

You're a kid, you play baseball. You are better at baseball than a human being has a right to be at anything. You're going to the pros, everybody knows it. But before it can become a reality, you hurt yourself, bad.

Things happen.

You wallow in your own misery and start hanging with the crowd of kids you would have nothing to do with before you shattered your leg. You do some drugs, break into some houses, get caught.

Things happen.

You trade baseball and petty crime for hot rods. You're a big fucking show-off. You crash your Mustang and your best friend is in the car and he sails through the windshield and you get to see what it looks like when a teenager's head explodes against a tree.

Things happen.

You go to college. You learn things, lots of things. You learn how things work, you learn some first aid, you learn some history and some books and some politics. All the things you didn't have time for when there was baseball. You meet a girl and move to New York City to be with her. She dumps you.

Things happen.

You learn to drink. You tend bar, you develop a drinking problem that's like the rest of your life: nothing special. Years pass. Blah, blah, blah. Boo, hoo, hoo.

Nothing happens.

Then everything happens at once.

A friend leaves something in your care, a cat. That is, you think it's a cat he leaves with you, but it's not. It's a key, a key at the bottom of the cat's cage. The key opens a door and behind the door is a prize, and lots of people want the prize. Who wouldn't want the prize when it's over 4 million clean, untraceable dollars? People come for the key. People threaten you and push you around and hurt you bad and try to kill you, and finally, they kill people you care about. Someone you love. And you kill back.

Things happen.

You stop drinking. You hide. You are severed from your life, huddled on a beach in Mexico, trying to pretend it's OK being a fugitive, cool being on the lam and living on a beach. The mysterious Americano. But it's not OK. It's not cool. And then you meet someone, someone who knows who you are. Someone who wants the money. Threats are exchanged. He threatens you, you threaten him, he threatens your parents. He dies. You run. Back home, to your parents, back to protect them. Bad call.

Things happen.

You lose the money. Lose it like an idiot. Lose over 4 million dollars. Lose the only thing that can save your parents' lives. You make moves. You play both ends against the middle, you make it up as you go along. You fail. Guns. Vicious dogs. Dead friends. Carnage, bloody and awful. You decide to die.

Something happens.

A man saves you. A man saves your life and offers you a new one. The money was his and you have lost it, but he has a use for you. He sees your talents. He sees the things you have done. He knows that you are better at violence than a human being has a right to be at anything. He has uses for a man like you.

Things happen.

But you don't want to think about them.

And that is how you lose your life. Because this is not your life. It is the life that has been allowed you. You live it, but it is not your life.

And then things start to happen again.

MY HANDS SHAKE.

They shake so bad I have to stab at the release button on the glove compartment three times before I hit it and the little door drops open. They shake so bad they turn the bottle of pills into a maraca. I fumble with it until Branko climbs into the car, takes the bottle from my hands, twists the cap off and looks at the pills inside.

—What are these?

—Vicodin.

He looks at me. I hold out my hand.

—My face hurts.

—It is hurting again?

—It hurts all the time.

He grunts, taps two of the pills into his hand and drops them in my waiting palm. I keep my hand out. He shakes his head, drops two more in my hand. I toss the pills in my mouth and dry-swallow them.

He seals the bottle and puts it back in the glove box.

—David wants to speak to you.

I flex my fingers, curling and uncurling them.

—He's in town?

—David is a man who likes to speak on the phone?

I shake my head.

—So where is he?

Branko jerks his thumb over his shoulder.

I look behind us at the reflective gold tower of the Mandalay Bay.

—Across the street?

—Yes.

He points at my hands.

—You can drive?

They've stopped shaking. Sometimes it's like that, just swallowing the pills makes me feel better.

—Yeah.

I stick the key in the ignition, turn it, and the Olds pops to life. I pull us out of the parking space and Branko starts fiddling with the radio. I stop at the exit, waiting for a break in the traffic. Branko hits Lauryn Hill singing "Ex-Factor" and stops spinning the dial. He taps his finger on his knee, slightly out of time.

—I miss Hal Jackson.

His Serbian accent makes it sound like Hell Jycksin.

—What?

—Hal Jackson. Sunday mornings. WBLS. I miss him from New York.

I had a girl back in New York once. She liked Hal Jackson. Sunday mornings reading the paper, coffee and bagels.

I pull us onto The Strip. Branko is looking at me.

—Sunday Morning Classics?

She's dead now. *Now.* As if it happened recently. It didn't.

I drive to the end of the block and stop at the light and wait for a green arrow that will let me turn left. Branko wants me to remember. He sings.

—*Listen to the Sunday Classics. Doubleyou bee ell esss. Hal Jackson. He's got a lot of soul.*

I get my arrow and turn.

—Yeah. OK. I remember.

He nods.

—Yes. Everybody knows Hal Jackson.

I have to wait again to make the left into the Mandalay's drive. A siren sounds from somewhere up The Strip. I glance into the mirror and see an ambulance pulling into the Happi Inn Motel lot. I look at Branko. He shrugs.

—I call the 911.

He holds up his hands.

—He would have to dial with his nose.

He taps the tip of his own nose.

I turn into the drive and join the long line of cars and cabs waiting to pull up to the entrance of the hotel. I glance once more back at the Happi.

—Guy was a cop.

Branko nods. I rub my right eyebrow, grinding away the last of the singed hairs.

—No one told me he was a cop.

Branko shrugs.

I watch the taillights of the car in front of us, flashing pale in the shaded drive.

—I'd like to've known he was a cop.

Branko nods.

—Next time.

Next time. Next time I'm supposed to bait a guy into a motel room with coke, they'll let me know if the guy's a cop. Color me reassured. We pull up to the valet stand and climb out. I take the ticket from the valet and follow Branko into the lobby where we get slammed by a wall of cocoa butter–scented freezing air and the screams of caged parrots and macaws. Branko points toward the elevator banks.

—Twenty-seven-twenty.

—You coming up?

—No.

—Where should I meet you?

—Nowhere. I will stay here.

—OK.

He sticks out his hand and I take it.

—Good today. Better.

I look at his hand holding mine.

—Thanks.

He lets go of my hand, slaps my shoulder and walks off toward the sports book. He'll sit there until David calls for him, watching the ponies and placing the occasional two-dollar bet. He disappears around a bar just off the lobby. Squat, balding and potbellied. He looks like any number of tourists in here. The cheap blue pants, the sneakers, the short-sleeve collared shirt and the Wal-Mart Windbreaker. He could be any Slavic American on vacation.

I step into an elevator and see myself reflected as the shining metal doors close. I don't look like anybody. I don't even look like myself.

THE DOORS OPEN on the twenty-seventh floor and I wander until I find the right room. I knock and wait and David opens the door. He smiles.

—Come in, come in.

He looks the same as ever. Buzzed gray hair, trimmed beard, silver-rimmed glasses, the slight belly and the hairy hands. I step past him and he pats my back as I walk ahead of him into the room. The gold tinting on the outside of the windows tinges the air green.

No one else is in the room. This is how I always meet with David, alone, in private. I am his ghost. The weapon no one knows he owns. No one but Branko.

He points at the honor bar.

—Something to drink?

—No, thanks.

—No. Something. You must have something.

He squats down in front of the bar.

—I am having Black Label. I know you will not join me. But a juice? Water?

I shrug.

—You will have juice, then. It is good for your blood sugar. My daughter tells me.

He looks heavenward. *The things young people worry about.*

He takes a bottle of orange juice from the bar, shakes it and hands it to me.

—A glass?

—No.

He points at a chair and I sit. He plops onto the bed and scoots his back against a small pile of pillows he's arranged. His jacket and shoes are off, and he sits there in slacks and socks, the knot in his designer tie loose at the collar of his designer shirt. He picks up the remote and points it at the TV, muting the hotel station that has been telling him how to play roulette. He drops the remote on the bedspread, picks up his glass of Scotch from the nightstand and takes a sip.

—When I was a younger man, the first time I was in a hotel with one of these.

He points at the honor bar.

—I drank everything clear. Vodka, gin, white wine, and filled the bottles with water from the bathroom and put them back just as they had been.

He smiles, closes his eyes, and shrugs. *Yes, I too was once young and stupid.*

He opens his eyes.

—It embarrasses me now because there was no need. It was not long after I had left the Soviet Union, but still, I could have afforded these things even then. But, we have all done things of which we are embarrassed. Things we regret.

I take a sip of my juice. He looks at the TV, at the silent figures of smiling people now rolling dice.

—Branko tells me you are still taking the pills.

I shift in my seat.

—My face hurts.

He looks from the TV screen to my face.

—Still it hurts?

My hand goes to the scar.

—Some days are worse.

He looks into his glass.

—I am sorry for that. If there had not been a need . . . But.

He looks back up at me, raises his eyebrows and tilts his head to the side. *Why talk about "buts"?*

I take my fingers away from the scar.

—It doesn't matter. I can live with it.

—That, I have never doubted.

He points at the window.

—And today? It went well?

I look out the window. Across The Strip I can see the purple-and-green sign of the Laughing Jackalope and, next to it, the tarpaper roof of the Happi. The ambulance is pulling away, but two LVMPD cars are parked in front of the room.

—The guy's a cop.

David swings his legs over the side of the bed, stands and walks to the window. He looks down at the police cars.

—This matters?

—What if he hadn't bit on the coke? What if he busted me instead?

He glances at me, looks back out the window.

—You would let that happen?

—It might have happened.

He faces me.

—And this is what it is that bothers you about this job? That you might have been arrested?

I look back out the window. I can see a blue uniform walking across the parking lot toward the Jackalope.

—You broke his hands?

I swallow.

—Yeah.

—You did it? Not Branko?

—Yeah, I did it.

—And yet you try to tell me you are bothered now because this man is a cop.

He hoists his glass slightly, sighting his eyes at mine over the rim. *Do we not know each other better than this by now?*

He sips his drink.

—This man, this cop. Do you know what he has done to make me so angry? So angry that I would have his hands broken?

—No.

—He is a cop that I pay. Every month he is paid money. It is a good arrangement. It is especially good for this cop because he is a man who knows that I can do him more harm than he can do to me. But still, still he abuses this arrangement. He takes more than is his fair share. He takes drugs from my dealers. He takes extra protection from my whores. He is especially greedy with the whores. Two nights past, the same evening after he has been paid what he is due for this month, that very night he shows up at the apartment of one of my whores. He wants money, yes, but he wants also to fuck. Well.

He lifts his shoulders. *What else are whores for?*

—But he is not a normal man. Fucking is not enough for this man. He likes also to beat my whores when he fucks them. This he has done before. And this night, two days past, he does it again. And he does this girl great harm.

His lips tighten. He sips his drink, exhales, and his lips relax.

—My family is from Armenia. This whore's family is from Armenia. She is from a family that I know from when I was born. Am I close to this family? No. If I were close to these people I would not let their daughter be a whore. But I knew her father and he was not a bastard. And she is, this whore, she is my daughter's age. Her hair. The same color.

He swallows the rest of his drink and places the empty glass on the windowsill.

—One whore beaten more or less. What is that? Nothing. But this cop has done it many times, and now he does it with a girl I have met. A girl who could be my daughter.

He rubs tears from his eyes, looks at his fingers, and then shows them to me. *You see, you see how I feel these things in my soul?*

—So I tell Branko what will be done. And I tell him you are to do it. Why? Because these are the things you are meant to do for me. You are meant to do difficult things. Things that would make most men throw up their dinners and crap like babies in their pants. This is how you are meant to pay your debt to me.

David reaches out, puts his hand on the side of my face, the tip of his index finger touching the scar, and gently turns my head to face him.

—But you do not do these things anymore. You fail again and again, and Branko must do your work for you. We have talked about this?

I can feel his fingers on my face, but not the one that rests on the patch of wrinkled, white skin.

—Yes.

—Yes, we have. And you try. I know this. I know you take these pills not just for the pain in your face. So today, this job? It was a gift for you. A man to hurt that truly deserved to be hurt.

He smiles at me, crinkles the corners of his eyes. *You see how I care for you, how generous I am with you?*

—But you must do better. You must get back the taste for this work.

His hand drops from my face.

—Soon.

He walks to the bed, sits.

—You understand this?

—Yes.

—That is why I ask to talk to you. So you understand this. I am being unreasonable?

—No.

—Good. That is good. Then.

He settles back into his nest of pillows, crosses his legs at the ankles and picks up the remote.

—The flight was long and I will take a nap now.

—Sure.

I get up and stand there looking for a place to put my nearly full bottle of juice.

—Take it with you. For your blood sugar.

He smiles. I nod and walk toward the door. I have it open when his voice floats up the hall.

—There will be more work for you this week. You are free?

I stand there with the doorknob in my hand.

—Yeah.

—Of course you are. Go home and rest. You are tired.

I nod back down the hall toward the room, where all I can see of him are his stocking feet.

—Yeah. Thanks.

I step out into the hotel corridor, and before the door is closed I hear the sound of the TV click back on, chattering about the artificial beach behind the hotel. I walk to the elevators and push the button and stand there wondering how long I have left before David Dolokhov sends Branko to kill me, and whether he'll send him to kill my parents before or after I am dead.

MY APARTMENT IS shit. But that kind of goes with the territory. The territory being my shitty life.

I shouldn't be doing this. But I can't help myself. I type in the address and wait while my shitty dial-up connects and loads the home page for www.sandycandy.com. It takes forever because the main feature of the page is a huge glamour shot of Sandy in one of her stripper outfits. Once the entire image of her embracing a chrome pole has resolved, I run the cursor down the menu. I start with public appearances. Not much. She's doing another Howard Stern, but things have certainly slowed up for her in the last six months. No more afternoon talk shows or Court TV interviews, and just the same entry that tells her fans to keep looking for her E! special, but still no date. That one was probably bull anyway. Like the *60 Minutes* interview that never happened. I skip going to the merchandise page, I've seen it all: Sandy Candy hats, T's, panties, DVDs. I could check out the discussion forum. It's been a week since I've been here and there will be plenty of new posts. Then I see she has a new entry in her diary. I click over.

Wow! Tough couple of weeks! I just got back from a tour of clubs in Florida. South Beach rocks! I was the guest dancer at

Club Madonna (no relation to Madonna!), Club Pink Pussycat, and Coco's Lounge Living on the Edge! I was dancing topless and totally nude (which you know I love. So much freedom!) And I had a great time and everybody was great! Special thanks to Sissy and Aura for letting me crash at their place! The fajitas were great! I just posted some pics of me on the beach in my bikini (don't worry, spf 30 for Sandy Candy's sensitive skin). Members can log on to the pay site and see pics of me with some of the other girls doing our thing! If you're not a member yet this is the time to join. Trust me, these Miami girls are hot! I also added links on the links page for all the clubs I was dancing at. Check 'em out when you're in Miami. So much fun!

On a more serious note. I want to thank all you guys who have been writing in to check on me and asking how my counseling is going. I still have some nightmares, but I really think I'm getting better and I'm learning to forgive and let go. Being kidnapped and seeing people killed just isn't something you get over easy. But having all you great guys (and girls) looking out for me sure helps.

Well, that's enough of the serious stuff. I'm gonna take a couple days off ("me time!"), but I'll be back out there real soon. All you guys in the Big Apple should keep an eye out because I'll be dancing there this weekend at Private Eyes, and then get ready for me out in Kansas City, guys, cuz I'm coming your way!

Everybody take care and I'll see you soon!

Luv,
SC

Kansas City. That's as far west as she's come since she moved to Pennsylvania. How far is it to Kansas City? I almost go looking for a map, but really, what's the point? After all, I'm the kidnapper she's talking about. Anyway, it's not like we were friends or anything. She was just a stripper with some connections, someone in Vegas who T thought could help us. So what if she ended up setting us up instead. She didn't know how bad that was gonna turn out. Besides, what do I think I'm gonna do? Drive out to KC, find her in a club and say, *Hi, remember me?*

I log off and head for the bathroom and my medicine cabinet.

The mirror on the front of the cabinet is broken. I broke it six months back when I mixed up my meds a bit too much. The Xanax I'd been taking was starting to bring me too far down so I'd started cutting it with some straight Dexedrine. I looked in the mirror one night and saw the face that isn't mine and got pissed at it and tried to punch it out. Proving yet again, thinking is bad for me.

So the mirror's still busted and I never got around to pulling the shards of glass out of the frame, just taped over them with black gaff tape. It worked out fine, now I don't have to look at myself when I go to the bathroom.

I open the cabinet and take out the two Ziploc bags full of pill bottles. I was right about going on Sandy's site, it was bad for me. Now bad thoughts are creeping into my head. Thoughts like, maybe I *should* contact her, just send her an e-mail and ask her what happened to T. That's all I really want from her anyway, to know where T is; to know if he's OK. But thinking about Sandy and T just starts up thoughts about New York, about what happened there. Thoughts about the people who've died. And that gets me thinking about what I've been doing since then. About the jobs for David. Next thing you know, I'm thinking about ways to get out of this shit. And those are the worst thoughts.

I have no business thinking that I could just cut and run. If I ever tried that, David would send Branko to my parents' home. That's the deal. So maybe the trick is to get rid of David and Branko. Except I don't think I could kill David and Branko. They would smell it on me the second I walked in the room. I could go find Mom and Dad and we could all run away together. I could make their lives worse than they already are. I could go to New York, find the money that started it all, the 4 million dollars. Except I have no idea where that money is. Tim hid that money. Hid it for safekeeping, to keep it safe for me. That was right before I killed him. I thought he'd taken the money for himself. How could I have known what a friend I had.

I could die. I could peel off a strip of this gaff tape, pry a shard of glass from the bent frame of the medicine cabinet door and start slashing my wrists. Just fall to the floor in here and bleed. But David has closed that door as well. He closed it the day we met when he spelled out our contract. My parents live, and I work for him for life. And I don't get to decide when that life is over.

And so here I am again.

Thinking.

Well, I know how to stop that.

I peel open the Ziploc that has the downs in it. I fumble through the bottles looking for something I haven't taken too much of lately, something that will work. The Vics took the edge off the pain in my face back at the motel and helped deal with the shakes I had, but I need something for my head now. I pop the cap on a bottle of Demerol, toss one in my mouth and swallow.

I put the bags back in the cabinet and close the door. I look at the mess of black tape, the occasional glimmer of fractured mirror peeking out. I pick at a loose end of tape and start to tease it away. It comes off, a few slivers of broken glass stuck to the back. I see my right eye and the patch of scar reflected back at me in mosaic. My face pulses once, twice, and I press the tape back down.

THE APARTMENT IS shitty, but it's still a step up from the Budget Suites of America. *That* was grim. A pay-by-the-week chain motel at the ass end of Las Vegas Boulevard. Half the tenants at the Suites were families, pulled to Vegas by stories of abundant employment and cheap housing, crammed into one bedroom. The other half were the families that had already crapped out and were trying to scrape together enough to get out. The Budget Suites, serving as the mouth and ass of Las Vegas. That was the first place David stuck me after the bandages came off. After the butcher he hired to give me a new look got done busting all the bones in my face and moving them around and slicing the skin and sewing it back up so it fit. Sort of.

It's not like I look like Frankenstein's monster or anything. He changed the shape of my forehead, moved my hairline back, broke my cheekbones and pushed them up, filed the point of my jaw down, flattened my nose and thinned my lips. It's not even that the face looks bad. Probably would have been a good job all the way around if I hadn't had those burns when he operated.

Turns out that performing impromptu plastic surgery on a man with a severly scalded face is a bad call. Things never quite healed as they should have. If I cover the outer half of my right eye with the palm of my hand it just about perfectly eclipses the scar. A patch of dead, white, wrinkled skin, its circumference cutting across my eyebrow, temple and cheekbone. The scar is a problem, not because it makes it hard to pick up chicks, but because it makes me easy to remember. The scar means David can't use me on many jobs. Only the kind that involve people you don't have to worry about identifying you later. Hard guys who fight back but know to keep their mouths shut when they come out on the losing side. Or people who just aren't ever going to talk to anyone again. I've met some of those people.

The scar is also why David stuck me in the Budget Suites. The Suites was perfect. Nobody looks at anyone at the Suites. Head down, mind your own business, that's the rules. Besides, there are so many scarred and gimped losers crawling in and out of that place, no one notices one more hacked-up face.

Anyway, the scar's not the issue. The issue is the nerve damage, it's the job the surgeon did when he reset the bones after he broke up my face. He didn't do a good job. Something in there is fucked up. Most of the time it hurts like a bad headache, but in your face. Sometimes it's worse. Like when a big guy crams my face into a mirror or something. So I take pills. I take them for the pain in my face. But I also take them to keep me from picking at the tape on that medicine cabinet mirror.

I sat on my shelf at the Suites and ate the pills I scored off one of the dealers who lived there. Some of the pills took care of the pain, some of the pills erased the nightmares from my sleep, and some of the pills got me in the car with Branko when he'd come by to pick me up.

We'd drive someplace where someone who was used to being the scariest dude around needed to be scared. And Branko would send me through the door first. And it was fine. The pills made it fine. I didn't hurt, I didn't care. And that was fine. Then the pills stopped working so good. Now I have to take so many of the god-damn things that I'm usually a zombie by the time I go in. Branko tries to sic me on some guy and there I am, leaning against the wall with little ropes of drool hanging out the corner of my mouth.

David doesn't like that.

David thought I had all-star potential. I was gonna be his ghost, the guy no one knows about. The secret weapon in his organiza-tion. And no one does know. Just him and Branko. I'm the gun he can pull and wave around, the gun that nobody knows he has. He thought I'd serve my apprenticeship with Branko and then I'd be able to go it alone. When he found out that I'd moved from Xanax and Vics to Demerol and OxyContin, he had me moved from the Suites and into this shithole in North LV. I just keep dropping by the Suites to score. I'd like to think David and Branko don't know I'm still popping the heavy stuff, but they aren't stupid. I'm the only stupid one around here.

And now I've started getting sent on the shitty jobs, jobs that are a little more visible. The kind of jobs Branko usually arranges with some guy they fly in from out of town. It's starting to feel like maybe David is less and less concerned about having me around for the long term. Like maybe he just wants to get some value back on his investment before he cuts me.

I try to care about that. I try to care whether I live or die. Be-cause that has an awful lot to do with whether my folks live or die. But the Demerol's kicking in now and I'm starting to stop caring about anything at all. Just the way I like it.

I go back into the living room. I flop on the couch and the De-merol makes it a slow-motion tumble from a rooftop into one of those huge air bags stuntmen use. I watch my hand pick up the stereo remote. I flick through the CDs in the changer until I find some Elvis Costello, and then song-hop, listening to the opening notes of each track until I find one that suits my mood: semi-suicidal, but chemically numbed. "Shipbuilding" seems to have it covered.

This is good. This is just fine. More to the point, this is as good as it gets for me anymore. Demerol, some tunes, and the hope of dreamless sleep. That's the mountaintop for me. How the mighty have fallen.

Used to be the mountain was swinging a bat, smacking a ball, watching it fly away, knowing it was a sure hit, and sprinting around the bases. That was a long time ago. That was another world. Baseball. I haven't played baseball since I was a kid. Shit, I can't even watch baseball. A bottle of Demerol wouldn't get me high enough to handle a ball game. I try to watch a baseball game anymore and I just end up rocking back and forth on the couch, arms wrapped around myself, whining.

The Demerol rushes.

I melt into the couch.

I SIT ON the couch with the little rule booklet, trying to figure out how it works. The Kid comes back into the room. There are strands of spaghetti in his hair and a mess of sauce on his face and neck. He's carrying a couple Buds. I look at the beers.

—Where'd you get those?

—My dad's.

—Won't he get pissed?

—He won't notice.

He hands one to me. I open it and take a sip. It's good. Only after the first sip do I remember how long it's been since I last had a drink. Shit. Fucked that up. Oh well. Gonna have to start from scratch anyway, may as well finish it. I take another sip.

The Kid sits down next to me and points at the booklet.

—You ready?

I toss the rules to the floor.

—No way. There is no way I can play this. I'm terrible at this shit.

—I thought baseball was your thing.

—Yeah, baseball, the real game, that was my thing. But this is different.

—But you were good?

—Yeah. Yeah, I was good.

—So this'll be easy.

—Look, can't we just go out back and have a little catch or something. I mean, if we're gonna play let's *play*.

He pushes open the curtain to show me the heavy rain outside.

—C'mon, just try it.

I groan, but I pick up my controller and he turns on the game.

He pushes some buttons and team logos start appearing on the TV.

—Who you want to be?

—Giants of course.

He pushes more buttons.

—Guess I'll have to be the Dodgers.

I groan again.

—Don't do that, man. You know you're gonna beat me. Don't do it with the Dodgers.

He laughs.

—Can't take it? Here, you can play a Giants All Star club. Ott, Mays, McCovey, Mathewson.

—No. No. Just give me the team.

—You want the last World Series team?

—No, I never got to see them play. Give me, give me that team that almost made the Wild Card. The one that had the one-game playoff with the Mets.

He pushes buttons.

—OK, you're up.

We play. I suck. By the third inning he's ahead 15–0.

He hits another homer and I throw my controller at the floor.

—This sucks!

He's laughing.

—OK. OK. Come on. We'll play something else. I got something that's more your style.

—Fine. Whatever.

He gets up from the couch. I pick up the rule booklet and try to figure out what he did to make his guy slide into my second base-man and take him out.

—Here we go.

I look up. He's over by the TV. He has a plastic gun in each hand.

—First person shooter. That's more your style, right?

I run my fingers over the glossy pages of the booklet.

—I don't know, man. Let's just keep playing ball.

—No, you were right. You suck. C'mon, you'll be good at this.

He lifts one of the guns and points it at his head.

—C'mon, you're a natural. Bang! Bang!

He pulls the plastic trigger, and smiling, turns around and shows me the huge hole where the back of his head used to be.

WHEN THE PHONE rings I'm sprawled on the couch in my underwear, one foot on the floor, resting on a cold, half-eaten pizza, a half dozen half-empty one-liter water bottles jumbled around me. I've been zonked on the couch for over forty-eight hours. The first Dem I took didn't keep the dreams away, so I took two more. Those were so sweet I decided to keep going.

The phone is still ringing. It rings and rings and rings until I figure out it's not an effect Moby mixed into "One of These Mornings." I come to, my nostrils clogged with snot, a huge gob of mucus at the back of my throat. I try to stand, my foot smearing the cold pizza onto the carpet, and get hit with a head rush that sends me dizzy to my knees. I hawk and spit the yellow wad of mucus onto the pizza box and crawl to the cell lying in the middle of the dirty shag carpet. The number of the incoming call is blocked, but only two people have this number and they both have blocks. The phone keeps ringing as I fumble the top off one of the water bottles and chug it down, easing the dryness of my lips and tongue and washing away the foul taste of my own phlegm.

Still the phone rings. I answer it.

—Yeah, I'm here. Branko?

—No.

It's David. David, who detests talking on the phone.

—Yeah. Hey. What's up?

—The phone was ringing a very long time.

I can see the look on his face as he says it, eyebrows pinched together. *I only mention this because I am concerned.*

—Sorry. I was in the bathroom.

—You sound hoarse. Are you unwell?

—No, fine. Just I was in the bathroom. Sorry.

—No. No. I am sorry to disturb you. My wife would not like me to mention this, but I turn the phone off when I am in the bathroom. So I will not be distracted. Irregularity is one of the curses of growing older.

The only thing I have to add to this conversation would be to tell him that the Demerol I've been popping will keep me from crapping for the next several days. But I don't think he wants to hear that so I just grunt instead.

He gives an embarrassed chuckle.

—You do not want to hear this. No one wants to hear the digestive problems of an older man except for another older man. I can tell you only this, roughage. Every day. Your later years will be so much more enjoyable.

—Sure. Thanks.

—But.

—Yeah?

—But this is not why I am calling you.

He's not calling me to talk about his constipation. Somehow I had a feeling.

—I am calling to talk about the work I mentioned to you. When we were talking earlier this week, I mentioned work to you?

—I remember.

—Yes. Good. This work then, this work begins tonight. Is your car clean?

—My car?

—You have. It is a Cutlass?

—Yeah.

—This is a nice car?

—It's, it's not fancy, but it's in good shape. I keep it clean. Clean enough.

—It will need to be very clean. Waxed. The windows will need to be washed. Vacuumed. Detailed, yes?

—Sure. Detailed.

—Good. And then you will drive it to the airport and pick someone up.

My head is still packed with Demerol-flavored cotton. I don't know if he means pick up, or *pick up*.

—I. David. Should we be talking about this on the phone?

He laughs. Once again I can picture him, shaking his head, a hand waving misunderstanding from the air. *No, I am unclear, forgive me.*

—No. Just to pick up. And to drive. You will pick up this young man and he will spend the evening in Las Vegas and you will drive him around and see that he gets in no trouble. That is all. A good job, yes?

—I don't.

—Yes?

I look at my right foot. Cheese and tomato sauce cling to my heel and a piece of pepperoni is wedged between my toes.

—I don't know if I'm up to this kind of thing.

—This kind of thing?

—People. Dealing with people.

He makes a little *tsk*.

—Dealing with people.

The sound again.

—We are on the phone, yes?

—Yeah.

—Yes, we are on the phone. And you know this is something I do not care for. To be on the phone. This job, I want you to have it. And I want you to know how important this job is. So I want to give you this job from my own mouth. But I am in New York again. So how to give you this job but on the phone? There is no other way. Do you understand?

—I guess. I mean.

—No. No, you do not understand.

He is scolding me now. Scolding me gently as a parent scolds a child, or a pet.

—I am in New York with my family. My whole family, we are on Long Island. My sister-in-law, she is here.

Oh.

—Yes? She is here and she is talking to me from the second she arrives. Asking me questions.

Oh. Shit.

—She is. The woman is a pain in my ass. Worse than constipation the woman is. Since her son was killed.

He doesn't say it. He doesn't have to say it. He doesn't have to say, *Since you killed her son*. It's not like I'm going to forget. I spin my mental wheels on the memory for a second; he keeps talking.

—She asks me again and again, when will I find you? When will she have revenge for her son? I tell her, I say, *Anna, he is most likely dead. There may never be revenge.* I say, *Forget, Anna, live your life. This will not bring you happiness.* But she is drinking.

She says, *No, if you will not find him, I will find him. I will have my nephews look for him.*

There's a sharp smack over the phone as he claps his hands in frustration. *This woman!*

—You see what it is I am putting up with? Two years I must have this from this woman. This woman I would not be in the same room with if she had not been married to my brother. Some days, I tell you this, some days I wish I could kill my brother for dying and leaving me this woman to deal with.

We are both silent a moment. I think about David's nephew. Mickey. The boy I killed in Mexico. Who knows what David thinks about?

He coughs, clearing his throat, signaling a change of tone.

—This is dangerous, this threat of hers to involve her nephews. They are here from Russia. They are here for their own protection. They are young and troubled and I do not want them involved in my business. There is a risk if she does this. A risk in my protecting you. And a risk can only be taken if there is something of value to be gained.

I tilt my head back and stare up at the cracks in the ceiling.

—This young man you will look after, he is an investment of mine. And he must be protected.

—Branko.

—No. *You.*

The cracks in the ceiling remind me of the fractured surface of the mirror. I look away from them.

—It must be *you.* Why?

—I don't know.

—Yes you do. It must be you because now is the time that I must know what is your value. Can Branko protect this young man? Of course he can. Better than any. But Branko is not, he is not . . . he impresses only those who know him. That is part of his great value. You. You will make an impression on this young man. You are a large man. And you have your face. You will pick him up not in a limo, but in your own car, you will look to him dangerous. This will be interesting for him. Fun. And you will have this chance to show me your value. To impress this man with yourself and keep him safe.

His voice drops.

—If I am to deal with my sister-in-law, this threat of hers, if I am to take that risk, I must see your value. Now. Show me your value. Do not let these trials be for nothing.

Help me to save you from yourself.

—You understand now?

—Yes.

—Good. Good. Branko will come to you soon with money and details. Then you will do this job and this will be all behind us, this unpleasantness. Yes?

—Yes. David?

—What?

I force the words from my mouth.

—My mom and dad.

—No.

—I. I need to.

—No. This we do not talk about. Not now.

I can picture his finger pointed at me. *There are lines not to be crossed.*

—But if.

—No. You want to talk about this? I am a businessman and will talk always about an arrangement. But first this job. Do this job and we will talk. Show me there is work you are still good for, and then we will talk. When we are face-to-face in a room, we can talk about this. Not now. Not now.

—OK. OK. Sorry.

—Do not be sorry. Be. Be the man I know you to be. This is a wonderful opportunity. Seize it and we may talk of many things. I have learned in my life that anything may be changed. Anything may be fixed. But now. Now I will go. My family is on the beach and I will join them. I am wearing shorts. I have white cream on my nose. You would laugh at me. You would laugh.

He says goodbye and I say goodbye and we hang up.

But I'm not laughing.

I pick up one of the water bottles, open it and pour it over my head. The water splashes off my face and I catch some in my mouth and I have a sudden flash of memory: the girls out front of the Jackalope dumping frozen blueberry daiquiris over themselves. The image is somehow crushing and I am hit with a childish depression, the kind you get when you see a kid who's just lost the scoop of ice cream from his cone. I sit, all but naked on the floor, my ever-growing gut rolling over the waistband of my dirty BVDs, pizza on the bottom of my foot, the dripping water bottle held over my head.

This would be a good time for it, but I don't get up and walk into the bathroom and peel the tape from the broken mirror.

BY THE TIME Branko shows up I've managed to get myself in the shower to hose off the two days of pill-sweat I've been wallowing in and pick the pepperoni out from between my toes. The Demerol crash is coming on strong and my eyes want to slide shut so I've popped a tab of x and that tilts me back the other way. It's dirty x. The euphoria of the MDMA is cut heavily with speed, which is what I really need right now to keep me on my feet. I'll drop another one right before I pick up this guy tonight and it might make me slightly more social than a corpse.

I still have the towel wrapped around my waist when there's a knock on the door. I know who it is, but I observe all the precautions out of habit. First, I peek out the back window to see if there are any guys with *FBI* blazed across their shirts hiding behind the cars in the back lot. Check. Next, I unlock the back door so I can run out it in a hurry in case something fucked comes in the front. Then I spend a minute going through drawers in the kitchenette until I remember that my gun is under the sink at the bottom of a bucket of cleaning products that I never use. I dig it out and walk to the front door, blowing Comet off the cylinder. I stand a couple feet from the door and move my head back and forth, trying to see the clear point of light through the peephole that will tell me no one is peering in from the other side waiting for me to stick my eye against it so they can send a bullet through. Check on the daylight. So I peek through the peephole, see Branko like I knew I would, and go to twist open the locks, none of which, I now realize, are fastened. I open the door.

Branko looks at me in my towel, the revolver dangling from my hand, and taps a fingernail against the door.

—Not locked?

I shrug.

—I remembered to look out back.

He steps in, closes and locks the door.

—Small miracles.

I drop the gun on the couch and head for the bedroom to finish dressing.

—The only kind there are.

He makes the little grunting noise that passes for his laugh.

In the bedroom I wiggle into a pair of size forty jeans that I bought a month ago and that are already getting tight on me. That's another reason not to have mirrors. Most of my life I wore thirty-fours. Not anymore. No gym memberships for wanted criminals. Not that I can fool myself into thinking that I'd go anywhere near a gym if one were available to me. There are people at gyms, and I don't really know what to do with people anymore. Except hurt them. I suck in my gut and button the jeans.

In the living room Branko has turned off the Cannonball Adderley I was listening to, swapping "Somethin' Else" for Cameo and "Rigor Mortis." He's bent over, adjusting the equalizer on the stereo he gave me when I moved into this place. It had fallen off a truck along with a couple dozen others just like it and he'd scooped up one for me because he hated the sound of the little boom box I used to have.

When I come in he looks over his shoulder at me.

—Your levels are wrong.

I sit on the couch and lace my sneakers.

—Thanks for taking care of that.

He frowns and turns back to the stereo.

—And your gun needs to be cleaned.

I don't know where the gun came from, but Branko gave me that, too. I was supposed to kill someone with it.

———

BRANKO SHOWED UP one night and we drove into Paradise, to one of the New Mexico–style housing tracts over there that look just like all the other New Mexico–style housing tracts in Paradise. He parked the car outside a house. We went in and I beat the hell out of a guy who had welshed on one too many bets, or stopped paying his vig, or cheated at cards, or didn't give a job to somebody's cousin, or something. Then Branko handed me this little revolver with the numbers filed off. I hadn't realized it was that. I thought it was a beating: beat the guy, make your point, get out. But it wasn't. It was a job with a gun.

Branko flipped the guy onto his stomach. I stood over the guy and pointed the gun at the back of his head.

The way you do it, you empty the gun, you wipe the gun, you drop the gun. The gun is a big fuck you. First it says fuck you to the guy who's getting it. Then it says fuck you to the cops. And finally, it says fuck you to all the guys out there who know why this guy got his head shot to pieces. The gun sitting next to the corpse says fuck this guy, fuck the cops who aren't going to catch me and fuck all you assholes out there that are thinking about fucking with David Dolokhov.

I've delivered that particular litany of fuck you's three times.

So I stand there with the .22 in my hand. It holds seven rounds. All I have to do is put them all in the back of this guy's head and drop the big fuck you.

But I don't. Instead I just stand there. Stand there and flex my trigger finger. But it never moves.

Branko gave it a minute, then he shot the guy with his own gun. Back in the car I tried to give him the little revolver, but he told me to keep it for the next time. But the next time I still couldn't do it. And then David stopped sending me on jobs like that, and I started feeling more and more that I had let him down, and that sooner or later, I'd have to pay for it.

But they let me keep the gun. A kind of promise to me that even if I have given up on myself, they haven't.

They know I still have it in me.

Killing still inside me.

I LOOK AT the gun. It's a Smith & Wesson .22 Magnum. A perfect gun for killing people. It's very small and very lightweight, but those Magnum loads still pack plenty of punch. I pull the cuff of my shirtsleeve down and use it to brush off the rest of the Comet. Branko straightens from the stereo and looks at me.

—This is what you will wear?

I look at my jeans, sneakers, and long-sleeve T-shirt.

—Is it wrong?

—For later. When you pick this man up. You must look better.

—A suit?

He thinks about it.

—Black jeans. A clean shirt. A jacket. And nice shoes. You have these things?

—No.

He nods.

—We will go detail the car now, and then we will shop.

WE STAND IN the air-conditioned waiting room and watch through the window as the Mexican kids detail my '91 Cutlass

Calais. Branko takes a sip from the cup of coffee he got at the mini-mart next door.

—Such an ugly car.

—You said I should get something unassuming.

—Yes, but this?

He angles his cup at the Olds.

—This is a piece of crap.

—It's a fast piece of crap.

He nods, giving my piece of crap its due.

They let me have a car when I was moved out of the Suites. Branko said it should be unassuming, reliable and fast. I clicked online and came up with a few options and we drove around to look at them. The Olds was a steal; a midsize, 2.3 four-banger with the Quad 442 performance package that cranks the horse-power over two hundred. The guy who owned it got it as part of his parents' estate and had no idea what he had. Fifty thousand original miles and we got it for under three thousand dollars.

The guy I'm picking up is a kid, a kid with a lot of money. Branko is concerned the kid won't think the car is cool enough. It's an ugly car, boxy and generic, aggressively uncool.

—You want to lend me your car?

Knowing he never lets anyone drive his car.

He drains his coffee.

—No. No one may drive my car.

Branko is a Toyota fanatic. Every year he pants over the new Camry, and every year he's behind the wheel of the new model by Christmas.

—Fine. Wouldn't want to drive that crap-box anyway.

He crumples his coffee cup and tosses it in the trash.

—Not a crap-box. Most reliable car on the road. My Camry will never break down. Safer than Volvo, and half the price. And *if* it ever breaks, it will not cost me my life savings to fix. Fucking Volvo.

Branko used to have a Volvo. It broke down while he was on the way to a job. He got there late. In the meantime someone had tipped the guy off. The guy was waiting for Branko when Branko came in the door. Things turned out OK, for Branko. But after that he swore off Volvos and pledged fidelity to Toyota.

The Mexican kids are waving their chamois over the red paint of the Olds. Branko and I slip on our sunglasses and push out the door into 100 degrees. If there was the slightest humidity in the air I'd sweat my clothes through by the time we reach the car. Instead, all the moisture is sucked from my body and into the atmosphere. Branko makes a show of looking the car over for any fingerprints or flecks of dry wax caught in the edges of the trim. I take a twenty from my pocket and hand it to the crew-boss and stir my finger in a little circle, letting him know to share the tip with his boys. Then I climb in the car, start the engine and blast the A/C.

THE GUY COMING to town likes to gamble. And he has money. That's why David has taken an interest. All I'm supposed to do is pick him up, drive him wherever he wants to go, keep him out of trouble, and act tough.

Branko takes a black jacket from the rack and hands it to me. I take the jacket off its hanger.

—Act tough?

—To make an impression.

—So?

—Tough. Say little. Look at everyone. Wear your sunglasses inside.

I shrug into the jacket and Branko looks me over.

—This will do.

We've only been in the mall for thirty minutes, but already I have three new shirts, some black Levi's that actually fit, a pair of black shoes, and now the jacket. We head for the register and I pull a roll of bills from my pocket. Branko pushes my hand down.

—Business expense.

He takes out a billfold, I pile the clothes on the counter, and he lays plastic next to them. The name on the card is Fred Durben. I don't know who Fred is. Could be he's a guy who handed his cards over in lieu of cash. Now he spends his sleeping hours having nightmares about the waste being laid to his credit rating; his waking hours a worse nightmare of watching the red-marked bills pile up. Could be he's a guy who never existed, just a name with a credit history and this one account. Could be he's in a hole in the desert, could be he's in several holes in the desert. All I know for certain is that the card isn't hot. If it belongs to a dead body, it's a body that's never been found and will never be missed. Branko would never trade in hot plastic. As it is, he'll probably clip the thing into a hundred pieces when he gets home, and drop each piece into a separate storm drain.

The cashier slides Branko the receipt and he signs it with a scrawl that might say Fred Durben, but that most certainly looks nothing like the signature he uses when he signs his real name. If he has a real name anymore. I pick up the bags and we head for the parking lot.

————

WE BUZZ UP the parkway into North Las Vegas.

—You have money?

—Some.

—How much?

—About eight hundred.

Branko pulls out the billfold again and produces a thick slab of cash. He thumbs through the bills, careful to count each one, peeling apart the new ones that have stuck together. It's a nice lump of cash, but not ostentatious, not for Vegas anyway. Having counted the money, he evenly divides it and hands half to me. I fold mine and tuck it into my back pocket.

—Pay for everything that is not gambling. Do not offer, do not ask. Just pay.

—Everything?

—You pay for food, drinks, strippers and whores.

Because what else is there to buy in Vegas?

—What if he hits the shops and wants a Rolex or something?

—He will not want to shop. He will want to gamble.

—OK. Where's his room?

—No room. He is here to party like a rock star and be on a flight in the morning.

He looks back out the window. I tap the rim of the steering wheel in x-time. Branko looks at the finger and then at me. I make an effort to stop tapping. I succeed, but it isn't easy. He points at the finger that I have to force to be still.

—David talked to you about this job?

—Yeah.

—He told you it is important?

—Yeah.

—He told you how important?

—Yeah, Branko, I get it. The kid is worth a lot of money and David wants his cut. He wants the kid not to be fucked with and he wants him impressed so that he'll use David's bookies. Got it.

—He told you how important this job is for you?

The finger taps a couple times. I stop it. Branko doesn't talk business with me. He talks detail. Where, when, who and how much to hurt them. But he doesn't talk business.

—He said some things.

—My friend.

I flinch.

Two years Branko's apprentice. Two years his charge. Two years this man's pupil, batboy, valet. He's never called me friend.

—My friend. This is an important job for you.

He points a rock-steady finger at my finger, which is tattooing the wheel again. I stop it.

We don't talk. Branko has commandeered the radio as usual and we listen to Billy T on KCEP 88.1. Billy T is getting his mellow on, turning back the clock, "Strawberry Letter 23" grooving us down the road.

YOU'D THINK I'D be losing weight. What with the pills, it's not like I have much of an appetite. But the amount of time I spend zonked on the couch or Web surfing seems to have taken the upper hand. That, plus I don't eat anything that isn't driven to my door or doesn't fit in a microwave. I also sleep over ten hours a day. Depression and self-medication are just bad for the waistline. But I'll be burning some calories tonight. The x will see to that.

It's just before six. The guy's flight gets in at a quarter to seven. I strip to my underwear and start tearing open the shopping bags, leaving ripped paper, tabs of sticky tape, and pins from the folded shirts scattered on the living room floor along with my dirty clothes. The jeans are stiff, but I can do the buttons without having to suck my belly into my spine. The shirts are all long-sleeve white button-ups. All my shirts are long-sleeved to cover the tattoos on my arms. The tattoos are some of the identifying features that predate, and survived, my surgery. There's also a lurid scar that bisects my left side, the remnant of a hole that one of my kidneys came out of. I fasten the buttons of the shirt with jittery fingers and then have to undo and redo them because I've done them crooked. I dump the shoes out of their box and that's when I realize we didn't buy any black socks. All my socks are white athletics. The only thing left to me that's athletic. Fuck it. I slip the shoes over my tube socks. The jacket is in a cheap plastic garment bag. I toss the bag on the floor with the rest of the trash and pull on the jacket. It fits fine in the shoulders and sleeves, but I can't button it without stretching the buttonholes. Whatever, I'll wear it open. A belt. I go back to the bedroom and find my only belt; black leather with a plain silver buckle and a couple extra notches I had to cut into it with a steak knife. I thread it through the loops and buckle it at the last of those homemade notches.

I gather my money, keys, cell, wallet with fake ID; the latest in a chain of fake identities that string back to New York, and I look at the gun. No. I slip the gun under one of the couch cushions and go to the bathroom.

I pull out the Ziploc full of ups, find the bottle of x and shake one into my hand. Then another. For later. In case it's a late night. Late night? Shit, a kid with money, this is gonna be an all-nighter. I shake two more into my hand. That leaves two in the bottle. Hell with it. I dump all but one back in the bottle, pop that one in my mouth, and drop the bottle in my left jacket pocket. For emergencies.

I look at the shattered mirror.

I wonder how I look.

I pick at a corner of the tape. Think about jagged glass reflecting blood as it cuts the skin. I smooth the tape into place, turn off the light and walk into the kitchenette. I turn on the overhead light and look at myself in the microwave door; a smeary, warped reflection in dark glass. I touch my face. Shave? No. Branko said I should look tough. Stubble is tough. I guess.

AT THE AIRPORT I stand with the livery drivers near the exits from the baggage claim area. I watch the crowds of weekenders jostling around the huge silver carousels, getting bombarded by the advertising throbbing from the massive digital screens hanging from the ceiling. I feel edgy and exposed. Standing here in my brand-new clothes, the package creases still in my unironed shirt, I feel like I'm posed on a pedestal, like every eye is gawking at me. They're not. To the rubes I'm just another driver in black, wearing his sunglasses inside and holding a sign with the name of some lucky stiff written on it. But I feel naked. Just like anyone wanted by the FBI and several police agencies for multiple homicides should feel.

Fuck, maybe there's too much speed in this x. Maybe that second hit was a bad idea.

—Arenas?

Or maybe I should do another one.

—Arenas?

Maybe I could cope better if I was just a little higher.

—Yo, man, Arenas?

—What?

I look at the guy in front of me. He's very young, my height, maybe a touch taller, with wide shoulders; built under the black DKNY suit and Ratpack-style open-collar shirt.

—Arenas?

—What?

He points at the sign in my hand, the name I wrote with a Sharpie on the back of one of the shirt cardboards.

—You here for Arenas?

—Yeah.

He points at himself.

—That's me. Miguel Arenas.

—Oh. Sorry, Mr. Arenas.

He puts out his hand.

—Mike. Call me Mike.

I take his hand. It's even bigger than mine, his wrists are thick with muscle.

I take my hand back, fold the sign in half and point at the doors.

—Right out here.

—Hang on a sec. There's some baggage.

I take a step toward the carousels.

—Would you like me to?

He puts up a hand.

—No, s'cool, it's coming along.

—Yo! Dude! Checking bags sucks!

He has a friend. His friend is maybe five-six on a good day, but also built under his black DKNY suit. He's passed on the Sinatra look and gone with a Hawaiian shirt, throwback Air Jordans, and a San Diego Padres sun-visor on top of his head. He's dragging a massive Nike athletic bag stuffed to bursting, the zipper popping teeth. He walks up to us and drops the bag.

He looks at me.

—This the bodyguard?

Miguel nods.

—Yeah.

—Sweet.

Miguel points at his friend.

—This is Jay.

Jay spreads the index and middle fingers of his right hand.

—Peace, yo.

Neither of them is twenty-five. Neither of them is twenty-three, for God sake. I point at the door.

—The car.

Jay bounces.

—Shee-at! The car!

He heads for the door. I pick up his bag and gesture for Miguel to go ahead of me. Out on the curb Jay is leaning against a white limo. He spreads his hands in Miguel's direction.

—I don't know, yo. It's classic, but on the tritish side don't ya think?

I walk past him to the Olds, pop the trunk and dump his bag inside. He spreads his hands wider.

—No. Way. Oh. Man. That. Car. Sucks.

He pumps a fist.

—Sweet.

I close the trunk. Jay runs his hand along the hood.

—Oh, man. This is some shit.

I open the passenger door and fold the seat back. Jay laughs.

—Dude. It's not even a sedan. This is hot.

Jay piles in. Miguel smoothly bends himself in beside him.

Miguel looks familiar. Not his face so much. His build. The way he moves. Something.

I walk around the car, climb in and start the engine.

—Where to, gentlemen?

Miguel puts a hand on my shoulder. I flinch. He takes his hand away.

—Let's hit Caesar's sports book first.

It's getting a little dark. I slip my shades off and turn my head to check my blind spot before pulling from the curb. Jay points at my face.

—Dude! Scarface! I mean total fucking Scarface.

FINGER FUCKER THROWS a haymaker at me. I lean back out of the way. Behind me, Uncle Fester is still taunting Miguel, trying to get him to take a swing. In the gutter, Jay is rolling around with Prince Valiant. Our only audience is the three guys doing blow by the back door of the Rhino, but that'll change if this isn't over soon.

The job is to keep the kid out of trouble.

Screwed that up.

Finger Fucker squares up to take another poke at me.

AT CAESAR'S SPORTS book, Miguel looks over the late West Coast games and starts to head for the windows. Jay grabs his arm.

—Yo.

Miguel taps his own forehead.

—Yeah, yo. Sorry.

He goes in his pocket, comes out with a rubber-banded roll of hundreds, and hands it to Jay.

—Uh, get me five on Oakland. A G on St. Louis and the over. And . . .

—That's plenty, yo.

—No, no. And, you'll like this, and five on the Pods, money line.

—That's a weak bet.

Miguel flicks Jay's Padres visor.

—Yeah, but you like it.

—Fuck you.

Jay walks to the window with Miguel's money and lays the bets. He comes back, hands Miguel the cash, but keeps the slips.

—What now, yo?

—Craps.

—OK, yo, I'll meet you there. Gonna see about some refreshments. Scarface, keep an eye on him.

MIGUEL LIKES CRAPS. A lot.

He fans twenty hundreds on the green felt and the croupier counts it and slides him his chips. He starts tossing them out and calling his bets. Jay comes back from his detour carrying a couple Cuba Libres. Miguel takes one.

—What took you so long?

—Yo. I was sweating this chick. She's gonna be at Cleopatra's Barge later with some friends. We should check that shit out.

Miguel takes a sip of his drink and nods.

—S'cool. Later.

Jay notices me.

—Scarface, yo, sorry, man. I didn't bring you a beverage. You want something?

I'm standing a couple feet behind them, trying to look inconspicuous and tough at the same time.

—No, thanks.

—No sweat, man, you want something, it's cool by us.

He nudges Miguel.

—Right, yo?

Miguel looks from the table to me.

—Sure, man, s'cool, whatever's good for you is fine.

I try to look like I'm calculating threat vectors or something badass and shake my head.

—No, thank you.

Jay clinks his glass against Miguel's.

—Scarface on the job, yo. Scarface lookin' out.

Miguel smiles.

—Quit fuckin' with him, man.

Jay spreads the fingers of one hand over his chest.

—Fuckin' with him? Yo, I got nothing but respect. 'Sides, Scarface don't mind me callin' him Scarface. Do ya, Scarface?

The x has settled down some and I'm feeling loose in my spine, perfectly balanced and relaxed. I could stand here all night just like this and be utterly comfortable. Do I mind him calling me Scarface? Hell, he could cut a couple new ones in my face and I wouldn't care just now.

—No, I don't care.

—See, he's cool. Scarface's mellow.

Miguel points at Jay.

—S'cool, man, you can tell him he's an asshole if you want.

Jay's jaw drops.

—Cold, man, that's cold.

I shake my head.

—It's OK, I'm fine.

—OK, but you don't have to take his shit.

—Harsh, yo.

Miguel smiles and turns back to the action on the table. Jay winks at me and gives me a thumbs up.

—Don't let no one fuck with my boy, yo.

—No problem.

Miguel cuts some chips from his stack and offers them to Jay.

—You gonna play, or you gonna fuck around?

Jay looks at the chips, takes them.

—Yo, I'm gonna play. Last hurrah. Got to play.

I look at the clock on my cell: 8:33 p.m.

By 10:00 p.m., they've maxed out the cash draw on Miguel's bank card.

He tosses his last black chip to the croupier.

—For the table, man.

The croupier tilts his head at him and drops the chip in the tip box. Jay sucks down the last of his fifth Cuba Libre and sets the glass on a passing cocktail waitress's tray. The tray tilts off balance and she has to do a sudden shuffle step to keep from dumping the whole thing. She gives Jay a nasty look and keeps walking.

—Baby, yo, I didn't mean it. Don't be that way. Don't be cruel. I love you.

She doesn't look back, but he watches the ass she has just barely hidden beneath a minidress-toga as it twitches away. He looks at Miguel.

—Cleopatra's Barge, yo.

Miguel drains the last of *his* fifth Cuba Libre and shakes his head.

—Palms.

THE ATM CARD was the tip of the iceberg.

At the Palms Miguel passes a black AmEx to the girl in the cage and says he'd like to open a line of credit. Before the vibrations of his words have left the air, a manager materializes from a trapdoor somewhere. He supplies Miguel and Jay with a bottle of Cristal, offers a comp room, passes to Rain a thick stack of meal tickets, and processes Miguel's two-hundred-thousand-dollar line of credit.

—You may, of course, extend it if you wish.

Miguel shakes the manager's hand.

—No, man, s'cool.

—Well, let me just say how happy we are to have you here. And congratulations, of course.

Miguel bobs his head; humble as all hell.

—Yeah, thanks, man.

I follow him and Jay into the casino, wondering what the fuck the manager was congratulating him for.

FINGER FUCKER SWINGS and I lean out of the way. I almost fall down because I'm so buzzed on x, and so fat and slow. But I keep my feet and watch as the momentum of his punch spins him around. I shove the back of his right shoulder as he rotates past me and use my right foot to scoop his off the ground and he goes down face-first and I hear a little crunch that might be his front teeth biting into the tarmac. I turn around and there's Uncle Fester, still in Miguel's face, wagging his head back and forth and bugging his eyes.

—What ya gonna do 'bout it? Gonna show me somethin', big man? I'm right here. I'm right here.

JAY WANTS TO go to Rain.

The line for the place snakes around the casino, circling the wall. A purgatorial conga line of twenty and thirty-somethings dressed in every possible interpretation of hip and cool, desperate to get inside the hottest club in Vegas. Miguel eyes the line and shakes his head.

—Uh-uh. Veto.

Jay protests.

—Yo, we got passes. All we got to do is cruise to the VIP entrance. Come on, yo.

He points at the line, singling out the girls sporting the most conspicuous absences of clothing.

—Bang! Bang! Bang! Can you imagine the talent that's inside? The shit they don't make wait in line?

Miguel takes the rate card the manager gave him from his pocket.

—Two hundred G's. Tonight's the night. Tonight we play big.

He holds out his glass of Cristal.

—Last hurrah.

Jay taps Miguel's glass with his own.

—My bad, yo. Let's gamble.

Miguel snaps a corner of the card.

—Let's get our drink on and let's gamble.

—It's on. It is on!

They drain their glasses and make for the tables. I trail behind, starting to get the idea that Miguel might be a new-money kind of guy.

MIGUEL STANDS AT least a half foot taller than Uncle Fester and is obviously in much better shape, but he keeps his open hands up at shoulder level and takes another step back, trying to create space between them.

—Just take it easy, man. S'cool. Nobody wants any trouble here.

Fester takes another step toward Miguel and gives him another chest bump.

—Looks like trouble's here, big man. What ya gonna do 'bout it? Gonna puss out on it, big man? Fucking showboat. Gonna puss?

I put my foot in his asshole. He squeals, lurches forward, and Miguel skips back out of the way.

I'VE NEVER SEEN two guys happier about being down a hundred grand. I watch Miguel lay two thousand on a hard six.

Jay snaps his fingers.

—Yo. That's a bet. That bet is coming in.

The dice come up craps and Miguel and Jay laugh and high-five.

—That was a for real bet, yo. Right, baby?

Jay's talking to the girl wearing the silver lamé bikini top and short red sarong, the girl glued to his left hip. He culled her from the Rain line a little while ago.

I saw him walking the line, flashing his club pass and asking who wanted to get in right now. Lots of hands went up and he drew a little crowd of spectators as he got the guys waiting in line to applause-o-meter each girl and pick the winners. He got three girls out of line and brought them over and dangled them baitwise in front of Miguel.

—Yo, let's lay off and go dance.

Miguel waved him off and kept rolling. At first the girls were pissed about losing their places in line and not being taken to the club, but then they saw the money flying and got friendly. Miguel's been friendly with the girls, throwing his arms around whichever one is near when he hits on a big bet, but they're clearly a sidebar to the dice.

Jay shoves one of them my way. She tries to chat with me, tells me she's an elementary schoolteacher from Flagstaff and *God! Does she need to blow off some steam.* I tell her I'm working and she goes back over to Jay. He whispers something in her ear. I see his lips mouth *Scarface.*

I look over the little crowd that's gathered at the tables. A few are playing, but most have been drawn by the big-spender show Miguel and Jay are putting on. A couple of beefy guys in baggy business suits are standing by the head of the table, Coors Lights in their hands, whispering to each other, pointing at Miguel, pointing at me. Sweat beads between my shoulder blades.

Are they planning to follow us out and rob Miguel? Are they sizing him up for a fight because they think he's a show-off? Or are they talking about him at all? Maybe they're talking about me. Maybe they're big true crime fans and they never miss an *Unsolved Mysteries* or *America's Most Wanted.* Maybe they're looking through the botched face job, the crew cut, the sunglasses. Maybe they see *me*.

They start walking around the table toward us.

If they confront me, if they try to finger me, I'll just laugh it off: *Am I who? Oh, not again. I get that all the time.*

They're around the table. Miguel has the dice now, holding them above his head, one in each hand, showing them to the crowd. The croupier is asking him to please lower the dice, but he's smiling. He's smiling, the pit boss is smiling, somewhere the manager is smiling. Miguel has dumped a hundred G's on this one table and no one who works this place is gonna stop smiling at him until they wring out whatever he has left in him.

The business suits are coming toward me. One is holding his beer bottle down at his side. It'll be easy for him to flip it and bring it up at my face. They're both rumpled and have their collars open and ties tugged down. They look exactly like a pair of early twenties business guys. Pals who knocked off early from their cubicle brokerage gig in L.A. and hopped the flight to Vegas for an overnighter. They look as inconspicuous as Branko.

They stop right in front of me. The one holding his bottle starts to bring it up. His buddy turns his head, looking at the crowd around us. All eyes are on Miguel, who has just rolled a four. The beer bottle moves higher. I take a step back and get ready to kick the guy in the balls. Why did I leave the gun at home?

The beer bottle is up. It goes to the guy's lips and he takes a drink.

—Uh, hey, man?

His buddy is still looking at Miguel, who has just made the point.

—Um, we don't want to bother anybody, but we were wondering.

The girls squeal as Miguel hits another point. The other guy is still watching.

—Would it be cool if we said hi to him?

The other one turns his face to me.

—Maybe get an autograph?

Uh.

The guy with the bottle holds up his hands.

—Like, we know you have a job to do and he's just hanging out. But? After he's done rolling?

I look past them to Miguel. He craps out. I look back at the guy.

—I guess I'd.

—Great, man. Thanks. We won't be a pain.

They don't wait for me to finish saying that I guess I'd have to ask, they just walk up behind Miguel and tap him shyly on the shoulder.

—Hey, hey. Sorry to bother you, Mike. We just. *Man*. Congratulations. And thanks for last year.

—You're not bothering me, man. S'cool. And thanks.

—Yeah, yeah. Hey, any chance we could get a couple autographs?

—Sure. S'cool.

Miguel grabs a couple cocktail napkins from the waitress who's been standing by to take his and Jay's orders, pulls a pen from inside his jacket and scribbles his name.

—Man, thanks. You're the coolest, man. Good luck this year.

Miguel shakes both their hands.

—Thanks, guys.

And the floodgates open. The crowd flows, its center point shifting from the table to Miguel. And I suddenly realize that all the whispering and pointing at the table hasn't been about Miguel's money or Jay's antics, it's been about Miguel.

I start moving into the crowd and I hear voices. I hear *MVP*. I hear *first round*. I hear *6 million*. I hear *gold medal*.

Jay's face pops up in front of me. He's got the three girls from the Rain line.

—Scarface, yo. Grab my boy. We're moving this party to the Spearmint Rhino.

And he's plowing his way out, towing the girls.

I put a hand on Miguel's shoulder. He turns from signing another autograph.

—Jay said I should get you out.

He nods.

—Yeah. S'cool, let's blow before it gets uncool.

Someone produces a disposable camera and I turn my head at the last second to avoid having my face photographed alongside Miguel's. I put my left arm over his shoulder, start making room with my right, and lead him out of the crowd. We dodge a couple people coming over to see what's up and Miguel picks up his pace, striding toward the exit. Behind us I hear a few people chanting *USA! USA! USA!* And the dots connect.

I don't have a TV, but I do pick up a paper sometimes. Miguel Arenas. Star of Stanford's 2003 College World Series–winning baseball team. Miguel Arenas. Star of the USA's 2004 Olympic gold medal–winning baseball team. Miguel Arenas. Out of school at the end of his junior year, the New York Mets' first round pick in this year's Major League draft. First pick overall. Number one.

I watch Miguel's back as he weaves smoothly through the packed casino. And now I know what's familiar about him. It's not his face or his accomplishments that I know him from. It's his walk, his grace. He moves like me. The way I was meant to move. The way I still move in my dreams. The good ones anyway.

I FOLLOW UNCLE Fester as he stumbles away and kick him in the asshole again. He screams and reaches back, but my next kick is already on the way. It lands on his fingers and his pinkie pops out of joint. He's reeling around now, reaching down between his legs with one hand, grabbing at his anus, and waving the other hand in the air, his pinkie sticking out at a right angle to the rest of his fingers. I grab the tail of his T-shirt and yank it up, dragging his arms up over his head. I push him to his knees and kick him three more times on the asshole and he flops forward, crying, blood starting to seep through the seat of his pants.

WE'RE ROLLING IN the Olds, cruising from the Palms to the Rhino. From the frying pan to the fire, Vegas style.

Miguel is up front with me. One of the girls, I think it's the schoolteacher, in his lap. Her legs are getting tangled in the stick shift and I keep having to push them to the side. It happens again and she takes her tongue out of Miguel's mouth.

—Sorry. Am I in your way? Sorry. Here.

She wiggles around until she's straddling Miguel's lap. He takes advantage of having his mouth free for a second and has a word with Jay.

—Screw the Rhino, let's hit some more tables.

Jay is in the backseat with the other two girls. He's been mak-

ing out with both and talked them into kissing each other, but he
was disappointed by the little peck on the lips they shared.

—No, yo. Like, kiss. Let's see it, get some tongue in there.

The girls start frenching.

Miguel slaps Jay's knee.

—Hear me, man?

Jay keeps his eyes on the girls as their tongues slide in and out
of each other's mouths.

—I hear you, yo, but I'm a little distracted.

The schoolteacher is chewing on Miguel's ear as he talks to Jay.

—Get undistracted. I want to roll some more.

Jay takes his eyes from the show and puts his face close to Miguel's.

—Yo, that was a hundred G's and change back there. Let's take a
break.

—Fuck the hundred G's. Last hurrah, man. Got another hundred
to get even with. I want to roll.

Jay puts a finger in his face.

—No. We're taking a break. Yo.

He points at the necking girls.

—Check this shit out. Get into this shit. Get your head in *this*
game, yo.

Miguel nods.

—Yeah, yeah, man. S'cool. You're right.

—Yo.

Jay claps his hands.

—I know what this party needs. This party needs some x. You
ladies know where we can score some x?

The schoolteacher in Miguel's lap detaches her mouth from
his ear.

—I'm from Flagstaff. But if you can get some that would be great.

Jay separates the girls in the back.

—Ladies?

They whisper in each other's ears, then the one in the silver top gives him their verdict.

—No, but we'll totally take it if you can get it. But don't think you're going to get us in a three-way.

—Yo. A three-way? What's that?

She laughs.

Jay's eyes go wide with innocence.

—No, seriously. What's a three-way?

He puts his face close to hers.

—*Explain* it to me.

She laughs.

—*Nooo*.

—Come on, baby. Here.

He taps his earlobe.

—Whisper it in my ear.

She puts her mouth close to his ear and starts to whisper. Jay puts his hand over his mouth.

—Oh my. You girls are naughty. Yo, Mike, these girls are naughty. We *got* to get these girls some x.

He leans forward.

—So, yo, Scarface. Know where we could score a little sumthin' sumthin'?

Do I know where they could score?

I reach into my jacket pocket and touch the unmarked brown pill bottle that contains exactly five white tablets imprinted with tiny smiling monkey faces. I wonder, will this qualify for keeping them out of trouble or getting them into trouble?

Fuck it. It'll be better than having them running around the Rhino trying to score off the strippers. I pull out the pill bottle and hand it to Jay.

There is a moment of utter silence. Then Jay grabs my neck, leans over my shoulder and kisses my cheek.

—Yo, Scarface!

And he leads the chant that fills the car.

—Scar-face! Scar-face! Scar-face!

JAY AND VALIANT are still at it. I walk toward them, looking at the ground for a weapon so I don't have to punch the guy and risk breaking my hand. I see a magazine. I pick it up and roll it into a tight cylinder and stand over the two writhing bodies. I take aim and slam the magazine across the back of Valiant's head. He goes cross-eyed and I grab him by the collar and drag him off of Jay. I hit him a few more times, the magazine cracking his cheekbone before I drop him.

WEDNESDAY NIGHT AT the Spearmint Rhino and the place is a zoo.

Jumping the line is easy, just a matter of a couple C-notes for the guys at the door, but it makes me even more of a hero to Miguel, Jay and the Rain girls. Once inside, the trick becomes moving. The only open space is around the huge rectangular bar. I make a stop there and get a thousand dollars in dance tokens and hand them to the guys. Miguel starts shaking his head, but I force them into his hand.

—It's part of the service.

Jay is doling out tokens to the girls.

—Yeah, yo, it's part of the service.

I order Cuba Libres for the boys and Stoli cranberries for the girls. There are booths along the wall where strippers are giving lap dances. The real action is in the other direction, but the crowd around the stages and tables is so thick that the only way you can see the dancers is by looking at the video monitors above the bar. Jay points at the crowd.

—Yo, Scarface. We want in.

So I get them in. It costs another couple hundred, but one of the bouncers plows into the crowd and comes back a couple minutes later and waves us to a table. The group he just kicked off of it stands to the side and gives us dirty looks.

The atmosphere is a touch less formal here than at the Palms. In less than half an hour I notice people starting to notice Miguel. Soon after they start coming by the table to shake his hand. He takes it in stride, and I try to look intimidating to anyone who might want to cause trouble. In the normal course of events, an MLB draft pick, even the first pick, would only be recognized by the most rabid seamheads. But Miguel is different. His achievements during last year's Olympics gave him unprecedented visibility for an amateur player. He's not superstar recognizable, and mostly it's the men who know who he is, but he still draws traffic. I keep my sunglasses on.

At first Miguel keeps pestering Jay about heading for another casino.

—There aren't even slots in here, man!

But eventually Jay pours enough booze down Miguel's throat, and he sees enough tits, that he gets into the spirit of the place.

Jay gets lap dances. Miguel gets lap dances. The Rain girls get lap dances. Jay pays the dancers to lap dance each other. Glasses pile on the table.

Hours pass like that.

Then Jay says something.

—Is that guy fingering that chick?

It's one of the guys who got kicked off our table. It's very, very late and he and his buddies have gotten a new table right next to ours. Jay is pointing at the guy.

—Seriously, yo. Is he finger-fucking that chick?

What the guy is doing is definitely spending a lot of time trying to get his fingers inside the dancer's g-string. The current song is almost over, his special moment drawing to a close, so she just keeps pulling his hand away. But then the song ends and she goes to get up and he grabs her wrist and holds out a fifty.

—Uh-uh, baby. One more dance. Come on, baby.

She cranes her head, looking for a bouncer, but the only one nearby is chatting up another dancer and not paying attention, not enforcing the no-touching-the-dancers-ever rule. She points a long fingernail at Finger Fucker.

—OK, one more, honey. But be nice. No touching.

—Yeah, yeah. No touching.

She starts writhing on his lap and he winks at his buddies over her shoulder and stuffs his finger into her G-string, yanking it to the side and almost ripping it off. She jumps back.

—That's it, asshole.

She makes a move toward the bouncer and Finger Fucker grabs her again.

—No way, baby. I still got some song left.

His buddies are laughing. One of them looks like Uncle Fester's long-lost son. The other has a perfect Prince Valiant haircut.

The dancer is still trying to get away, calling for the bouncer, who looks like he might finally have noticed a customer getting out of hand.

—Hey, mister.

It's Miguel.

—Lay off.

Finger Fucker looks over.

—Wha'd you say?

—Said lay off the talent, guy. Let the lady go.

Jay stands up.

—And stop trying to stick your fingers up her action.

—Say what?

Finger Fucker lets go of the dancer's wrist and stands up and the bouncer and three of his cohorts pile into him and his buddies and wrap them up and drag them toward the front door. They go out, shouting back at us, Uncle Fester pointing at Miguel.

—Fucking asshole. Fucking big shot. Fucking take our table. You ain't shit. Mets suck!

They get stuffed out the front door.

Everybody still in the place is looking at us now. Talking about what happened.

The bouncer who got us the table is coming over.

—You guys cool?

I nod.

—Yeah, but we need to split. Can we use the back door?

He points toward the bathrooms. Miguel and Jay are already up and moving. The girls are gathering their things to follow us. I pull out a C and hand it to the schoolteacher.

—Party's over ladies. You can get a cab out front.

The girls don't like it, but they take the cab fare.

The bouncer leads us past the bathrooms, out to the rear parking lot. The Olds is about thirty yards away. Three guys are standing in a circle, taking turns dipping their keys into a little bag of coke. They ignore us as we walk past.

—Hey, big man.

Fuck.

—Hey, Mr. Baseball.

Fuck me running.

They're coming around the side of the club, on a path to cut us off. I put a hand to Miguel's back, then Jay's.

—Just walk to the car. Don't say anything.

—Big shot. Fucking table stealer.

Uncle Fester is doing the talking, but Finger Fucker is the first one to arrive. I stop and turn to face him and he puts his hands up.

—Oh, the bodyguard. I'm scared.

Valiant starts sprinting and moves to cut in front of us. I see him put a hand on Miguel. Jay jumps, lands on Valiant's back and takes him to the ground. They start rolling around, grappling. Fester plants himself in front of Miguel. Finger Fucker starts hopping around, his fists up just like he was taught in his boxing class at his gym.

I hate the Spearmint Rhino.

JAY SPRINGS UP from the gutter, a rip in the right knee of his suit pants and a scrape on his chin. He points at me.

—Yo, Scarface fucked 'em *up*.

Miguel is looking at the three men on the ground.

—Should we call someone?

I shake my head.

—The doormen at the club will call someone. Let's get out of here.

Jay grabs Miguel and starts dragging him toward the car.

—Hell yeah, yo. You don't need this kind of shit on you now.

I lead them to the car, looking back over my shoulder to make sure no one is coming after us. The guys who were standing out back doing blow are starting to walk toward the three assholes on the ground, asking if they're alright. None of them are answering.

MIGUEL WANTS TO go back to the Palms and hit the tables again, but Jay shows him his watch. It's almost 6:00 a.m.

—Flight's in a couple hours, yo. Time to chill.

—Man, we still got a hundred Gs credit at the Palms.

—So, that's like going home up. Put that shit on your hip, yo.

Miguel shakes his head like a little boy being told it's time to come in and get ready for bed.

—Yeah, OK, man. But this sucks.

He rolls down his window and leans his head into the hot breeze.

—You're right, but it sucks.

SPORTSCENTER PLAYS ON the main screen in the empty Caesar's sports book. Miguel and Jay watch the highlights while they fill out dozens of keno tickets. They've commandeered one of the few cocktail waitresses on the shift. She shuttles back and forth between them and the keno lounge, dropping their slips off and bringing them fresh drinks.

Jay points at the screen.

—Yo, here it is again.

Miguel and I look up and watch Sean Watson make a sliding, run-saving catch. Miguel goes back to his keno slips. Jay shakes his head.

—Fucking Watson.

Miguel sips his Cuba Libre.

—He's a stud.

—Yo, he's a stud. Fucker's looking to build permanent housing in center field.

—S'cool. I ain't in a hurry.

They have the same conversation every time the highlight comes on, and it's been on a lot. I didn't even know who the guy was, but it turns out Sean Watson is the Mets' Gold Glove center fielder. The same position Miguel plays.

—Long as he's there they can keep you down, yo.

—S'cool. I'm just starting. There's shit to learn. Gotta hit that big league curve.

Jay looks down from the screen and at his friend.

—Bullshit, you can hit the curve. You *are* big league, yo. You are ready.

In the last hour I've seen more baseball than in the last five years. It's strange, kind of like the dreams I sometimes have about people I've killed. Seeing the dead walk again. But this is different. For the first time I can remember, I'm watching baseball and it doesn't make me want to curl up in a ball and feel sorry for myself. Must be the x. Whatever it is, I like it.

—Yo, Scarface, my boy ready for the bigs or what?

Is Miguel big league ready? No one is big league ready straight out of college. No one. Everyone spends a few years in the minors. Rookie ball, single A, double A, triple A. Even a top pick like Miguel? It'll be a major achievement if he ends the season in double A. Hell, *I* would have had to spend a few years in the minors. Of course, I was going to go in straight from high school. If I had played in college, I might have been ready to hit big league stuff. Sure I would have. I was practicing with a wood bat every day. I was born big league.

—Scarface?

I come back to earth. Big league? I was never even bush league. Just a hotshot high school jock.

—Scarface?

—Sorry. What?

—My boy ready or what?

—Sorry, man, I don't really know anything about baseball.

Jay slumps back in his seat.

—Oh damn, just when I was thinking you might be the man. Mike, Scarface doesn't like baseball.

Miguel fills out another keno slip.

—S'cool. He's got other virtues.

He looks up from his slip, smiles at me.

—Like keepin' my ass out of trouble. That was good lookin' out back at the club. I don't like to see no one get hurt, but that was good lookin' out. Man can feel safe with a dude like you watchin' his back. No lie.

—Thanks.

—When I get up there, when they move me to The Show, gonna be lookin' for you. I'll give a call. You can be my man maybe.

—Sure. Maybe.

I point at the screen.

—Shouldn't you be playing now?

Miguel shakes his head.

—Had the College World Series. We just got knocked out last weekend.

Jay snorts.

—Yo, that was bogus. Texas sucks. And the ump was fucking blind.

—S'cool.

—Yeah. Anyway, yo, that shit's behind you now. Now's the real deal.

Jay winks at me.

—Anyway, that ain't the real reason why Mike hasn't reported yet. Real reason's business. Gettin' paid business.

Miguel smiles. His teeth are perfect.

—Man's got to get paid.

He clinks glasses with Jay.

—Anyway, contract took a little while to sort out. But it's on now. Kingsport tomorrow. Pro ball.

Jay shakes his head.

—Fuckin' rookie ball.

—S'cool. Everyone starts in rookie. I'll get up there.

He watches the players on the screen; spectacularly gifted young men making their bodies do things that no one else can do.

I look at him. His plane takes off at eight. He'll touch down on the East Coast around three in the afternoon and report for his first day of professional baseball. Young and fit, relaxed and smooth, just the slightest of rings under his eyes to say that he's done anything but get a good night's rest.

The cocktail waitress comes by with another round and picks up another stack of keno tickets. The drink in front of Jay is still all but full. He slides the new cocktail over to me.

—So can you have a drink now, yo?

I look at the glass.

—I don't drink.

He shakes his head sadly.

—Damn. Doesn't like baseball. Doesn't drink. That is some sad shit. Wasn't for that car and the way you were all MacGyver with the x, I don't know what I'd do with you.

Miguel leans back in his chair and yawns.

—And that ass-kicking he delivered.

—Oh, yo, that was intense. You laid some hurt on those assholes. Check it. What's the most fucked-up thing you've ever done to someone?

A short film starring all the fucked-up things I've done screens inside my head.

Miguel puts a hand on Jay's arm.

—Lay off. Man's a professional.

—But I want to know.

I shrug.

—Nothing too bad.

Jay squints one eye at me.

—See, yo, I expect that to be your answer, but I bet you've done some seriously fucked-up shit. Like, where'd you get the scar?

Miguel gives him a little shove.

—Cool it, bro.

I touch the scar, remember a guy no older than Jay, remember sitting on top of him while scalding water pounded down on both of us, remember pushing the barrel of his own gun into his mouth, and pulling the trigger.

—It was in an accident. No big deal.

Jay holds up his hands in surrender.

—That's cool. I'll back off. You got your secrets. I won't push. But next time we come to town I want some stories, yo. I want to hear the gangsta shit.

He lays out his hand. I slap it lightly. He nods.

—That's what I'm talking 'bout, yo.

A half hour later I drive them to the airport. I offer to stick with them until they board, but Miguel says it's cool. Jay grabs a baggage cart, drops his enormous bag in it, climbs on top of it and curls up.

—Yo, Mike, I'm finished. You're gonna have to push me.

Miguel flips him off and turns to me.

—So we cool? We owe you anything, or what?

I shake my head.

—All taken care of.

He nods.

—Cool. So.

He puts his hand out. I take it and we shake.

—On the real though, you took care of business tonight. I want to thank you. That shit had blown up? That would have been bad news. Last thing I needed would have been cops and reporters. So thanks.

He offers me his fist.

—Respect.

I bump my fist against his.

—Sure.

He flashes me a peace sign, and I watch him push the luggage cart, loaded with his friend and his friend's baggage, through the automatic doors.

At home I pop four ludes. And still I dream.

I dream about baseball.

And wake a few hours later, wanting things and people that are long dead.

mantracker45: sandy, there's a rumor that he's been in touch with you.

scandy: where you hear that mt???

bigdangle: sandy, i think ur hot.

scandy: TY big!!! you buy the calendar yet?

mantracker45: it was on danny lester's site.

bigdangle: my favorite shot in the clandar is the one with you kneeling on the chair and looking back over your shoulder. its HOT :)

scandy: I don't know what danny lester has on his site and I cant really talk about him because of my lawsuit but i have not been in touch with him and ty again big, I like that shot 2.

mantracker45: you worry about him coming for you?

bigdangle: what u wearing sandy?

scandy: I used to worry, but i cant live mny life like that. I cant live in fear. thats what my therapist says

bigdangle: what ru wearing sandy??

scandy: sweats and a tanktop, big. but come see me dance some time and i'll be wearing the stuff I feel most comfortable in. n othing ;)

manwhogotaway29: hello sandy

bigdangle: im not wearing anything. i'm alone with my big cock and your calendar and I'm thinking about fucking you in the ass. do you like it in the ass?

USER BIGDANGLE HAS BEEN BOUNCED
FROM THE SITE

mantracker45: what a dick.

scandy: hi manwho

scandy: yeah, mt, what girl wants a big "dangle" anyway.

mantracker45: lol.

manwhogotaway29: it's me sandy.

scandy: who do you mean manwho?

mantracker45: just bounce him, sandy.

manwhogotaway29: remember the el cortez, snady? remember your house on jewel and what I did? remember what the dog did to your boyfriend's dick? I know where you are sandy.

**USER MANWHOGOTAWAY29 HAS BEEN
BOUNCED FROM THE SITE**

mantracker45: another dick. you ok sandy?

scandy: i'm fine.

mantracker45: is it the same guy?

scandy: I think so. I bounce him and a couple weeks later he reregisters as manwhogotaway67 or something.

mantracker45: he scare you?

scandy: not any more.

mantracker45: i could take care of you sandy.

scandy: ty mt. that's sweet.

mantracker45: i could strap you to a fence and cut your nipples off and saw your head open and put your brain in a bag. I could take care of you good WHORE!!!

**USER MANTRACKER45 HAS BEEN BOUNCED
FROM THE SITE**

USER SCANDY HAS SIGNED OFF

Pretty standard stuff for one of Sandy's chat sessions.

I watch the empty screen for a couple minutes to see if she'll come back on, but she doesn't. I click the sign-off button and **billybob44** disappears from the list of signed-on users. My screen name hung up there all through the chat along with a couple others, never popping up in the main window with a message for Sandy. Just another heavy-breathing scroller, eavesdropping on the chat, but never participating.

It's the middle of the afternoon and I still haven't been able to get back to sleep. I think about going to Danny Lester's site and checking on this rumor that I've been in touch with Sandy, but I just turn off the computer instead. Why bother? It will be like every other lie on Lester's site, just juicy enough to bump up his hits for awhile and keep his advertisers happy. Besides, I have to take about five Xanax to be able to look at Lester's site. The home page centered on my FBI wanted poster; his account of how he "flushed me from cover"; his bullshit memorials page to my victims. Thinking about it gives me hives.

Of course. Thinking about Lester makes me want to climb on a plane, fly to his home, and wrap my hands around his throat. No reason why I should feel that way; other than the fact that he's the one who let the world know I had come back to the States in the first place, the one who stalked me from San Diego to my hometown, the one who forced me to run from my parents, the one who plowed his truck into my childhood friend. No reason at all I should want to kill the asshole who has made it his mission in life to find me and "bring me to justice."

In any case, I'd never be stupid enough to actually join a chat.

But I think about it.

I've typed a couple messages before and placed my cursor over the private message button, but I've never clicked it. I've typed stuff only I could know.

> billybob44: sandy, it's me. remember "Place to Be" on the radio at the El Cortez?

> billybob44: sandy, where is T?

Where is the last friend I had in the world?

She would know. She would at least know where she left him before she found a lawyer and turned herself in. If she told me that, maybe I could find him. I could find him and maybe he would help me again and I would have a friend and someone I could trust.

I'm staring at the blank computer screen. Something is on my face. I touch it and my finger comes away wet. I'm crying. Fuck, when was the last time I cried? No, I'm not crying, I'm sobbing. I'm choking and gasping and moaning. I roll off the chair and start crawling down the hall, snot pouring out of my nose and drizzling on the carpet. I make it to the bathroom, get to my knees and reach over the sink and open the medicine cabinet. I clutch at the two Ziplocs and pull them out and one of them isn't sealed and plastic bottles and loose pills scatter across the scummy floor. I fumble around, still jerking and wailing, sobs like an epileptic fit, trying to collect the pills. I curl up on the floor, still wearing my new jeans and clean white shirt, and I dump pills into my hand. What are these? I don't even know. I shove a handful in my mouth, but they get caught at the back of my throat and the next sob chokes them back out and they spray the room and rattle off the shower stall door.

Fuck this.

I can't do this anymore.

I grab the towel bar and use it to pull myself to my feet. I stumble to the other side of the bathroom and clutch the edge of the sink with one hand while I rip black tape from the mirror with the other. Tiny flecks of glass rain down into the sink, but the larger pieces, the ones I need, remain lodged in the frame. My fractured reflection stutters across the face of the mirror. I pick at a scythe-curved shard, slicing the tips of my fingers. The blade of glass comes free and the entire mirror rains down into the basin. I let go of the sink and the sobs drop me to my knees. I fall back on my butt, one leg folded beneath me, the other splayed across a dingy bath mat. I bite the buttons from the left cuff of my shirt and tug the sleeve up with my teeth. On my forearm is a tattoo: six black slashes. Once an accurate accounting of the lives I had taken, but now hopelessly out of date. Blood from my fingers is already dripping from the tip of my mirror knife. I dig the point into my skin, blood wells around it. It's as if the little scrap of glass were made for this: A single hard yank and it will open my forearm from wrist to elbow. Then I can do the other one.

I yank.

But nothing happens.

I yank again. And still my hand doesn't move.

The sobs subside. I sit on the bathroom floor, staring at the blood reflected in the shard of mirror, just as I always pictured it, and I don't kill myself.

Who knew there was anything left I couldn't do.

————

I WAKE UP on the bathroom floor. The sun has gone down. Blood is clotted around the hole in my wrist. I stand up. I run water in the sink and splash my face. The pieces of broken mirror rest at the bottom of the sink, reflecting pieces of me. I walk out of the bathroom, pause in the hall to brush away pills that have stuck to the bottoms of my feet, and go into the kitchen. I find a package of Eggos and throw them in the microwave. A minute later the microwave dings. I take out the Eggos, the steam burning my cut fingertips when I open the plastic pouch, and dump them on the one plate I own. I get an old packet of McDonald's syrup from the fridge, pour it on the Eggos and eat them with my one fork. They'd be better toasted, but I don't have a toaster. When I'm done I wash my plate and fork. I go into the living room and turn on the stereo. "Boots of Spanish Leather" plays and I listen to it.

I look at the hole I poked in my wrist.

That was close. I was stupid and I got very close. It was the baseball. It was being around Miguel and Jay and their friendship. It was checking on Sandy and thinking about T. It was cramming too many different pills into my system at the same time.

I have to start doing my job again. No more choking in the clutch. David wants me to drop the big fuck you, I need to drop it. No more getting sent out on gigs like last night. Jobs like that make me think. I have to do my job and I have to do it clean. I have to remember. I have to remember I quit drinking because I couldn't control it. I can't use the pills to get by, I don't have the discipline. I have to start from scratch.

I have my own people to worry about. I have my mom and dad.

I keep fucking around and I may as well go find them and put the bullets in them myself.

The bullets myself.

I SPEND THE rest of the evening cleaning. I clean myself and I clean the shitty apartment. I clean the broken mirror out of the sink and I bandage my wrist. I go through the pills. I flush the Demerol and the OxyContin and the Quaaludes and the Lithium and the Xanax and the Percocet and the Darvocet and the Morphine and the Klonopin and the Librium and the Adderall and the Dexedrine and the Desoxyn. It's not the first time I've flushed an addiction down the toilet, but it needs to be the last.

By eleven the place looks half decent and I'm thinking about going to the twenty-four-hour supermarket to buy some real food for a change.

Then David calls and tells me that he wants me in New York.
—Branko is on his way to pick you up. It will be good for you. Almost a homecoming, yes?

After I hang up I go in the bathroom and stare at the toilet. I get as far as taking a wrench from my tool kit and turning off the water pressure, but I stop myself before I can unbolt the toilet from the floor and check the bends in the pipe for any pills that might have gotten stuck.

PART TWO

GAME ONE

—Henry.

That's me, that's my name. Henry Thompson.

—Henry.

But no one uses it anymore.

—Henry. You must tell me.

No one uses it because Henry Thompson is a man most everyone would like to see dead.

—Henry. How does it feel to be here?

But David is using it.

—Henry? To be home?

I don't answer. Because this is not my home. Not even close.

BRANKO PICKED ME up at the crappy apartment.

He comes in and sees the bandage on my wrist, but says nothing. He uses my bathroom and sees the broken mirror, but says nothing. He takes me out to his car and drives me to the airport. And finally he says something.

—You cleaned your apartment?

—Yeah.

—It was dirty?

—Branko, it was filthy.

—Yes, but it is always filthy.

—I got tired of it.

He points at the bandage on my wrist.

—You hurt yourself cleaning?

—Yeah.

He nods. William DeVaughn croons "Be Thankful for What You Got" on the Camry's CD player.

—You packed no contraband?

—You watched me pack.

—The security, it is very strict.

I haven't flown in the U.S. since 9/11 and Branko is worried that I left a toe clipper in my bag or something.

—There's nothing.

—Good. You need money?

—No.

The song plays. We turn off at the airport and Branko takes us down the departures lane.

—If they pull you out of line, it is nothing. Go with them. They will open your bag and ask you to take off your shoes. In case there is a bomb.

He grunts laughter at the ridiculousness of a shoe-bomb, knowing better places to hide explosives.

—I know.

—You will fly coach. First class I would have booked, but people, they walk past you and stare at your face. The people in coach, they hate the people in first class.

—No problem.

He starts to say something else. Changes his mind and pulls the car to the curb at the United gate. He puts the car in park.

—You need money?

—No. You asked.

—Yes.

He looks past me, through the car window and the glass doors, into the nearly empty terminal. It's just after midnight, Friday morning. A few people who were in town for midweek specials are taking a red-eye back east, but the real traffic will be coming into the airport around eight when the weekenders start to arrive.

—Branko.

He doesn't say anything.

—What's this about? Me in New York. That's.

He shakes his head.

—You have somewhere else you would go? Yes? No. Go to New York. Do as you are told.

—Yeah. Sure.

He fishes a credit card out of his breast pocket and hands it to me.

—At the automatic kiosk, you zip this. The ticket will appear. In the name on your driver's license. The card, you throw away.

—Right.

I open the door and climb out. Branko gets out as well and comes around the car to my side. He reaches into the backseat, grabs my bag and hands it to me.

He takes out his billfold and offers me a stack of cash.

—I have plenty left from the other day.

—Take it.

—Branko.

—Take the money.

—Sure. Thanks.

I take the money. He nods, puts his billfold away and walks back around the car. Before he gets in, he points at me.

—Do as you are told.

Then he gets in and drives off.

I walk through the automatic doors, find the ticket machine and swipe the card. I take my ticket to the security line and show it and my driver's license to a polite woman in a blue blazer. I shuffle through the short line and my baggage is X-rayed. No one asks to look inside. I board the plane and find my window seat. A middle-aged man sits on the aisle and when the door is sealed without anyone having claimed the seat between us he gives me a tired half smile, tilts his seat back and falls asleep. I stare out the window, watch the ground fall away, and try to remember what it was like the first time I flew to New York. Try to remember being very young and starting something new. But I can't. I look at the sleeping man. I could be sleeping. I could be chewing down a couple Ambiens and sleeping dreamless and long. Instead I grind my teeth and watch the bad movie with the other insomniacs who lost their shirts in Vegas.

THE PLANE BANKS and Manhattan appears outside the window.

Coming back here.

Coming back here makes me want a pill. But then again, so does breathing.

—How does it feel? Being back, how does it feel?

David's Brighton Beach office is the living room of an apartment above the Winter Garden Restaurant, right on the boardwalk. It's a strange corner turret. The exterior is corniced at the top, an old salmon pink building at the dead end of Brighton Street. El Marisol is spelled in black tiles outside the front door, harking back to some time before the Russian immigrants had taken over the neighborhood.

—It feels weird.

He comes over and stands next to me. He points out the window.

—You can see Coney Island.

I press my face close to the glass and look to my right. Far up the boardwalk, past the aquarium, I can see Deno's Wonder Wheel, the red-and-white pillar of the observation spire, and, further on, the tower of the abandoned parachute drop. Coney was one of the last places I saw before I ran away from here.

David taps the glass.

—They have a baseball team now.

—I heard something.

He puts a hand on my shoulder and steers me away from the window.

—Baseball I know less than nothing about, but the park is nice. A baseball park on the beach. When my daughter is married and has children, I will take them there.

He places a hand over his heart. *I long for this more than anything.*

He points at the brown leather couch. I take a seat and he sits in the matching overstuffed chair to my left.

The office is crowded with furniture. The couch and chair, a coffee table, two end tables with identical ceramic lamps, a desk and office chair and two chairs facing it, a small sideboard with a selection of liquor decanters and soft drink bottles, three antique filing cabinets, a magazine rack, two floor lamps with shades wrapped in plastic, and an actual divan with a price tag still stuck on it.

—You like it?

—Sure.

He smiles and tilts his head to the side.

—You do not have to lie with me. It is tacky.

I start to say something but he holds up a hand, blocking my words before they can come out of my mouth.

—It is my wife. She does this to me. Buys these things and brings them here. She wants me to be comfortable. My guests to be comfortable. At first I tell her, *Marya, no, it is too much. A desk, chairs, this is all a man needs in his office.* She tells me my office must impress. So.

He holds out his arms, inviting me to look at the clutter. *You see who wears the pants.*

—So this is fine. I do not care. I care only about these.

He points at the walls.

The walls are covered in family photos. Behind the desk is the centerpiece: a poster-size soft-focus image in a massive gilt frame. David with a short round woman wearing large Gucci glasses, and an almost pretty young woman who is obviously fighting a pitched battle with her mother's stocky genes and her father's flat features.

—These are my treasures. Everything is for them.

He lays a hand on my forearm.

—This you understand.

He pats my arm.

—Do not answer. It is not a question. This I know you understand. To do everything for one's family. This is what it is to be a man. And you are a man, Henry. Of this can there be any doubt? The things you have done to prove it.

He takes his hand from my arm and touches his whiskers with his fingertips.

—And now there is more to do.

—Yeah. David . . .

—Yes? There is something on your mind? You must speak it.

—David. I don't even know what you want here. You want me to? What?

He laughs.

—What I want? No. Henry. It is what you have done.

—Yeah, but.

—Would I bring you to New York? No.

He clutches his head with his hands. *The insanity.*

—I still don't.

—It is your national pastime. This game. You, you can explain to me.

He gets up and picks through the furniture to the magazine rack, comes back with a copy of today's *Daily News* and drops it in my lap. The headline is something about someone blowing up something in the Middle East.

—I don't.

—No, not this.

He picks up the paper, flips several pages and drops it back in my lap. I look at the page, trying to find what it is he wants me to see. He taps his finger on the Mets Notebook and a small item headlined in bold type.

—This.

Mets Top Pick Moving Up

Miguel Arenas, the Mets' top pick and the first pick overall in the Major League draft, is already moving up. Having spent one day in rookie ball, the Mets will move Arenas to the single-A Brooklyn Cyclones. Arenas is expected to see playing time in this weekend's season opening series against the Staten Island Yankees. The move was instigated by injuries that have plagued the Mets' farm system this year, requiring the early advancement of several players, but it certainly won't hurt Cyclones' ticket sales to have the darling of last year's Olympics playing at Keyspan Park.

David sits in his chair and gazes at the photo of his family while I read about baseball.

—You understand all of this?

—Yeah.

—Yes. I remember you like baseball.

—Yeah. But I still don't . . .

—Henry. It is not clear?

He takes the paper from me and points at the article.

—This boy, he is coming now to New York. Now. And he asks for someone. For you. So now it makes sense, why you are here?

It makes no sense. But I get it. And it's a bad idea.

—I can't do it. I can't be this guy's bodyguard. He's. There's gonna be press. It's. How can I?

David turns his head to the side and puts up both hands, palms outward. *Stop! You are going too fast.*

I stop. He lowers his hands and looks at me.

—I will explain.

He pauses, collects his thoughts.

—This boy, he has a disease. He has the disease that he must gamble. Yes?

I nod.

—And so. And so he gambles. He bets on everything. Cards, dice, lottery, a spinning wheel with numbers, horses, dogs. Men are ahead of him in the bathroom, he will bet which will finish pissing first and take an over and an under on how many will wash their hands. He is sick. And while he plays for his high school and his college, Stanford, a school my daughter was accepted to, he gambles. When he plays for the USA at the Olympics, he gambles. And he bets on all things. He bets on baseball. Never on his own team, but he bets. And he bets only with the same bookie. The same bookie who was his father's bookie, I think. A man who is a friend. He can trust this man not to take advantage of him, not to sell this information to a newspaper. *The Olympic hero who gambles!* He is protected from such headlines. But he is not protected from himself. He gambles, and what happens to all gamblers is what happens to him. He loses more than he can pay.

David shrugs with just one shoulder. *And what else can one expect?*

—His friend can no longer afford to take these bets. But he is a talent, and from a young age there are many who have faith in him, faith in his talent. And faith that this talent will earn money. And where there is that kind of faith, there is also credit, and many many IOUs.

He lifts his hand slowly to show me the growing stack of IOUs.

—Baseball, I told you, baseball means nothing to me. But I employ people who know this game well. Someone must set the odds, someone must make the spread. I am told. And one of these men watches when the boy plays baseball in the Olympics. You saw this?

I didn't. The summer of 2004 I was in my shitty apartment finding out how much Demerol I could take at once.

—Missed that one.

—I understood very little, but it was stirring. And this man, the odds-setter. He has heard of the boy's gambling. And he asks questions. And he finds things. Among the things he finds are the many IOUs. And he suggests something to me. And I say yes. And so he starts to buy these IOUs. This is good paper. These are debts that one expects to have repaid. But a bookie will always rather have cash. Quietly he buys these IOUs. And then he has them all. Do you know how much, Henry?

—No.

—Guess.

—I have no idea.

—That is fine. You could not guess it anyway. Nearly 2 million. Nearly 2 million in paper. And I have bought all of it.

He bugs his eyes slightly at the notion. *Can you believe my foolishness?*

—Tell me, who is the worse gambler here, Henry, this boy or myself? Nearly 2 million. That is a great deal of money. I will tell you honestly, that is money I can not afford to lose. But life is a gamble. And sometimes even a businessman must gamble. It is how one stays on top. A risk from time to time is necessary. To prove to yourself that you do not fear the fates. But still, having bought all this paper, I am constipated for weeks.

He winces.

—And then.

He smiles.

—You know what happens, yes?

—Sort of.

—First pick. A number one. And he sets a record. Do you know what record?

I shake my head.

—He sets a record for the largest rookie signing bonus ever in baseball.

He briefly raises his fists about his head. *Yes!*

—Over 6 million. This is a good record to have, yes? But it is maybe not so much.

He makes his right hand into a blade.

—There is to be this much for the agent.

He slices the air.

—This much for the manager.

Another slice.

—This for the government.

A very thick slice.

—And so. I call him. I explain to him who I am. And I tell him of the paper I have bought. And I have a conversation with Miguel. In person, yes, but very private. In San Diego, where his home is. We talk about . . . everything. We talk about family and life and being young, we talk about love and women, we talk about New York City and what it will be like for him when he comes to live here. All of this. He also talks about baseball, but this I do not understand. And then, we talk about gambling. I tell him that I could ask for my money. But what then? He will have so little left. Where will be the house for his mother, the new car for himself, the many things a young man desires? I tell him this does not interest me. I will want my money, but not now. He wants still to gamble? Good. I will help. He will place all of his bets through me. If he wants to play cards, I will find him a game. If he wants to roll dice, I will find him a table. If he wants to bet on two men pissing, I will find him a toilet.

He smiles at his joke.

—And if he wants to go to Las Vegas, I will give him an escort to be sure there is no trouble for him. And he listens and he says, we will *try* it.

He widens his eyes. *Everything should be so simple and pleasant.*

—And so this paper has led to another investment. I have invested in this boy's future. I have kept my money on the table and will spin the wheel once more to see where this boy will land. But I am not stupid. If the wheel falters, I will pull my paper back before it can all be lost. This is making sense?

It's a long-shot bet David is laying. Does Miguel have what it takes? Can he make the bigs? Once there, can he stick? If he lives up to a slice of the potential he's supposed to have? Jackpot. Give him a couple years and he'll sign a free agent contract in nine figures. And huge chunks of it will be carved away by the spread every time he places a bet. And that's not even the big payoff. If David can get his hooks in deep enough, if Miguel compromises himself in the right way, we're talking fixes. A dropped ball here, a strikeout there, getting picked off first on occasion. Do it right and it doesn't have to even be about throwing a game, just making sure the right team beats the spread.

I nod.

—It's making sense.

—Good. Now he comes the first time to play in New York. A young man with all that money. Many mistakes can be made in New York. So I call him, I tell him, this boy, I tell him he must have someone. And he says yes, that is fine, he will have you.

David mimes a phone at his ear, pulls it away, looks into it. *Did I hear right?*

—I say to him, *Miguel, I have many good men. I will get one of them for you. You will have a magnificent time. You will be a prince and do anything you wish.* But he says no. He will have only one man. He will have only you, Henry. This boy, he knows already what I know, that you are a good man. Already, this boy, he loves you. So this is good. You will escort this investment, keep him from harm, help him to have his fun.

He wags his hand loosely. *And help him lay his bets. And keep other bookies from him. All of those things.*

Keep him under David's thumb.

—You can do this?

Can I do it? Can I help fuck up this guy's life?

Of course I can.

It's not that hard really, put your mom and dad on the other side of a scale and you'll find the guy doesn't weigh anything at all. Even if looking at him is like peering through the looking glass right into What Might Have Been Land.

Besides, it's better than killing.

—Sure. Sounds good.

My left hand rests on the arm of the couch. David wraps both of his hands around it.

—Good! Good. You have done your job so well in Las Vegas, it has brought you here again. And this, this is not chance, I think. This is fate. You are meant to be here. I want for us to work together, Henry, for us to work with trust between us. It can happen.

He tilts his head at the huge family photo.

—Between two men who love their families as we love ours, there is always understanding. Where there is understanding, yes? Where there is understanding, there is always room for trust.

Still clasping my hand, he leans his face very close to mine.

—So you will look after this young man.

He lets go of my hand and stands up.

—This and one thing more.

He turns to his desk and speaks to me over his shoulder.

—You will kill my fucking sister-in-law.

THE FIRST TIME was The Kid.

I HAVEN'T FORGOTTEN any of them. Far as I know there's no way to; forget about the people you've killed for hire.

I remember Branko knocked on the door and he answered. The Kid. Sixteen, maybe seventeen. He must have known Branko from business or something because we went in and he asked if we wanted something to drink. Branko said yes and followed The Kid into the kitchen. I stood there in the living room and looked around.

Just your average suburban home. The Kid's mom must have been a neat freak because there wasn't a speck of dust anywhere. Other than that, average. I was just standing there, wondering how we were gonna do this, wondering if The Kid was in on it, or if we'd just call it off. I mean, if the guy we were supposed to deal with was The Kid's father, we couldn't just do it in front of him. That's what I was thinking. I stood there.

There was a frozen image of a baseball player on the TV screen. I thought for a second that it was real. Then I remembered that it was winter. Then I saw the big EA Sports logo on the bottom of the screen and the game controller lying on the floor and I figured it out. Then I heard a sound from the kitchen and Branko stuck his head around the corner and told me to get in there.

I nodded and walked in and The Kid was lying on the linoleum in front of the open fridge, a bunch of soda cans and a Tupperware container of leftover spaghetti spilled around him. Branko grabbed his arms and flipped him over onto his stomach. I looked around the kitchen and saw how well kept it was, just like the living room. I was wondering if it was a good idea to have let the kid see us. I mean, what did I know, I was a beginner. Branko took a Beretta Tomcat from his pocket, chambered a round, clicked off the safety, and handed it to me.

Branko told me to hurry and I looked at him and he shook his head and said something in Serbo-Croatian that I didn't understand. He pointed at The Kid. Dots connected. I pointed the gun. His mom and dad were gonna come home and find him.

There were some loud noises and I stood there and looked at the pattern the spaghetti sauce had made around The Kid's head. It looked like someone had shot him. Then I realized it wasn't just spaghetti sauce anymore and that *I* had shot him. Branko took the gun out of my hand and did things to it and dropped it and led me out of the kitchen.

We walked through the living room to the front door and I looked back over my shoulder and saw the screen of the TV with the frozen baseball player and one word flashing at the bottom of the screen.

RESUME?

RESUME?

RESUME?

———

ANYWAY, THAT WAS the first time.

DAVID TAKES HIS seat behind the desk. The time for socializing over.

He places his hands palms down, flat on the leather blotter his wife picked out.

—Time has passsed. Many things are ready to be forgotten. People forget. Either because it is too painful to remember, or because they no longer care, or because life changes things. Between you and me, everything is ready to change. But some people do not forget, Henry. Some people cling to the past as if it were still in front of them. You, sometimes I have thought you were one of these people.

A person who lives in the past, a person who can't get over things that happened a couple years ago; he thinks I might be that kind of person. He doesn't realize I'm the kind who hasn't gotten over things that happened when I was sixteen.

—With these pills you take.

—I got rid of the pills.

—I know. Branko, he looked in your apartment. He called me, told me the pills were gone and that you did not bring them with you.

He pats the desktop lightly with his right hand. *Bravo.*

—This tells me something. The work you did with Branko at the Happi Inn, the good impression you made on Arenas, they tell me things. But getting rid of the pills tells me more. You are no longer willing to live in the past. You want a future again.

I think about a future. I think about living another thirty-seven years. It's not something I've been thinking about much lately, so it takes a little effort.

—But not everyone has grown up, Henry. Not everyone is ready as you are to move forward. Some people dwell. It is not healthy, but some people do not know what is good for them. My sister-in-law, she is such a person.

I think about thirteen thousand mornings, give or take, waking up and breathing.

—Her son. Always now, everything is about Mikhail. Her darling Mickey. This nosey little shit who got himself killed.

He drops his head and presses his fingertips to his temples for a moment. *I should not think these things about the dead.*

He looks up, puts his hands back on the desk.

—She cares only for one thing now. You. Your death is all she lives for.

Thirteen thousand mornings, waking up and wondering if I will have to kill anyone that day so that my parents can stay alive. And somewhere else, this woman waking up, staying alive one more day until she can find me and kill me. Irony tries, but doesn't really cover it.

—She has pleaded with me for this revenge. *Where is he? Why can you not find him? If he is dead, I need proof. Show me where is his grave so that I can spit on it.* And I tell her always, *You must forget, Anna. Forget and live your life. We may never find him. And if we do? His death will not give you peace.* For years she pleads, but now she demands. *I want him, I must have him. You do not care. You never loved my son. Your daughter, she is alive. You cannot understand. Find him, or I will have my nephews find him. Find him.* I tell her, *This will create havoc in my business, Anna. It is no good.*

And then, Henry, she tells me, my sister-in-law tells me, she says, *I do not care about your business. Find him.*

He makes a fist and bangs it once against the desk. *Enough.*

—She does not care about my business? Her husband's business it was. The business that feeds her. And so there is no more talking to be done. She was my brother's wife, this is true. But he is dead from cancer. She was my nephew's mother, true, but he is dead by his own stupidity. So now, there is no blood between us. Now, she is nothing. She is not family.

He circles his finger in the air, taking in the photos.

—We understand family, Henry. We understand what one must sacrifice for family. So you will help me with this woman. And in helping me with this, Henry, you will help yourself, and you will help *your* family.

He stands.

—This threat, this childish threat to your mother and father that has hung over both our heads. This threat of which I am ashamed.

He comes around the desk.

—Make it go away, Henry.

He pulls me to my feet.

—Deal with this woman who is no longer my family.

He embraces me.

—And your mother and father will be at last safe.

He spreads his arms wide. *Could you hope for anything more?*

DAVID SHOWS ME out but does not walk me to the elevator. I stand in front of it alone and watch the numbers light up one by one as it crawls closer to me.

The elevator stops and the door slides open. A very attractive woman in black steps out and walks up the hall. I step into the elevator, but something about her curly, just-graying hair reminds me of someone, and I peek out before the door can close. She's standing outside David's door.

I want her to be David's elegant and aristocratic mistress, the woman he spends his afternoons with when he is not at home with his wife, the woman he talks to the way he would never talk to the whores he and his business partners fuck on the weekends. But I suspect I am wrong. I suspect this woman passed her curly hair and almond eyes to her son. And that I met him in Mexico. And that I killed him. I suspect that this woman is David's sister-in-law.

The elevator doors try to close, but I am blocking them and they make a noise. She turns her head and looks at me looking at her. I pull back into the elevator and the doors close.

Well, that can't have been good.

DOWNSTAIRS A LIMO is parked out front. The driver stands next to the car, smoking. I've seen his type before. Young. Blond spiky hair, meaty but not fat, Ralph Lauren sportswear, oversized pop-star sunglasses on his face. I've seen his kind shooting at me. I've seen his kind bleeding in the street. I have more than a slight premonition that I'll see both again.

We ignore each other. But not really.

AS I WALK down the boardwalk, I think about The Kid. I think about killing sons. And about killing their mothers.

Past the Winter Garden and the Moscow Café; past the Tatiana Restaurant with fluorescent green and orange napkins accordioned and tucked into water glasses on the tables; past all the little boardwalk places where Russians and tourists sit at umbrellaed tables, eat pierogies, and stare at the ocean. And past all the many families out in the early Friday sun.

It's hot in my black jacket and jeans. I take the jacket off and stuff it under the strap of my shoulder bag. I'd like to roll my sleeves up, but the tattoos would show. I feel on display again, walking down the middle of the boardwalk, no cover to cling to, but no one seems to pay any attention to me. I walk past the Brighton Playground, past the handball courts, past the sculpted and textured wall of the aquarium, styled to look like a lower-depths seascape.

I've had only the few hours' sleep I got after I took Miguel and Jay to the airport yesterday morning. My face aches and the hole I put in my wrist feels hot and itchy. But the sky is blue and the breeze is soft, and if David isn't lying to me, I only have one person left to kill.

And I already killed her child, so how hard can this really be? It takes me about twenty minutes to reach Coney. The Cyclone is clanking up its track, getting ready to drop, the Wonder Wheel spins, "Celebration" booms from the bumper cars. A nice Friday crowd is building.

—Scarface! Yo!

I stop. Miguel is sitting at one of the picnic tables in front of Ruby's, a crappy carnie-dive version of the Russian places up at Brighton, sipping from a plastic cup of beer and surrounded by shopping bags. "Crazy Train" is playing on the jukebox inside.

———

—Sorry we didn't grab you at the airport.

—No problem.

Miguel stuffs half a hot dog in his mouth.

—We came up on a midnight flight after the club sent word I was moving.

Jay comes back from putting money in the jukebox.

—Moving up, yo.

He slaps hands with Miguel and starts digging through the dozens of plastic shopping bags. Bags from the NBA store, Niketown, the Sony store, Macy's, and more.

Miguel stuffs the other half of his dog in his mouth and talks as he chews.

—Had late dinner with my agent, got checked into the suite. All that. Then we hit the hotel bar. Had to sleep in. Then we had some shopping to do. And then I called the guy. You know.

He makes a vague gesture that means David.

—And he said you were on your way, so we waited here.

Jay sticks a bubble-wrapped gadget in my face.

—What the fuck is this, yo?

—I don't know.

—Yo, Mike. What the fuck is this?

—I don't know, man. You bought it.

Jay laughs.

—Shit, yeah. Man, I was still fucked up this morning.

Miguel laughs, inhales another hot dog. He chews, his face smooth-skinned, surrounded by his toys, hanging with his best friend. He is a boy.

He eats the last of his four dogs, drains his beer, wipes his mouth with the back of his hand and then offers it to me. I take it and he pulls me close on the bench and puts his other arm on my shoulder.

—Good to have you here, bro. We're gonna have fun. Gonna be cool.

—Yeah, thanks.

He lets me go. I think about how much he's fucking up his life. I think about how that's not my problem.

—What now?

He smiles, a blob of mustard at the corner of his mouth.

—Ballpark. Gotta get fitted. Game tonight.

Steely Dan comes on the juke. Miguel stands.

—Let's jet.

Jay pulls his head out of a shopping bag and points into Ruby's dark interior.

—Yo, "Kid Charlemagne."

He points at me.

—Played this for Scarface, yo. Old skool for my old motherfucker. He's a hood, just like The Kid.

He punches me on the shoulder.

—Don't forget, yo, I want to get into some of that gangsta shit this time around.

IT'S A BEAUTIFUL ballpark.

I sit with Jay in the field-level seats between home plate and the home dugout. Beyond left field we can see Deno's Wonder Wheel and the Cyclone rising above Astroland and the rest of Coney's midway. Right field is backed by the ocean. The sun shines down and a breeze blows in off the water.

A ballpark on the beach. What's not to love?

Jay is pulling a brand-new pair of Nikes out of a box. He dumps the box in the aisle for someone else to clean up.

—Nice place to play ball, yo.

I nod.

He kicks off his old shoes and leaves them next to the box.

—Bet there's some Annies hangin' round here. Some *beach* Annies. Love it.

I nod.

The park is empty except for us. It's early, but the trainer and the equipment manager wouldn't let us into the clubhouse while Mike gets fitted.

Jay tilts his face to the sun and closes his eyes.

—Won't be here long, though. My boy's moving up. Mean, it's cool to hang at the beach a couple weeks, but my boy needs to get up and out. Can't be wastin' talent down here. These single-A guys, they put 'em up in a fuckin' dorm. Fuckin' dorm rooms. Mike just got done with college. Fuckin' watch, they bring 'em here in a bus. Mike told his agent, told him, *No fuckin' way, yo! Need wheels, need a pad. Hook it up.* Told him, *I'll pay the tab, just hook that shit up.* Got off the plane from Tennessee, from my boy's *one day* in rookie ball, there's the Escalade waitin' for us. Got a suite in the City, yo. One of those downtown places. *Boutique* hotel. My boy says he didn't come to New York to live in Brooklyn.

A couple groundskeepers have appeared. They start peeling the tarps off the infield dirt.

—Stick it out, Scarface. Mike takes a shine to you, stick it out, yo. He takes a shine and nobody can talk him out of it. And he's startin' to shine on you.

He opens his eyes and looks at me.

—Got anything to say to that, yo?

—I like him, too.

Jay sits up.

—That a joke?

—No.

—Good. Cuz Mike likes you. He liked your moves in Vegas. Liked how you were smooth with the crowd at the Palms, liked how you eased us in at the Rhino, and he sure as shit liked that no-nonsense you laid on those yokels in the parking lot. Said to me on the plane back, *That guy's the kind of guy a man wants around to take care of shit.* Said, yo, said he felt *safe* with you. Safe. You get that?

—Sure.

—Do you? Cuz that, yo, that's some deep shit, someone says they feel safe with you.

He moves into the empty seat between us and drops his voice.

—See, I know *all* Mike's shit. Right, yo?

—Right.

—We go back. Grew up in San Diego together. Little League. We go back like that. Kids together. Played on the same teams to-gether. School together. When his dad, when he split on the fam-ily and went back to Mexico, back to some other family turned out he had goin' down there, Mike's moms couldn't support him and his brothers and sisters on her own. He came to live with me. Moved into my home when he was thirteen. My mom and dad, they took him in. I know *all* his shit.

He shakes his head.

—People don't know. His agent told him to get rid of me, said I was trouble. He don't know, cuz he don't know Mike. Mike likes trouble. Me, I like fun. That shit in Vegas, that *last hurrah*. That was a deal we had. I told him he's in too deep already. Got to stop the betting. But that contract dropped and he had to spend, had to play. So I put him on a budget. Two hundred G's. Throw it around like you don't care. But that's it. In *pro* ball now. Got to get square with the guy who has the IOUs. Can't have shit like that hangin' over his head now. That's just beggin' to be Pete Rosed. But Mike has what they call *poor impulse control*. That hundred grand we split Vegas with? That's already gone. Twenty-four hours and it's gone. That Russian set him up with his own *personal* bookie. Like giving a junkie a on-call dealer who delivers the best shit in town.

He pulls off his Pods visor, runs his finger around the outline of the picture of a friar swinging a bat, keeping his eyes from mine.

—And now you. The man says Mike needs someone while he's here, to keep an eye on him, help him out. I don't like it, but as long as the man is holding Mike's paper, he gets his say and we can't push too hard. Got to have someone? OK. I say to Mike, *Ask for that guy from Vegas*. Ask for Scarface.

He looks up from the visor.

—*I* asked for you. Cuz I think Mike might be right. You could be the kind of guy he needs to have around. You know how to take care of trouble and you don't take shit. Could be, yo, you're just what Mike needs.

He pulls the visor back on.

—Mike got himself in this shit and all I can do is help dig him out. I got one mission, that's watch my boy's back. He wants to bet, he's *gonna* find a way. That doesn't mean I have to help. You, yo, you have to make that call for yourself. My boy knows what's best for him, even if he don't always do it. He'll see what side you're playing. He sees you're part of the solution, you could end up with a new team, whole new livelihood.

He holds out his arms, taking in the ballpark and the ocean.

—Spend your time watchin' ball games, hookin' up with Annies and hangin' with us, yo. Instead of fightin' with guys in parking lots or whatever the hell you're used to. Could be sweet. Could even learn to like the game.

He lowers his arms.

—Anyway, I'm just talkin'. But this could be an opportunity, yo, to change your life. You just got to decide the right thing to do.

He holds out a fist.

—Cool?

I bang my fist against his.

—Sure.

—Alright. See, that's the shit. Now we're all in the open and we just get to be ourselves and everybody gets to see what everybody's made of. Gonna be sweet, yo.

He slips his feet into the new Nikes and bends to lace them up. I look at the back of his head. I see what I usually see when I look at the back of someone's head, I see exactly how it would look if I put some bullets in it. He straightens, and I look at the water.

Miguel comes walking up out of the home dugout. He's wearing the white-and-red Cyclones uniform, red socks worn up and out, old skool.

—S'cool, right?

Jay jumps up, runs down the steps and vaults the wall.

—Sweet, yo. Need some help though.

He reaches up and twists Miguel's cap to the side.

—That's the shit.

He pulls a cell phone out of his pocket and tosses it to me.

—Scarface, snap a picture.

I flip the phone open, push a couple buttons until I figure out the camera and point it at them.

—Wait a sec, yo.

Jay jumps up and Miguel catches him in his arms.

—Snap it.

I take the picture and Jay jumps down.

—It good? Need another one?

I look at the picture on the phone's tiny screen.

Miguel is tall and straight. The uniform fits him perfectly, like second skin. He looks born to play the game. He looks like a ball-player, looks like just what he is. Jay is cradled in his arms, looking like a child in an adult body, looking like what maybe he wants you to think he is.

I look up from the phone.

—Yeah, it's fine.

THE PLAYERS ARE over Miguel before they even see him. They pulled up, saw the Escalade parked next to the players' entrance, and word got around quick who it belonged to. Not what you want to see when you're getting bused to work and living in a dorm. They tap fists with Miguel and say *yo*, but no one hangs out with him. He makes it worse because he doesn't seem to care. Just does his thing, lets the publicity guy take his photos, talks with the GM, does some jogging, meets the manager and coaches, everything smooth and professional and with the air of a guy who knows this is a pit stop. All the while Jay tags after him, whispering in his ear, blatantly pointing at other guys on the team and talking shit about them.

There's press around, and the Staten Island players are starting to drift onto the field to stretch. First game of the season, everyone's early. This may be single A, but add the Mets farm vs. Yankees farm matchup to that first-day vibe and throw in Miguel's debut. It may not be a game for ESPN, but local interest is high. There are reporters from all the city papers, and TV cameras are set up to do a cable broadcast of the game. I decide it's time to lie low.

I duck past a couple of the visitors and cut through their dugout into the tunnels. Down at one end I can see an Aramark vending truck pulling up to the loading dock. I turn in the other direction, past a stack of boxes filled with player photos; a guy walking around in a seagull suit carrying the mangy head under his arm.

THEY HAVE A little museum devoted to Brooklyn baseball. I go in. There's a bench just inside the door. I sit down and lean my back against the window and watch a young woman as she leads a group of kids around the place, showing them relics of the Brooklyn Dodgers.

I try to relax, try to enjoy the air-conditioning and let myself be soothed by the woman's voice as she tells the kids about the importance of Jackie Robinson. But all I end up doing is grinding my teeth and wishing I'd at least kept some Xanax.

I'm itchy and antsy and sweaty and my face hurts and I'm thinking about the thirteen thousand. All those mornings I might have if I kill Mickey's mom.

I think about going back to Mexico, back to my beach. It

wouldn't be the same, I wouldn't have the 4 million stashed away. But Pedro might still be there running the bar I gave him. He'd give me a job. A place to be. A home. And shit, of course he's still there. Where else would he be? Pedro and his wife Ofelia and their kids and his brother Leo, and Bud. Bud. Yeah, Pedro will still have my cat Bud. Shit, I'd sure like to see that cat again.

I THINK ABOUT working at the bar and taking swims in the ocean, getting tan and fit again. I wonder if my bungalow is still there. Pedro probably rents it out. But he'll get rid of whoever's in it if I come back.

I think about the sun and the impossibly blue ocean and the jungle. I think about not worrying over my mom and dad. Thirteen thousand mornings spent waking up and not worrying that I'll fuck up and Branko will appear on their doorstep.

Thirteen thousand mornings.

To spend however I like.

A better stash than the 4 million ever was.

Someone bangs on the glass my head is resting against. I jump and twist around to see Jay.

—Yo, Scarface, snap out of it. Batting practice is starting. You want to see this shit.

FANS ARE COMING into the park for batting practice. These are the hard core, the folks wearing authentic Cyclones jerseys and jostling around the white-board on the concourse, copying the starting lineups onto their scorecards. I follow Jay down the steps to our game seats behind home. We settle and Jay gives me a jab with his elbow.

—Yo, these people don't know. Watch this shit, they're gonna freak.

I don't say anything, just push my sunglasses against my face and watch the players as they parade to the plate one by one and take their hacks. The pitching coach pours low-key fastballs down the middle and the players slap them to short or pop them up or send easy flies to the outfield. The first baseman has some power and actually puts a couple over the left field wall, just above the 315-foot mark. None of it matters much. The fielding in single A is almost as bad as the hitting; just making contact with the ball is enough to put a guy on base half the time. Then Miguel comes up.

The atmosphere changes. The feeling from his teammates is less, *Now, let's see what the star can do,* than, *Man, I can't wait to watch this asshole flailing at this shit.* He sets up in the right side of the batter's box. The pitching coach puts a little extra on the first one and the ball cuts, coming in on Miguel's hands. He's looking middle of the plate, he swings anyway and shatters his bat. It doesn't just break at the handle, it explodes into four or five pieces.

Jay shifts in his seat and Miguel goes for another bat.

—Oh, this is gonna be good.

Miguel sets, the pitch comes down the pipe and his bat hits it. The ball soars into center, and keeps going. It slaps into the huge black screen in dead center, just over the 412-foot mark.

—Yo, Mike. Get one over! I want to see a Green Monster shot!

Another pitch. The ball goes to the same place, only higher this time.

—Stop topping the ball, bitch, I said I want one *over* that shit!

Miguel glances at him, adjusts his cap with the middle finger of his right hand, making sure Jay catches the gesture, then steps back into the box.

Jay laughs.

—This is it. This one is a goner.

The coach rears back, puts everything he has into it this time. Miguel swings free and easy, getting all of the ball this time. And the ball climbs and climbs, and clears the top of the screen, cutting through the wind coming off the water.

—That my boy! Now give me another!

Another ball goes over.

—Another one!

Over.

—Give it to me.

Over.

—Again!

And again and again and again. Seven in a row go over the screen, Major League homers all, moon shots. ESPN Top Ten material, every one.

—That's my boy! Yo! That. Is. My. Boy.

Then Miguel switches sides of the plate, sets up to hit lefty, and does more of the same.

THE COACHES AND players have a bit more enthusiasm for Miguel when he comes up during the game. Not that he seems to care. Not that he seems the least aware that he is playing in his first game of pro ball.

And it may be a silly game for children being played by grown men, but when he comes to the plate in the bottom of the ninth, having single-handedly kept the Cyclones in the game, and swats an RBI double to tie it up, I jump out of my seat and cheer.

And I almost give a shit when they lose it in the tenth.

—Yo, we tried to find a shitty Olds for you, Scarface, but the Caddy was all they had.

We're in Mike's Escalade, driving across the Brooklyn Bridge. Mike stares out the window at the lights of the Manhattan skyline.

Jay sticks his face between the seats.

—Sweet. You see that shit on TV, but it's not the same, yo.

Mike nods.

—Can you fucking imagine if the Mets hadn't grabbed me number one?

—Don't even, yo. Playing for the Dodgers would have sucked.

I shake my head.

—Dodgers suck.

They look at me.

—Yo! Turns out Scarface knows some baseball after all.

Shit.

—Not really. My dad, he was a Giants fan. I just know enough to know the Dodgers suck.

Miguel tugs at the bill of his Cyclones cap.

—Well that's the basics, man.

Jay laughs.

—No shit. Get that down and the rest of the game is easy. So, yo, where we gonna get our drink on?

Drink. Are any of the places I used to know still here? Shit, would they want to go to any of those dives?

Miguel adjusts the A/C.

—What about that Hogs & Heifers spot? That's by our hotel, right?

Jay reaches between us for the stereo volume.

—Yo, Julia Roberts got topless in that place or some shit. I'm in.

He cranks the bass and "Bombs over Baghdad" shakes the car.

THEY ALMOST GET me clean.

I come out of the hotel and start toward the restaurant the concierge told me Miguel and Jay went to for breakfast. A car is parked a little ways down the street. Two men in the front seat. The passenger gets out, a young guy in expensive jeans, his black hair heavily gelled and styled back from a sharp widow's peak. He flicks a cigarette butt into the gutter and walks briskly around the car with his hand out and a smile on his face.

—David wants you.

His accent is thick. Russian. I stop for a second, long enough for him to get a couple steps closer. Then I see the one still in the car. Another young guy. One with spiky blond hair and pop-star sunglasses.

They'll have guns.

I don't.

I run.

I WAKE UP on a couch, jet-lagged and groggy. I grab my bag and take it to the bathroom. I turn on the light and my hand reaches automatically for the medicine cabinet. I tug on the edge of the mirror a couple times, trying to open it, thinking about starting the day with a Percocet maybe. Then I remember where I am. Miguel's suite at Soho House.

No one else is around. The bedroom is empty, no sign of Miguel or the bartender he brought back. The other couch looks like Jay and his girl spent the night having a rabid pillow and champagne fight. Thank God I was so wiped out. I can't imagine having to lie there sleepless and witness that.

I shake my head and try to open the medicine cabinet again; and again go through the process of remembering my pills going down a toilet in Vegas. Right, Henry, you're in New York and you have no pills. OK, at least that's settled. Then I realize that this mirror isn't shattered and covered in black tape. I close my eyes. But it's too late, I've already seen myself. And I look like shit. Fine, let's get it over with. I open my eyes. Yeah, I was right the first time: I look just like shit. Eyes bagged and bloodshot, hair sticking up on one side, my skin nearly as pale as the scar on my face. I lean closer. I hadn't realized how much gray there was in my stubble. I knew I was getting old, but no one wants to see the evidence of it right there on his face. That just sucks.

I go to switch off the light, but stop and look at myself again. Cleaned up, I look a little better. Could I spend the rest of my life looking at this face? Strange thought. I still haven't gotten used to the idea that I might have one of those, a rest of my life. Besides, if I want it, I still have to kill Anna Dolokhov.

I find a note next to the phone, written on thick hotel stationery.

> *Yo! Went for breakfast. You were laid out like a bitch so we left you alone. If we're not back you can call my cell and come watch*

us drink bloodies. Mike's worried about getting the party bus. Will
you check that shit?

J

PS

Good looking out last night.

Good looking out last night. I guess so.

HOGS & HEIFERS sucks.

It's packed with tourists hoping to catch sight of a star, not realizing that a true celebrity hasn't stooped to dancing on top of the bar here for a good many years. It's a sad scene until Miguel and Jay get the party started. Within an hour Jay is on the bar with his shirt off dancing to "The Devil Went Down to Georgia" and Mike is getting lessons from one of the bartenders on how to spray Bacardi 151 from his mouth and light it on fire. Miguel does get recognized, but the response is pretty temperate. I mean, most of these people came hoping to see Julia Roberts's tits after all.

I find a corner by the pool table and try to stay out of the way. Miguel comes by on his way to the bathroom.

—Man, hey, man. This place is great, right? I love this shit.

He's having the night of his life. Why shouldn't he be? He's a twenty-one-year-old millionaire who just had a monster game, and everybody loves him. I'd feel good, too.

—So, do me a favor.

He glances at Jay, dancing a two-step on the bar.

—Slip me your phone, bro.

I look at him.

He leans against the wall next to me.

—Jay has mine and I need to make a call.

Jay looks in our direction and hoots. Miguel hoots back, trying to look like we're talking about nothing at all. He looks at his watch.

—I have to make this call.

He wants to make a bet. He wants to call his personal Russian bookie and lay a bet and get deeper into David's hole. Fine. Jay can say what he wants to say about having an easy life, about getting in on something good, having friends and all that shit. But David's already made me an offer. All I have to do is kill someone. That, and don't fuck up with Miguel.

He has his hand down low, open and waiting.

—The phone, bro.

Not my fucking problem.

—No problem.

Not my problem, his problem. Just the one problem he has in his superstar life. The one huge fly in the otherwise perfect ointment. Let him ruin his life. Me, if I had had the chance he has, I would never have pissed it away.

So I put my hand in the pocket where my phone is, and I wrap my fingers around it, and I nod my head.

—Sure thing, Miguel.

Not my problem *at all*.

I take my hand out of my pocket. And it's not holding the phone. And I point at Jay.

—Except the thing is, your mom over there? He says you aren't allowed.

He looks at Jay and back at me.

—That's harsh.

I shrug.

—Take it up with him.

So he walks to the bar, grabs Jay by the ankles, and pulls him down.

I RUN. THE Russians chase me.

If they catch me they'll kill me. If they kill me I'll have broken my contract with David. If I break my contract he'll kill my mom and dad.

If they catch me David will kill my mom and dad.

I run faster.

MIGUEL AND JAY are rolling around on the beer-soaked floor. The fat, hairy bouncer who gives people shit at the door grabs the seat of Jay's baggy jeans and yanks. The jeans pop off Jay's hips and the bouncer falls backward over a table, crashing into a pyramid of empty PBR cans. Now Jay is topless and his pants are tangled around his ankles and one of the bartenders has started spraying him and Miguel with her soda gun.

Miguel is on top of Jay, his knees pinning Jay's shoulders to the floor.

—What the fuck, man?

Jay tries to kick him in the back of the head.

—Yo! Yo! Yo!

Miguel has a fistful of Jay's hair.

—I could kill you right now. I'm that mad.

—So do it, yo.

Miguel nods his head, his mind made up.

—OK, man.

He yanks Jay's hair, forcing his head back, and starts hocking up a loogie from the back of his throat. Jay twists and thrashes.

—Don't do it, yo.

Miguel hocks again.

—Say you're gonna mind your own business.

—No way, yo.

Miguel positions his face right over Jay's, lets the loogie slip from his lips, and sucks it back in.

—Gonna be eatin' it. Say it.

—No.

—Open wide.

The bouncer is being helped up.

A couple tourists are going for their cameras.

The rope of spit is dropping toward Jay's face.

I grab Miguel's collar and pull him back and the spit drops on Jay's chest.

—Gross! Yo, sick!

Miguel shrugs me off easily. Jay kicks free. I get a grip on Miguel's arm.

—Chill. We have to go.

A flash goes off. Another.

He looks at me. Another flash. Looks at the people looking at him, and at the bouncer crossing the room. Jay stands up, pants around his ankles.

—Yo, let's jet.

He starts to waddle toward the door. Miguel grabs him and throws him over his shoulder. The bouncer gets closer, realizes how big Miguel is, slows down. I put a hand in his chest. He looks at it, sees the C-notes and takes them. I toss a couple more on the bar and follow Miguel and Jay out the door, flashes popping around us, making our escape.

SOME THINGS CAN'T be outrun.

The Russians catch up to me a little over a block from the hotel, right out front of Hogs & Heifers as fate would have it. The car screeches around the corner and cuts me off, and the guy on foot tackles me and sends me face-first into the hood. Heat flashes in the bones of my face and a vice clamps my skull. I want to fight. I need to fight. But the pain is followed by a wave of nausea and instead of fighting I puke up a little fluid onto the hood of the car. My arms are pulled behind me and something is wrapped around my wrists and I hear a zipping sound. I'm jerked back off the hood and hauled toward the rear passenger-side door of the sedan. The one behind me has a hand on the plastic bindings he zipped around my wrists, pulling my arms up and back, and the other clamped on my neck. The driver with the spiky hair reaches into the backseat and pushes the door open. I plant my feet. The one behind me pushes my arms higher and something grates in my right shoulder as it threatens to dislocate. I lurch as the pain leaps up my neck and meets up with the agony in my face and he trips me into the back of the car. My upper body flops onto the seat. Spiky grabs the collar of my jacket and pulls while the one on the sidewalk pushes on my legs. I roll, land on my back in the footwell, pull my feet free of the one on the sidewalk and kick him in the neck. He stumbles back.

———

MIGUEL RUNS AROUND the block toward Soho House where we left the Cadillac, Jay still draped over his shoulder. I trail them, making sure no one follows. Halfway to the hotel Jay slips from Miguel's shoulder, lands on his feet, and hops up the street pulling his pants back on.

—Yo, I left my shirt.

He turns and starts back toward the bar. I put out my arms and herd him in the other direction.

—Uh-uh. Bad call.

—Yo, my nippies are hard. I need my shirt.

I take off my jacket and hand it to him.

He looks at it.

—Little big.

—Roll the sleeves.

He pulls on the jacket and rolls the sleeves, but still he's swimming in it.

—This sucks.

Miguel points at him.

—Makes you look . . .

He points at me.

—Like his bitch.

He starts laughing. Jay shakes his head.

—Harsh, yo.

We pass a bar on Ninth Ave.

—Yo! I need a drink.

Miguel pulls the door open.

—Let your new girl buy you one.

He goes inside and lets the door swing shut.

Jay opens the door and smiles at me.

—See, yo, how hard was that?

They get silly drunk. Miguel picks up the bartender and Jay picks up her friend. We stay after closing. I drink seltzer and try to calculate the hours since I slept. The bartender tells us about the party bus.

—It's, like, exactly like a limo, but it's, like, a bus.

Jay and Miguel love it.

—We have to. Yo! We *need* one to pick us up after tomorrow's game.

Miguel looks at his watch.

—Today's game.

They drink more.

On the way back to the hotel, the girls walk together whispering in each other's ears while Jay walks right behind them, still wearing my jacket. Miguel puts his arm around my shoulder.

—You know I wasn't really mad, right? About you not giving me the phone?

—Sure.

—You know, I know what's right. I know Jay's right about that shit. How I'm a little out of control. I just get a little pissed when he sticks his nose in it. Telling other people and shit. But that's, you know, man. That's kinda why he thought you'd be good to have around, I guess. Anyway, we're cool. OK?

—OK.

—Cool.

He pats my shoulder once and runs up to the girls and throws his arms around them.

—What's the big secret? Jay, what's the big secret here?

Me, I follow behind, watching their backs, trying to figure out why the hell I *didn't* give him the damn phone. But knowing the answer. It's easy enough after all. I like the guy. Fuck me.

I HAVE TO get out of the car. If I stay in the car they can take me anywhere and kill me. I have to get out of the fucking car, Mom and Dad.

I heave myself up and scoot on my ass toward the open door. Spiky tries to grab my hair, but it's too short. He reaches for something in his pocket. He's going to do it. He's going to shoot me right here in the car. The one on the sidewalk is coming back, a hand held to his neck.

I can't get out of the car.

I have to do something.

So I scream.

AFTER I'M CLEAN, before I go down to see if I can find Miguel and Jay at the restaurant, I pull the phone book from the desk and flip to the pages for limousine services. My eyes drift over the open Yellow Pages. I see a small ad in the lower right corner. It's black with yellow lettering in gothic script.

Mario
Personal Car Service
sweet

And a phone number.

Mario. Looks like he's moved up in the world some. Good for him. But nothing in his ad about what I need. So I turn the page and keep looking. I find it and make the call. A woman comes on the line and asks me what I need.

—Yeah, uh, do you have a party bus available tonight?

They do.

Then I go downstairs, the concierge tells me where she sent the guys for breakfast. I walk onto the street into a beautiful day, feeling far from the worst I've ever felt.

And they almost get me clean.

SPIKY SWINGS SOMETHING at me. I flinch and it hits me in the shoulder that was almost dislocated. Pain jumps to my wrist and the arm goes dead.

I scream.

The one on the sidewalk is trying to get a grip on my legs as I kick and thrash. Spiky swings his sap again.

I scream.

The sap hits the top of my head.

I'm going to die. I've done these things and I'm going to die. Oh, God. Oh, no. Please. Save me please. Someone save me. I don't want to die.

I scream.

The sap comes down again.

I stop screaming.

A DOOR OPENS. Closes. Footsteps. Three people, I think.

There's pain in my right arm and shoulder, something digging into my wrists and ankles, a hard ache at the top of my head. And my face, the bones behind my face feel cracked. I open my eyes.

The light makes the pain worse, but I keep them open. It takes several seconds for my vision to clear, for the living room to resolve.

I'm facedown on a couch, my arms bound behind my back and my ankles strapped together. A man, the guy with the gelled widow's peak, is sitting on a flowered armchair across from me, smoking. The spiky blond driver is standing behind him, sunglasses on. Between us, perched on the edge of the chair's ottoman, is a beautiful woman dressed in black. She is very small.

I remember Mickey telling me his mother was once a dancer. She must have been a ballerina.

She's looking at me.

—You killed my son.

It seems pointless to say I'm sorry.

PART THREE

SATURDAY, JUNE 25, 2005

GAME TWO

THE SECOND TIME was The Rep for the Culinary, the Vegas union that handles restaurant and hotel workers. The bulk of the Culinary's members are Mexican. The Rep was Mexican. He was helping more Mexicans join the union. Big deal. That's how things work. You have a choice between helping out someone who's familiar to you, someone you understand, as opposed to say, some Russian guy, and you're going to help the one you understand, the one from your country who was recommended to you by your cousin's husband. That's what he did, and he kept doing it. David kept sending people over, trying for Culinary jobs that this guy controlled, and he kept helping Mexicans instead. He was offered money. He didn't take it. He didn't care about the money, he cared about helping people from his country. So David sent me and Branko.

He worked as a cook in a restaurant inside the Bellagio. He made enough money to own two cars, a house in a gated community, and to send his two kids to a private Catholic school, not to mention health insurance for the whole family. That's how good those Culinary jobs can be. Shit, I would have liked a job in the Culinary.

It was a parking lot deal. Parking lots are popular for this sort of thing. It's easy to be anonymous in a parking lot. Easy to get a moment's privacy. And you're close to your car.

He worked the swing, 5:00 p.m. to 1:00 a.m. We sat in a used car Branko had bought for cash. I don't remember what model or make. I don't remember the color. By then I was too high to remember shit. Xanax, Darvocet, and Dexedrine, I think.

The Rep came out an employee entrance, into the underground parking lot. He started toward his 4x4, walking slow, stretching his back after the long shift. We got out of our car and started walking toward him, Branko in front, me right behind, both of us wearing ball caps, sunglasses, and fake beards for the security cameras. A couple more people came out the employee door. One of them called to The Rep and he turned and waved. We slowed a bit, but he didn't stop to talk, just reached in his pocket for his keys and pressed the button to turn off his car alarm. The alarm beeped as we came abreast the truck, blocking his passage. Branko turned sideways to let The Rep by. He waited politely at the hood of his truck, gesturing with his arm that we should go by him first. Branko gave a little nod, stumbled, and I bumped into his back. His keys fell out of his hand and skittered toward The Rep. Branko turned to me and I told him I was sorry. Behind him, The Rep bent to pick up the keys, and I nodded. Branko turned, grabbed The Rep's neck, and rammed his head into the fender of the car parked next to his truck. The Rep grunted, tried to stand, and Branko rammed his head again. The Rep went limp and Branko dropped him.

I was carrying the gun this time, but for a second I forgot what came next and Branko had to pull it out of my pocket and put it in my hand. I don't remember the car we drove, but I remember the gun. It was a Ruger, a Rimfire .22. I remember because it had a ten-round magazine. And I was supposed to use all the bullets. And I did. Branko had drilled little holes down the length of the barrel to vent gases as the pistol was fired, an integral silencer. But the shots were still loud in the enclosed garage. Branko watched the first two bullets go in, then he started for our car as I pulled the trigger.

There was a hesitation between the fifth and sixth bullets. Branko paused halfway to our car when he heard it. If he had turned just then, he would have seen that I had raised the gun, bringing it up to point it at either the back of his head or the front of my own. I'm not sure which. But I lost my nerve, kept firing into The Rep, and Branko got into the car. I wiped the gun, dropped it, and Branko pulled the car up in front of me. I got in.

The new rep opened the book to a few Russians and David got his first toehold in the Culinary. And I went and saw my dealer the next day and told him I needed something new. He said Demerol. I said I'd take all he had.

—*You* killed *my* son.

This time the words aren't addressed at me, but at the floor, as if she's trying to put it together, make sense out of how *I* could have killed *her* son.

She looks up. Her brown, curly hair is shot with gray, her eyes are bloodshot and dark-ringed, a weary tension pulls at the corners of her mouth. She licks her dry lips.

—How?

She gets that one word out. I wait for another, but if there was anything more it's caught inside her. I wonder if she really wants to know how I killed Mickey. How I pushed him from the top of a Mayan ruin and watched him tumble down, spilling blood on the steps. No, she must surely know. She must know how her own son died. I say nothing.

She finds the words in her throat.

—How could you . . .

She breathes.

—Do that?

She is breathing through her mouth now, her chest heaving, hyperventilating.

I don't know what to tell her. I try to think of the answer that will keep me alive the longest, the one that will give me the most time to try to get out of this. I try to think. I think the top of my head feels cracked and itchy, like the sap split the skin and a scab has formed. I think my right shoulder hasn't been seriously damaged, but it hurts like hell. I think the plastic handcuffs zipped tight around my wrists are cutting off the circulation to my hands. I think my face has had nails driven into it and I want something to make the pain go away.

—How?

There is more, but she can't get it past all the air rushing in and out of her lungs.

I think I have something I want to say. It's hard to speak. It hurts to say things. But I try.

—I don't want to die.

Whatever was to come out of her mouth next doesn't.

I say it again.

—I don't want to die.

She shakes her head.

—Shut.

It is less a word this time than a gasp. Air shaped like a word, but carrying none of the weight of spoken language.

—Up.

But I won't.

—I don't want to die.

She starts to rise on trembling legs, strong dancer's legs weak with rage.

—Shut. Up.

But I can't.

—I don't want to die.

She takes a step toward me. Her fists balled at her sides, arms shaking. Tears hot, spilling from her eyes.

—Shut up.

But it's true. What I am saying is true.

—I don't want to die.

She crosses the space between us, and her fist crashes down on the side of my head.

The nails in my face are driven deeper. But I don't shut up.

—Please.

Her other fist slams into the back of my neck.

—Shut up.

No.

—I don't want to die.

She swings her arms, pummeling me, hammering at my back and shoulders and head and neck. Sobbing.

—You shut up. Shut up, you. You. Shut. Shut. You don't. No. Never. Shut up.

And me.

—Please. Let me live. I don't want to. I can't die yet. I want. Don't want to die.

Both of us begging in whispers.

She's falling to her knees, wheezing, her blows have no strength.

—You shut up. Shut up. Please shut up.

She's on her knees next to the couch, her face a foot from mine, her hands clenched together, pounding on my back.

—Please shut up.

Spiky says something in Russian. She stops hitting me, says something in Russian. He walks to her and offers her something. She stays on her knees, takes it from his hand. I see what it is.

—Please. I don't want to die.

She puts the gun below my chin, presses it into my throat.

—Shut up.

I open my mouth. Something comes out; a noise, the tail end of a years-long sob.

—Please.

She digs the gun into my flesh.

—Shut up. Please shut up. Please shut up. Please shut up.

They are whispers. Pleas.

I shut up.

She breathes.

She looks at my face, the face I was not born with.

She breathes.

The barrel of the gun is deep in the hollow beneath my chin, shivering.

She breathes.

Her mouth opens wide, mirroring my own, and a sound, a ragged wail like the one that escaped mine, comes from hers.

She slumps, the gun falls from her hand and thumps on the carpet. Spiky touches her shoulder.

—Tetka?

She looks at me, closes her eyes.

Whispers.

—No. It is all right. Everything is all right.

But it's not. How could it be?

—How do you kill?

She speaks English beautifully, just the trace of an accent to let you know it is not her native tongue, so I know there is no misunderstanding. I know it's not what she means, but still, I think of all the many ways I have killed.

—How?

And she is not speaking to me in any case.

—How can you kill another human being?

She is speaking to the wall-to-wall carpet.

—And a boy?

She gestures to the carpet, trying to eke an answer from it.

—How do you kill a boy?

She shakes her head.

—A simple boy. A beautiful boy.

She looks at the ceiling now.

—You. You have killed so many people. A boy, more or less, what was he to you?

She puts her hand to her chest.

—But he was everything to me.

She clutches a handful of material at her breast.

—Everything.

Her eyes fall back to the carpet.

—You have killed so many.

Her hand goes to her forehead.

—And I cannot kill even one.

And now she looks at me.

—Not even if that one is you.

She spits on my face.

—A murderer. A killer of boys.

She stands, gets up from the floor where she has been sitting right next to me.

—I cannot kill you.

She is straightening her dress, her hands scuttling over her body, tugging at wrinkles.

—But I know who you are.

She steps to the ottoman and picks up the small black handbag sitting next to it.

—I know who you are.

She opens the bag, takes out two pieces of paper and unfolds them.

—I know who you are.

The papers have been handled much, and she smooths them against her thigh.

—See, I know who you are.

She separates the papers, holds them one in each hand, and sticks them in my face.

—This is who you are.

The paper in her left hand is a photocopy of various pieces of ID: my driver's license, a library card, a credit card, a gym card. They are mine, really mine. They say Henry Thompson. These are the pieces of identification I left with a forger named Billy.

The paper in her right hand was torn from today's *Post*. It's a fragment of Page Six, a photo of Miguel, half-naked Jay tossed over his shoulder. But that's not the best part, the best part is me, right behind them, pushing them out the door of Hogs & Heifers.

She drops the papers on the floor and wipes her hands on her thighs, cleaning away any trace of me that might have clung to them.

—They told me.

She points at the two young men.

—They told me you were alive. And that David knew. They told me, *Go to David, go see your brother-in-law. Ask him.* But I did not believe them. It was too much. Too much.

She brings her hands to her forehead and turns her back to me. She stands like that, hands pressed to her forehead, holding something terrible inside. The blond walks to her, starts to whisper in Russian, but she takes one of the hands from her head and holds it out, silencing him. He shrugs, bends, picks up the gun she dropped next to the couch, puts it in his pocket and goes to stand behind the chair.

The guy with the widow's peak just sits there watching, chaining cigarette after cigarette.

Mickey's mother drops her hands to her sides. She is still now, only her eyes move, skipping around the room, occasionally touching on me, but never looking into my own.

—I went to see him yesterday. To apologize to my brother-in-law. To my son's godfather. To tell him that things had gone too far. I wasn't thinking clearly. Since my son died, since he was murdered, I have not been able to think clearly. I.

She's starting to lose it again. She stops for a moment, gets it back.

—And I walked past a man in the hall. Then I looked. And, *you* were looking at *me*. And I. Something. But. How could I think? Impossible. I talked to David, but I told him nothing. Nothing. And when I came home, I looked at this again.

She's pointing at the photocopy.

—And I looked and I looked. But I couldn't see it. And I can't sleep. I can never sleep. I want to. When Mickey . . . I would dream about him. And it was. He was with me. I could feel him. It was the only time he was with me anymore. But I can't sleep now. I have to take pills and they won't let me sleep. And I take other pills and I sleep, but they don't let me dream. And I want to sleep. I want to dream about my son. I. I. I.

Tears again. She is furious at them. She presses the heels of her palms into her eyes and whisks the tears away.

—But last night. I slept. And I dreamt. But it was about you. You son of a bitch. I can't dream about my son, but I dream about you. You. And this morning. I see that.

She points at the page of torn newsprint.

—I sit with my tea and I flip the pages of the newspaper. I see nothing. Flip, flip, flip. Nothing. Until I see this. And I looked. I looked at that picture. And I looked at the other pictures of you. And I.

She presses her hands flat together and holds them in front of her chest.

—I knew.

She squeezes her eyes shut. Muscles on her forearms flex as she pushes her hands one against the other.

—I knew.

She opens her eyes and drops her hands. Air sighs from her mouth.

—I knew.

She bites her lower lip.

—But I can't kill you. I can't. I can't. I can't. And I want to. So badly I want to. I. But I can't. But you.

She points at me.

—You can kill David.

—She's our aunt.

She left without saying another word. Picked up her bag, went to the door, waited while Spiky opened it, and went out with him following. She never looked at me again, and I never had a chance to tell her what me trying to kill David would mean to my parents.

Then Widow's Peak gets up and starts pacing back and forth in front of the couch. A pair of legs in very blue jeans, bleached nearly white down the fronts of the thighs, scissoring past me. As he paces and talks, he smokes, flicking ashes, letting them drift onto the carpet.

—Tetka Anna. Our mother's sister. A beautiful woman. Even now.

His hand dips in his pocket and comes out with a flick-knife. The blade pops open. He bends over my back and there's a snap as he cuts the plastic bindings on my wrists. I sit up slowly, a rush of blood making my hands tingle and my head throb even worse. I sit and massage the deep red welts on my wrists.

—She brought us over last year.

He takes a seat in the flowered armchair.

—We had to leave Russia.

He takes another Marlboro Light from the box on the table next to him, sticks it in his mouth and lights it from the butt of his last one.

—Trouble.

He stubs the butt in a glass dish full of glass marbles.

—Our father. Our mother. Do you know what a *Shakhidki* is?

I shake my head.

—It is a Russian word for a word in Arabic. It is a female word.

He has one of those thin beards that trace the line of the jaw, a moustache just as thin arches from it to cross his upper lip. He traces it with a fingertip.

—You know anything about Chechnya?

I shake my head, still massaging my wrists.

—But you know what it is? A country? Part of the old USSR?

I nod. I press my hand to my forehead and find a residue of saliva. I wipe it off.

—You know there are rebels?

I nod.

—Yes. It is like the Middle East for Russia. Shit. It is a great pile of shit.

I gently run my hand over my face. Sometimes it helps. Sometimes it eases the pain. Not this time.

Widow's Peak points at the door Mickey's mother and Spiky went through.

—My brother, his name is Martin. I am Adam. Those are our American names. In Russia, we would be called something different. But here, these are our names. Tetka Anna thought of them for us.

He blows a smoke ring, watches it dissolve, thinking of his real name maybe. He stops thinking about it and looks back at me.

—Our father. My brother Martin and me, our father. He was an intelligence officer. In Chechnya. Very high up. Very important. He. Everybody must serve in Russia. Not like here. Everybody. My brother and me, we did not wait to be drafted. We served. Volunteers. In Chechnya. With our father. Intelligence.

He picks up the box of cigarettes. Holds it out to me. I shake my head. It hurts.

He shrugs and chains another.

—Intelligence. Interrogation. An interrogation unit we worked in. Our father put us there. To keep us out of combat. But it was.

He smokes.

—It was hard work. I think sometimes. Sometimes I think we would rather have fought. Martin would rather have fought. I know this.

He pulls the knife from his pocket and his thumb snaps it open and shut. Open and shut.

—OK. So. Yes. It was hard work. But it was over. Like all things. It was over.

Open and shut.

—I know English. I was almost. I could have taken another post. In Moscow. Somewhere. A city. I could have stayed in intelligence. But no. When we had served, we were done. Our father. He understood. Chechnya.

Open.

—He stayed. His duty. And our mother.

And shut.

—She stayed. Of course. And. There are people there. These women. They have lost husbands. Sons. So.

Open.

—So one of these women. She has a bag. A knapsack. She walks into a café. She sits at a table. She takes off her knapsack. She reaches inside of it. And the bomb inside goes off. And the intelligence officer sitting at the next table is blown up. And his wife he is having lunch with is blown up.

And shut.

—And this woman had lost men. Her husband and her boys. And so she became a *Shakhidki*. A holy warrior. The newspapers, they call them also black widows.

He slips the knife back in his pocket.

—And now you know what this is. And you know also.

He draws the last cigarette from the box and lights it.

—You know also, I think, that she is one, too.

He points at the closed door.

—Tetka Anna. A *Shakhidki*.

THERE'S MORE.

—Martin wanted to stay. To fight. He wanted to reenlist and fight in Chechnya. No interrogation this time. Guns. Battle. But he would have died. We both would have died. They knew who we were. The rebels. They knew our father. We would have been assassinated as soon as we returned. Anywhere in Russia we would be assassinated. And family. We still had family. Here. Tetka Anna.

Out of cigarettes, he has begun pacing again.

—After Mikhail was killed, she was calling all the time. To talk to our mother. She was so sad. When our mother was killed, she was more sad. And I told my brother, *If we stay here we will be killed.* He did not care. But I did. I told him, *We can still do something. We have family. We can take care of Tetka Anna. For mother. For mother.* He likes this. Taking care of someone else, it makes him. He does not forget, but it makes him better. We came here. And she is. There is only one thing she talks about. Yes? No. Two things. Her son. And you. We can do nothing about her son.

He returns to the chair, sits, and pokes at the butts in the glass dish. He finds one not quite half smoked and lights it.

—But maybe we can do something about you.

He takes a drag from the stale butt and makes a face, but he keeps smoking it.

—She told us that David believed you were dead. OK. We investigate. There are books. There are old TV programs. There is the Internet. And we find that there is no body. Something is wrong. In Chechnya, if a rebel is not there when the soldiers go to capture him, often the family says he has died. The soldiers say, *Where is the body?* And if there is no body, or if it is the wrong body, they bring us the family and we ask them questions. But your family, where are they? We do not know. We need. We need someone to ask questions. No. Someone we can ask questions. There are these things.

He points at the papers at my feet, at the photocopy of my ID. I pick up both papers.

—This was bought from a forger. He heard of Tetka Anna. Brought her these and sold them to her. She thought they could help. How? I do not know. But, the man who sold them. That is a man my brother and I must talk to.

I look at the photocopy and think about Billy. A young guy. A freelancer. A guy with a talent for computers and pieces of plastic.

I put the papers together and fold them between my hands.

Adam sucks a last bit of smoke from his butt, crushes it and begins digging for another.

—We went to him. Martin and I. The things. The things he knew. We had no idea.

He finds a suitable remnant, straightens and lights it.

—He does work for everyone. His work is valued. He does work for David. Not just forgery. But information. He has a gift for this. Like us. But different. His is with machines. Ours, not so. But we can learn what he knows.

He makes a noise, like a cat quietly coughing up a hairball, and drops the butt back in the dish. He sniffs at his fingertips and makes the sound again.

—And we do. We learn.

He closes his eyes.

—Too much.

He opens them.

—David. He is our uncle. By marriage only. But he is our uncle. But this man. He is shit.

He stands and paces once more.

—The forger tells us he has done a job for David. Identification for a man in Las Vegas. He showed us the pictures. He showed us the changes. He told us what he thinks. But we do not need him to tell us. We can see it. But there is more. If you wait, if you are patient, there is always more. He has met our cousin. Mikhail. And he knows something.

He stops pacing.

—Mikhail had lost his passport. He was to travel soon and he had lost his Russian passport. This is not a easy thing to replace. But it is something David could help with. He was a artist, our cousin. You know this? A filmmaker. A student.

I nod.

—Yes. He wanted to make a film. For school. NYU. I remember when my mother received the letter from Tetka Anna. She was so proud. She told us what it was, NYU. One of the best. And expensive. They do not give you the money to make your films. He wanted money for this film. He went to his uncle. He had plans. He would go to Europe. Take time from school and travel Europe. Russia. See family. Then back and start this film. But David, he thinks a man should work. He offered the money, but Mikhail must work for it. *Do not go to Europe,* David said to him, *go to Mexico. Have fun in Mexico. Relax. But look for this man.*

He points at me.

—You. David told his nephew to go to Mexico and look for you. *Do not do anything,* he said. *Just look.* David promised the money whether Mikhail saw you or not. Ten thousand dollars to go to Mexico on vacation and to look. Why not?

He stops pacing.

—And the forger can tell us this story because Mikhail had lost his passport. So David had sent him to the forger. And he had bragged to the forger. About his uncle. About the job he would do. And how he would be paid. Paid by his uncle to go to a foreign country and look for a killer.

He makes the hairball sound. But this time he is not smoking.

—So now we know. We know you are alive. We know you are in Las Vegas. We know David is protecting you. And we know how little he cares for his family. Is there need for more?

He waits.

I shake my head.

He nods.

—But there is more. We cannot make Tetka believe. She will not believe this is David. That he would do these things. She thinks we are wrong. Until she sees you at his office. And the picture in the paper. And we show her the forger's pictures again. And she believes. So then. She wants you. And we know where to find you. Because in the news article there, it says the man you are with is a baseball player. And people at newspapers are weak and make little money. For a little more, they will tell you where someone is. They told us where the baseball player was. And so we found you.

He sits. Picks at the cigarette butts again, but finds them wanting.

—And now. You are here. And Tetka Anna wants David to die. And she wants you to die. So you will do the first.

He scratches his beard.

—And we will do the second.

I look at the papers in my hands. I fold them over again and tuck them inside my jacket.

—If I try to kill David he'll have my parents murdered.

He nods.

—Yes. He will. He knows where they are. They are in a small town in Oregon. On the coast. This is something the forger found out for him. He found out from the Internet, from all of the men who talk about you. The forger told us this last. Told us where your parents are. Before we killed him. Because he was so broken. He wanted to die. That is what will happen if we go to Oregon. To them. You see?

—David. It's me.

He makes a sound, the kind you might make if your favorite player did something unbelievably boneheaded on the field.

—I need to see you, David.

—Yes. You do. But I, I have seen you already this morning. Do you know where? In the paper, yes? In the newspaper I saw you.

He will be making a fist and bouncing it lightly against his forehead. *What have I done to deserve this?*

—Yeah, I know. I need to see you.

—Yes. Yes, you must see me. How is the boy?

—He's fine. It wasn't a real fight, just him and his friend.

—Are you with them?

—No. They went to breakfast. I went to meet them and saw the paper on the way.

—Where are you now?

—The West Village. A coffee shop.

—Good. That is good. Stay away from them. This photograph. Someone might see something in this, yes? The surgery is good in its way, but someone could see something. There is nothing they can prove if you are gone. No way to ask you questions. I will have someone talk to the boy. If anyone asks him questions, you will be someone his agent hired. A simple bodyguard.

—Sure.

—Come to my office. We will talk. You will take care of this other business of ours. And then, then it will be time for you to leave.

He'll be looking at the ceiling, searching it with his eyes. *I have no words to describe how disappointed I am.*

—Come to my office. Wait for me there. Yes?

—Yeah. Sure thing. David?

—Yes?

—I'm sorry about this.

—Sorry will not help this. Come to my office and we will fix things. Things can always be fixed. I have told you this?

—Yeah.

—So we will fix.

He hangs up. I drop the phone in my pocket. I look out the car window as we hum over the George Washington Bridge. Martin is driving. Adam sits next to him, turned sideways, watching me in the backseat as I hang up the phone.

I lean my head against the window. I found some Motrin in Mickey's mother's bathroom. They made my face feel a little better. I was hoping to find some of the pills she had been talking about, but I'm sure it's better I didn't.

We come off the bridge and pull onto the West Side Highway. Déjà vu hits me. Right, I made a trip like this before. Coming back from Jersey in the DuRantes's car. They were brothers, too. Ed and Paris. They wanted me to set someone up. That didn't work out very well. Not for them. In the long run, not for anybody.

—What does he say?

I take my head from the glass.

—He said come over.

He looks at his watch.

—Good. He will be taking tea. There is a café below his office. The Moscow. He takes tea there. Do not go to his office. Go to the café. If you walk to him very quickly, talking to him. Saying you are sorry to be early. If you do this and move quickly, you can shoot him in the face. I have seen it. It will work.

—He'll have bodyguards.

—Yes.

—They'll kill me.

—They will kill you, or we will kill you. Someone will kill you, yes. Either way, Tetka Anna maybe will be able to sleep.

He peels the cellophane from a fresh pack of cigarettes.

—And we will not have to go to Oregon.

It's a long drive. Every bump hurts. I think about a town on the

Oregon coast. A place we used to go when I was a kid. We'd go up every summer. There was a campground near the beach. We'd bring the dog we had when I was a little kid. We'd go to the beach and watch the dog chase the waves. I stopped going when I was in high school. Summertime, there was always a baseball camp, always something more important. But my folks went without me. And they always talked about how they'd like to retire there one day.

We stop at the intersection of Brighton Beach Ave. and Brighton Road. Adam hands me a paper bag with a gun and a handful of bullets inside. I get out of the car. And then they drive away.

I heft the paper bag. That was smart of them, giving me the empty gun. If it had been loaded I would have shot them.

IT'S ANOTHER BEAUTIFUL day at the beach, just after twelve and the coastal haze is burning off. I walk the two blocks to the boardwalk. Right there, where the street dead-ends into the boardwalk, is a place called the Smoothie Café. My stomach rumbles, reminding me I've not eaten since the dogs I had at last night's ball game. I walk past the café and up the steps to the boardwalk.

The Brighton Towers, a sixties-styled modern apartment building, rises above me on my right. American flags dangle from several of the balconies. Coney and the ballpark are off in that direction. The Cyclones have a day game. Miguel and Jay will be there. Batting practice is probably ending. I would have liked to see Miguel play again. He's good at the game. I look the other way.

I can see the colored awnings of the four or five Russian cafés that cluster together about a quarter mile away. The beach is just starting to fill. People walk past me, across the boardwalk and down to the sand. They carry their blankets and coolers and umbrellas toward the water, their children running ahead of them. I go to one of the benches that face the sea, walking past an older Russian couple reclining on beach lounges, little squares of white cardboard tucked under the bridges of their sunglasses to protect their noses from the sun.

I sit on a bench.

I want to lie down on this bench. I want to pull my jacket and my shirt open and feel the sun on my skin. I want to find a bag of ice and lay here with it sitting on my face. I want to sweat and feel the poison leaching from my body. Instead, I open the paper bag.

There's the gun and five bullets. The gun is a Norinco. It's a mass-produced Chinese knockoff of a 1911 Browning. It's a very bad gun. It is legendary for both its inaccuracy and its utter lack of reliability. Anything over five yards is long range for this gun. Walk right up to someone, stick it against their heart, and there's still a good chance you'll miss. That's if you can get the thing to fire without jamming. I put my hands in the bag, eject the clip and snap the rounds into place.

I look to my left and catch the Russian woman with the square of cardboard on her nose looking at me. She quickly turns her face back toward the water. She's wondering what I'm doing with my hands in the bag. She's wondering if I'm fiddling with my lunch. The bag is in my lap; maybe she's wondering if there's a hole cut in the bottom of the bag so I can play with myself while I look at the girls on the beach. If only.

I push the clip back. It clicks, but when I turn the gun over it drops right out. I push it in again, hear the click, give it another tap, and hear another click. It stays in this time. I point the gun down and work the slide, chambering a round. It's sticky, but the bullet seats itself without going off. So that's something. I flick the safety up and down several times, making sure it doesn't have a nasty habit of flicking itself off. It seems OK. I take a look at the woman. She snaps her head back to the ocean again. I stand up, turn my back to her, and, as I walk around the bench, I take the gun out of the bag, tuck it into my waistband, and pull my jacket over it. I drop the empty bag into a trash can.

I start walking toward the cafés.

I'm holding the jacket closed over the gun. I have to do this because I can barely button the jacket over my fat gut. If I walk up to David with the jacket buttoned over the gun, he and his bodyguards will see the huge bulge it makes. Why'd they have to give me such a big gun? Something smaller I could have carried in my pocket.

I walk past a big concrete shelter: open on all four sides, stone tables with chessboards set into the tops, wood benches. A few people play, moving their pieces around the boards. One man reads a book patiently as he waits for his opponent to finish studying the game and make his move. I keep walking.

I'm trying to come up with a plan. It's hard because I've never really planned to kill someone. The people I've killed on my own, it always just happened. The ones I killed for David, Branko always made the plan, explaining to me carefully why he had set things just so, preparing me for when I would do this on my own. And here I am on my own, but this is not the way anyone planned it.

I've passed the Brighton Playground. The first café is just ahead. It's the Volno Café, a blue awning with yellow letters, a handful of people at the tables. A gull screams overhead.

I can walk up to him with my right hand out, ready to shake. It will give me an excuse to get very close. But I'll have to shoot with my left hand.

There are a few apartment buildings before the next café. I walk past a Parks Department "comfort station." The smell of urinal cakes is blown toward me.

The Café Tatiana is next, a blue awning with silver letters. The same tables, same people, the same signs with Russian letters. What do they call that? Cyrillic?

I can pull the gun with my right hand as I walk to the table, start shooting from several feet away, hope the bullets don't go awry, hope the terrible gun doesn't jam.

Right next to the Café Tatiana is the Tatiana Restaurant. One imagines a dispute between former business partners. A dispute that ended in an act of spite as one of them bought the space next to the original and opened a place with a nearly identical name. A very Russian strategy, meant to drive the former partner not so much out of business as out of his mind. Beyond them is the Winter Garden. And pinched-in before that, the Moscow Café.

I slide the jacket from my right shoulder. With a bit of maneuvering I'm able to take it off while keeping the gun concealed, then slip the gun into my left hand, the jacket draped over it. It's already a hot day, I can feel the sweat in my pits dribbling down my sides. It will make sense that I have the jacket off. If only the gun weren't so big.

I'm walking past the Tatiana Restaurant, the one I fancy was opened by the spiteful partner. I see again those fluorescent green and orange napkins blossoming from the water glasses on the tables. They remind me of caution signs. Markers warning of some peril in the road ahead.

Such a big fucking gun. Don't they know a small gun will kill just as well from two feet as a big gun will?

I see the red awning of the Moscow Café. It is the smallest of the cafés, only five or six tables on the boardwalk, a few more inside, and a short bar. Above it, where it abuts the Winter Garden, I can see the little corner turret window of David's office. His castle keep. Laundry lines are strung between the buildings behind the Moscow. Someone has a window garden of nothing but sunflowers.

I look at my left hand and forearm, draped under the jacket. The huge gun makes that arm look nearly a foot longer than my other one. Maybe I can walk up to David and tell him what has happened. Maybe he will be grateful. He will send people to protect my parents from Adam and Martin. I'm in front of the Moscow.

I see David.

He's alone.

There are no bodyguards anywhere. He's alone. I look around for some sign of Adam or Martin. I can't see them.

There are no bodyguards. I can do it. I can kill David. And Adam and Martin? Without bodyguards to take care of, I'll have bullets left. I can handle them. I can handle them and I can get away. David sees me.

I walk toward him.

I put out my hand.

He starts to rise.

Words are coming out of my mouth, something about being early. Something about being sorry for making trouble.

His hand is out.

Branko walks out of the shadows inside the Moscow Café, a glass of tea in each hand.

BRANKO AND I had a conversation once.

I was still at the Suites. It was after my face had healed. We had worked together a couple times, but it was before The Kid. We had just come back from beating someone. Branko had watched, I had beaten. The knuckles of my right hand were swollen and the skin over them split and bleeding. Branko looked at them, then filled a bowl with ice water and had me soak my hand.

—If you are going to beat someone with your fists, you want always to have gloves. Leather work gloves are best. Better is to beat a person with a tool. Something that will not break. Something that will not break bones, unless you want to break bones. A shoe. A rolled magazine. A book. Bars of soap in a sock. These are all good. If you use your hands, always you will break your fingers. You see?

He showed me his hands. Large working hands, but no scars or knobs on the knuckles; signs he had already taught me to look for, indications that *this one is a fighter*. Branko wanted no one to know he was a fighter.

—I have always protected my hands. My hands will never fail me when I must hold a knife or a gun. When you are holding a knife or a gun, these are the times you must be able to trust your hands. Save your hands for these times.

He took my hand from the ice water and inspected it, blotting the blood with a dishrag.

—David tells me you have killed men.

He put my hand back in the water.

—He says you have killed some the TV does not know about, but not all they say you have. Do you know how many?

I did. And I told him the number.

He nodded.

—It is likely you will never meet someone who has killed more.

He leaned back in his chair.

—I have killed more. But that is different.

He took off the reading glasses he had worn as he inspected my hand.

—Do you like to kill?

I told him I didn't.

He folded the arms of his glasses and tucked them away inside his Windbreaker.

—Few men do. Only the sick. But all men, I think, get used to it.

He leaned forward again.

—Have you gotten used to it?

Under the ice water, I made a fist of my hand. It felt tight and I could only close it halfway. I told him I was starting to.

He stood up.

—That will make it easier.

He went to the door, stopped, pointed at my hand.

—Keep it in the water as long as you can. Next time, we will try it with a shoe.

BRANKO WALKS OUT of the shadows inside the Moscow Café, a glass of tea in each hand.

He sees me. I freeze. David sees me freeze. Sees what is in my eyes as I look at Branko.

David looks down. I look down. He is not looking at my left hand, at the ridiculously obvious bulge beneath the jacket. He is looking at my wrist, at my right wrist sticking out of my shirtsleeve. He is looking at the red welts on my wrist.

—Henry?

And then Branko is between us, the glasses of tea still in his hands.

—Go inside, David.

And David does. He turns and walks quickly into the Moscow without another look.

I look at Branko. He is looking at the welts.

David is gone.

I have failed.

Branko sets the glasses of tea on a table.

I run.

I RUN PAST the cafés and the comfort station and the shelter and the park. I'm winded. I'm worse than winded, I am fat and covered in sweat and gasping. I quit smoking long ago, but my lungs burn. My legs feel wobbly and unwilling to move. And every pounding step I feel in my face. I should have taken more Motrin. I should have never flushed the pills. I should be sitting on the floor of my shitty apartment zoned on Demerol, listening to music and staring at the carpet with spit running down my chin. That would be nice.

People look at me as I run past them, a man in black jeans and shirtsleeves running on the boardwalk, sweat rolling down his face. I pass the handball courts. My lungs are still heaving.

I look back over my shoulder. There is no sign of Branko. Of course not. He would never run after me, never risk attracting attention. Where will he be? The streets? He will be *thinking*. He'll be thinking about me on the boardwalk, lost, panicked, not knowing what else to do but keep going straight. He'll be on the streets parallel to the boardwalk, checking the breaks between buildings, making certain I stay on my course. I should get off the boardwalk. No. *That's* what he's thinking. He's thinking *I'll* think too much and head for the streets and he'll be there, looking for me. Or he's not on the street, he is behind me. Right behind me. I stop and spin and a man on Rollerblades behind me makes a sharp cut. He skates past, flipping me off. I have to cool down. I have to get it together.

Branko is in New York.

Why?

To kill me.

And it's not because of the fucking picture in the paper. There's no way Branko could have gotten here since that picture came out. They wanted to use me to kill Mickey's mother and then get rid of me.

I stop running. Running, I am an easy target.

I stroll toward Coney Island and the thick crowds around the amusement park. I watch the faces. The further I get from Brighton, the fewer are stamped by Russia. I'm past the Aquarium, just ahead is the fence surrounding the Cyclone.

Hiding in that crowd won't be enough. I need to think. I need a Percocet. I need a plan. I need a Darvocet. I need to know what Branko is doing, where he is. I need—

Shit.

Oh, shit.

Branko isn't hunting for me. Branko is in a car going to the airport. Branko is calling the airline and booking a flight to Oregon.

I turn around and start heading back.

I have to kill David. I have to find a way up into his office and kill him. I. No. I have to go to him and beg. I have to explain. No. Kill him. That's. Wait.

Branko won't be on a plane. They can't have me running around. There's too much I can tell the police if I'm caught. David won't just kill my parents. He'll use them. He'll. What? He'll.

I lean against the chain-link around the Cyclone. I tilt my head back and close my eyes, letting the sun fall on my face.

They will call me first. They will call me and tell me to come to them or Branko will leave for Oregon. That is what they will do.

My phone rings.

It's nice to be right about something every now and then.

I answer the phone.

—Henry, what is this? What is this you are doing?

I stand with my back to the fence, my eyes still closed, the sun still on my face.

—Why are you calling, David?

—Henry, Henry. What is this? Why am I calling? Why are you running? What is the trouble? Someone has been talking to you, yes? Yes? This, you do not need to answer. I know.

—Where's Branko?

—Branko, Branko is here.

He will be pointing at his own forehead. *Think, Henry, what else would Branko be doing?*

—He's not on his way to my parents?

—Henry.

His mouth will have dropped open. *You could think such a thing?*

—Are we children? We are not. We can talk. Is Branko on his way to your parents? No. No, Henry. What sense is there in that? None.

My hand is still stuffed inside the balled jacket, sweating on the gun.

—Let me talk to Branko.

—First, we talk.

—Now, I want to talk to him now.

—Tell me.

—Where's Branko?

—Branko is here.

—Let me talk to him.

Silence.

—I want to talk to him.

—Of course.

More silence. I stand there waiting. I stand there waiting while David takes his time getting Branko.

I'm standing here waiting, while David takes his time. My eyes snap open and I look down the boardwalk toward Brighton. I don't see Branko.

But Adam and Martin are ten yards away and getting closer.

More running.

I BREAK AROUND the corner. The Cyclone roars past, burdened with screaming passengers. As I run I unbutton my shirt, peel it off and stuff it in a trash barrel. Now wearing just a wife-beater, the tattoos running down my arms exposed to the sun, I cross the street toward one of the arcades. I unwrap the jacket from my hand. I stuff the gun in my waistband and tie the jacket around my middle so that it hides it. I walk into the arcade. There is a rack of sunglasses. I find a huge bug-eyed pair that sit on my face like goggles and all but cover my scar. I walk to the counter. A teenage girl wearing a blue shirt with the clown face of the Coney Island mascot silk-screened across it stands there making change for the kids playing video games. Behind her is a display of base-ball caps. I put the sunglasses on the counter and point at a red and white cap with I ❤ NY on the front. She takes the hat down and puts it next to the sunglasses.

—Forty.

I hand her two twenties and grab my purchases.

—Want a bag?

I rip the tag from the hat and put it on.

—No thanks.

I peel the sticker from the lens of my new sunglasses, put them on and head for the arcade entrance. I look down the street back toward the Cyclone. Adam is coming. He's alone. Martin will be up on the boardwalk in case I try to circle around. The arcade's other entrance opens on the midway. I turn around and head out that way.

I walk past a couple rides, spinning cars mounted at the ends of giant pinwheels. Barkers man the shooting galleries and penny pitches and ringtosses. They talk into microphones, calling for people to join in the fun and win a sawdust-stuffed Bugs Bunny. I cut straight through it all, making for the Stillwell exit. I come out into the street, walk to the corner and look across Surf Ave. at the subway station. It is shrouded in construction scaffolding, a huge sign announcing that it will reopen next summer.

Down Surf I see Adam standing next to the entrance to the Cyclone, peering up the street. I turn, and at the end of Stillwell, I see Martin coming down the steps from the boardwalk. I cut back onto the midway, walk up to the nearest game and put a ten down. The barker picks up the money.

—How many?

I'm looking back toward the street.

—As many as I can.

—Start with these.

No sign of Martin yet.

—Mister?

—Huh.

—Start with these.

He's offering me three baseballs.

—Got to knock all of them off. Completely off.

I look at what he's pointing at, the three wood milk bottles stacked in a pyramid on a little table.

I look at the balls in his hand. Take them. Stare at them. I wonder if the universe does this to everyone or if it's just me?

—You're up, mister.

—Right.

I look back at the street. Still clear.

I toss a ball. Miss everything.

—One down!

I look again. Clear. Toss. Miss.

—Two down.

Still no one. Toss. Miss.

—Three down. Got plenty left.

He offers me three more balls. I'm still looking for Martin. No sign. OK, time to go. I take a step toward the street.

—You got more balls coming, mister!

—That's OK. I.

Martin comes into view. I step back to the counter, take the balls and look at the bottles. I look only at the bottles. I do not look up to see if Martin has seen me. And I throw three misses. Shit. I should be able to hit those things.

—I got more?

—Ten buys nine.

He hands me three more. I throw one and knock the top bottle off. OK, that's more like it. The barker resets the bottle. I toss a ball up and down, enjoying the feel of it landing in my palm. And not, absolutely *not* looking up for Martin. The bottles are set. Now, the trick here is to hit them low. The bottoms of the bottles are weighted with lead or something. That's why it's so hard to knock them completely off of their little table. I throw hard and hit them dead center. The top bottle flies, but the bottom bottles just get knocked on their sides and spin around a couple times. The barker resets them. I focus on the target, not looking at Martin. Do not look. Let him pass on by. Yeah, I can do this. Shit, if there's one thing in life I have ever been able to do, it's throw a goddamn baseball. I throw and miss again.

—Shit. I got more?

—That's it.

I pull out a twenty.

—Let me get a few more.

I take a look to make sure Martin has moved on. He hasn't. He's twenty feet away, looking at the crowd and talking into his cell phone. Then he looks at me. He sees me seeing him, and starts talking a little louder into his phone.

—Balls, mister.

I grab the three balls and start firing them at Martin.

The first one hits him in the thigh and he stops and curses and does a little hop. The second one whizzes past his head and he instinctively covers his face, dropping his phone. The last one plunks him in the chest and he gasps and coughs. I run straight at him, drop a shoulder, and plow him to the ground. I keep running, the crowd parting for me, the barker yelling after me. I hit Stillwell and look over at Surf. Adam is coming around the corner. He sees me. I go straight across the street. A flea market has been set up on a parking lot. I run into it. I start making for the far side of the market, thinking I can cut back out to Surf and maybe grab a cab, but all I find is a chain-link fence. On the other side is a motor pool for the New York Department of Education or something, a couple acres of yellow school buses packed tight. I look back at the entrance of the flea market. Adam is working his way toward me; Martin is right behind him, rubbing his chest. I start to climb the fence. A man working a booth stocked with VHS tapes waves at me.

—Hey. Hey, man. You can't do that.

At the top of the fence are three strands of barbwire. I boost myself up so that both my feet are on the top bar of the fence. I balance there for a second, then push off, driving with my legs.

—Hey! I'm gonna call a cop, man.

I clear the barbwire and belly flop on top of the nearest bus.

—Hey.

The wind knocked out of me, I worm to the edge of the bus and push myself over. I drop to the ground and lay there for a second, trying to get my wind back. Sprawled on my stomach, I can see under the bus and through the chain-link. I see two sets of feet run up. One of them starts to climb. The feet of the VHS guy come around his booth.

—Hey! That's city property. You can't go in there.

I see the VHS guy's feet leave the ground, and then he's lying on his back, holding the side of his head. The other feet are going up the fence. I stand, one hand held over my stomach, and start working my way into the maze of yellow school buses. By the time I realize I've lost my gun, Adam and Martin are over the fence.

I STAY HUNCHED below the level of the windows. It's easy enough because my gut still aches from slapping down on the roof of the bus. Crap. That's where my gun is, either on top of that bus or on the ground next to it. I can cut back, circle back to that spot in the fence. No. Think. There are two of them, they'll be spreading out. I can't circle back. I need to lose them in here. Maybe go to ground. Find a good spot to hunker down and wait them out until they give up. I look around for a good hiding spot. It's all buses, the same hiding places over and over. I keep moving, heading toward what I think is the farside of the yard. I hear something. A voice? I stop. There are footsteps. They crunch in the gravel and then stop. I get down on my hands and knees and look under the buses, back in the direction I came from. Several buses back, Martin is lying on the ground, his phone pressed to his face. The footsteps crunch after me. I stand and start running. He's spotting for Adam, tracking my legs under the buses. I need to put a few more between us so he loses sight of me in the jumble of tires.

I dodge back and forth randomly, losing all sense of where I came from or which way might lead to the edge of the yard. I stop. I hear nothing but "99 Problems" blasting from the bumper cars. I'm sandwiched between two of the short buses that used to bring the special education kids to my high school. Straight ahead is the rear of one of the big buses. A ladder runs up past its emergency exit, bolted there so a guy can climb up and clean the roof. I run to it, climb on top and flatten myself on the sunbaked steel.

The hot metal feels good against my sore stomach. I rest my face against it. It burns for the first second and then starts to ease the pain beneath my skin. I crane my neck to get a look around. The Coney midway is to my left, the boardwalk and the ocean straight ahead.

The buses are packed tight. There's just enough room between them for a man to walk, just enough room for him not to have to turn his shoulders to get through. What I can do, I can stand up and run across the tops of the buses to the fence. By the time these guys realize what I'm doing I'll be halfway there. I can be over the fence and back on the boardwalk, back where there are people. That's what I need. People. Coming in here was stupid. I need to get back to where there are people.

I get up to my hands and knees, ready to jump to my feet and start running down the length of the bus.

—Hey!

I flatten.

—Hey.

It's coming from below.

—You! Hey, you! Hang on there. Hang on.

I twist my head from side to side, looking for who is calling to me. But nowhere does a head poke up above the level of the bus tops.

—Hang on, hang on!

—What? Yes. We are. Hello.

Adam's voice. He's below me.

The new voice comes closer.

—Yeah, you. Who the hell do you think I'm talking to? Hold on there. And tell your buddy to hold on.

—Uh, yes. Da. Yes.

Adam says something in Russian.

—You guys see the No Trespassing signs around this place?

—We are sorry. What?

—The signs. No Trespassing?

—No. No. Sorry.

—This is off-limits in here. Verboten, like.

—Sorry. No. We did not know.

—Yeah. Well there's a guy over in the flea market says you gave him a shove. Want to explain that to me.

—We. No. A man. He tried to.

He mumbles to himself in Russian.

—He tried to *grab* my brother.

Martin starts chattering loudly in Russian.

—Whoa. Fucking whoa! Tell your brother to settle down.

Adam says something else in Russian and Martin is quiet.

—The guy grabbed your brother?

—Da. Yes.

—The little guy out there shoved your bigass brother?

—He. Bigass? He grabbed him. Da.

—OK. Well, that's not his story.

—He is. He is bigass! We. We do not.

He starts rattling off Russian again.

—Whoa! Fucking shut it.

Adam shuts it.

—OK. Whatever happened, you guys are not supposed to be in here. What we are going to do, we are going to walk to the exit. We are going to go talk to the guy in the flea market and sort out who grabbed who. We're gonna take it all very easy, 'cause no one has been hurt. And if you and the guy out there can settle your differences without any charges, and that is how I'd really like to handle this, I will give you a citation for trespassing on city property. OK? Sound good? You get all that?

—Citation?

—Like a ticket. Just. Just come on. Come on.

Adam talks in Russian, Martin answers, and footsteps start walking away.

—Hey! Hey! Where's your friend?

—Friend?

—Tavarich. Right?

—Yes, I know what a friend is.

—Great. So where is he? Guy said there were three of you.

—No. *Nyet.* No. Only us.

Silence.

—Yeah, OK, fine. Just. Let's just get out of here, it's hot as hell.

I scoot to the edge of the roof and look down and see Adam and Martin threading their way through the buses, followed by a cop.

And my phone rings.

I pull it out of my pocket and press the power stud. The phone turns off, but not before emitting one final loud chime to let me know it won't be ringing again. I wait. The footsteps don't come back.

OK. Good. That was good. Sometimes a cop is good. Now I'll. They were going that way. So now I'll just go the other way and

I'll. I'll. Shit. I don't know what I'll do. I'll get out of here. I dangle my legs over the side of the bus and drop to the ground right at Branko's feet.

I try to run. Branko trips me. He's on top of me. His arms dragging mine behind me, his legs twining around mine.

—Calm down.

I jerk and writhe, trying to break free.

—I cannot talk until you calm down.

I open my mouth wide and scream. Branko pulls a racquetball from his pocket, stuffs it in my open mouth and holds his hand over it.

—Stop! We must talk. We will go someplace where we can talk. Out there.

He jerks his chin in the direction of the midway.

—We will go someplace where there are people. You will feel safe and we will talk.

I'm screaming through the ball, trying to force it out of my mouth with my voice.

Branko squeezes my face.

—Stop this. There is no more of this to do. You are not saving your parents this way. Think.

I stop screaming.

I think.

—Yes, think.

I think.

—You see now?

I think.

—Yes, you see.

He takes his hand from my face and holds it below my mouth.

I push the ball out with my tongue and it lands in his palm. He wipes it off on his pants and puts it back in his pocket.

—These things, you never know when you may need them again.

I WAIT WHILE Branko buys the tickets.

He waves me over and I go stand with him. We wait side by side, saying nothing. Our turn comes.

We get into our car and sit on opposite benches facing one another. The operator closes the door. It latches, he pulls the big lever that releases the brake and the Wonder Wheel spins, carrying us slowly into the air.

Branko looks out the side of the car, watching the ground drop away. I shift in my seat and the car rocks back and forth.

He looks at me.

—I cannot kill you here.

—I know.

—But you must be killed.

—Sure. That was the plan, right? I kill David's sister-in-law, and that's it. Hey, why not? I'm a fucking mess.

He shakes his head.

—No.

I watch his eyes as they gaze down at the midway.

—No. You are a mess. But no. You were not to be killed. No.

He looks at me.

—No.

—Bullshit, Branko. You're here. You are here.

—Yes. I am here. And I have something for you. Look what I have for you.

He reaches into his pocket and comes out with the Smith & Wesson .22.

—I am here to help you. With Anna. To help. Because you are a fucking mess. But the baseball player wants you. So David wants you. So I must help you. But now. Yes, now you are fucked.

Oh, crap. Wrong again, Henry.

The Wheel stops as the operator lets one couple off and puts another on. And then it spins again. We are near the top.

He puts the gun back in his pocket. He points over my shoulder, back toward Brighton Beach and David's office. Toward David.

—He is not unreasonable.

—Sure.

—But you had a gun. Those marks.

He points at the welts the bindings left on my wrists.

—These mean you have been held. Threatened. And you came to see David with a gun.

—His sister.

—Yes?

—She. Oh, shit, Branko. His sister-in-law and her damn nephews.

He nods. He looks at the ocean. He nods again.

—I cannot kill you here.

—You said that.

—We will go somewhere else. You will tell me about Anna and her nephews and what they told you.

He touches his upper lip, scratches a slight itch.

—And then I will kill you.

Behind Branko I can see the Cyclone's ballpark. The stands are full. The players are on the field. A game is being played.

—And what do I get?

—Your mother and your father. What else is there left?

—Right.

The Wheel spins again, carrying us toward the ground.

—But it must be now. You must go with me now. I know David.

He grunts.

—And he likes to have his way.

—Right.

We dip down, and the ballpark is lost to view.

The Wheel spins.

I AM EVIDENCE.

This is what I saw while I was being held down in the dirt with the ball in my mouth. Branko cannot kill me anywhere that he cannot safely dispose of my body. Nor can he march me down the boardwalk, or even out to the street and into a car. He can do none of that unless I am willing, unless he knows I will not start yelling for the police.

I am evidence.

My body and its fingerprints and its new face. The fingerprints will lead to Henry Thompson. The face will lead to the photo in the paper. The photo will lead to Miguel. And sooner or later, after the questions start, Miguel will lead to David.

He has to be careful.

But I don't.

OUR CAR CIRCLES to the ground. The operator opens the door and we climb out. Branko leads me past a cluster of kiddy rides and back to the boardwalk. We turn left and start the long walk to Brighton Beach.

We walk past the fried clam shacks and the beer booths and the Cyclone and the Aquarium. And then I turn left, heading for the walkway that will take me to the Aquarium subway station. Branko catches up with me and walks by my side.

—This is not the way.

—This is the way I'm going.

—David is waiting.

—You should go then. You can tell him I'm not coming.

—I cannot let you go.

—What are you going to do, Branko? You can't drag me screaming. You can't kill me here. Go back to David. Tell him I said no.

—I cannot leave you.

—OK.

We get to the station. There are two cops standing next to the token booth. I walk up to them.

—Excuse me, officers?

—Yeah?

I point at Branko.

—This guy wants to know which train to take to get to Queens.

One cop looks at me.

—Sorry, I'm from Staten Island.

The other cop points at the map on the wall.

—Let's take a look.

He walks to the map, taking Branko over with him. I wave.

—Good luck.

Branko smiles.

—And to you.

He keeps the smile on his face and follows the cop to the map. I buy a MetroCard from the booth, walk upstairs and get on a

Manhattan-bound F train. Cops just when I needed them, twice in one day. Go figure. Maybe things are turning my way at last. But probably not.

I HAVE TO talk to Mom and Dad. I have to tell them I didn't kill David. And that means Adam and Martin will be coming, coming to interrogate them.

I never wanted to talk to them again, never wanted to see them. There are no explanations for the things I have done. No way you can tell your mother and father that you have murdered people to keep them alive.

So while I sit on the train, I try to figure out how I'm going to tell them all of that. But, oh yeah, first I have to figure out how I'm going to find their damn phone number.

—What city please?
—Port Orford, Oregon. A residential listing for Thompson?

I get two Thompsons. The first is picked up by an answering machine. The voice is not my mother or my father. The second is answered by a small child who tells me that her daddy is not home and her mommy is in the bathroom. Each time, as the phone is ringing, a pit with no bottom opens in my stomach and I fall into it. I am so relieved. Then I dial information again and try it with my mother's maiden name and my father's middle name and every variation I can think of. None of them work. But I'm not done. I remember what Adam told me about how they found out where my folks live in the first place. I get off my bench, walk out of Washington Square Park, and go looking for an Internet café.

> MagickBulletMan: No way! I've been to the El Cortez in Las Vegas. I tried to stay in the room Thompson and Sandy Candy were in and they told me it was closed off.
>
> MrTruth: That's because you didn't bribe the security guard like I did. You think they're going to let you in there if you ask nice? Don't be an asshole, MBM. You want something you got to go get it. Just like Henry.
>
> MagickBulletMan: A) Don't curse at me! B) You don't know anything about Henry. C) YOU'RE LYING!!!
>
> MrTruth: FUCK YOU, MAGICKBOWELMOVEMENT!
>
> Robert Cramer: No shouting in here guys.
>
> MagickBulletMan: Sorry, Robert. I'm just sick of MrTruth acting like he's the only one that knows anything about Henry and pretending like he's been everywhere Henry was when we all know he's lying.
>
> MrTruth: MBM wouldn't know the truth if it fucked him in the ass. Henry Thompson was captured at the El Cortez by a Special Forces Black Ops Squad. They then manufactured evidence to make it appear that he had escaped. They want to maintain a fiction that he is at large so they can use him as a cover story for state killings in the future. In the meantime, Henry was reprogrammed and sent to the Middle East to hunt for terrorists and insurgents.
>
> MagickBulletMan: OMG! That's what I'm talking about. Every time he comes here he has a new story. Last time he said Henry was working a fishing boat in Alaska.
>
> MrTruth: My story changes because I am constantly gathering

evidence and trying to get to the heart of the greatest crimi-
nal mystery this country has ever known and unlike some
assholes I care about Henry and what happened to him so I
work to find out what really happened instead of just parrot-
ing the crap that the police and the FBI would have us think.
FUCK FACE!

Robert Cramer: I said no shouting, MrTruth.

MrTruth: FUCK YOU ASS CRAMMER! Just because you
wrote a couple books about Henry you think you own him.
That's bullshit! Henry's story is an American narrative that
belongs to all of us. It's part of our heritage and you can't
shut up the truth!

USER MRTRUTH HAS BEEN BOUNCED
FROM THE SITE

MagickBulletMan: Thanks, Robert. That guy drives me crazy.

Robert Cramer: Well it is an open forum, MBM, so you need to
be patient with all points of view.

SF Giants Fan: You think there's anything to what he says?

MagickBulletMan: No way, SF. All that conspiracy stuff is crap.

SF Giants Fan: What about the Alaska stuff?

Robert Cramer: The truth is, Henry Thompson is most likely
dead. In <u>The Man Who Came Back</u> I wrote about the many
enemies he had made. More than likely one of these killed
him during the Las Vegas rampage and his body was dis-
posed of.

MagickBulletMan: Who do you think killed him, Robert?

Robert Cramer: I have a theory, but you'll have to buy my new
book when it comes out. I don't claim to know the truth, but
I think when <u>The Man Who Got His Due</u> is released it will

answer pretty much all the key questions about Thompson's crimes.

SF Giants Fan: I was asking about Alaska because I heard that his folks had moved to Oregon. That's not all that far from Alaska. Maybe that's where he really is.

MagickBulletMan: where did you hear that, SF?

SF Giants Fan: On another site.

MagickBulletMan: Which one?

:

:

:

MagickBulletMan: SF?

SF Giants Fan: sorry. I think it was Danny Lester's site.

MagickBulletMan: Danny Lester sucks! Ru one of his goons?

SF Giants Fan: No I just went to his site.

MagickBulletMan: Danny Lester floods other sites with links to his. He lies all the time. and he's notorious for logging onto sites under assumed identities. Ru Danny Lester?

SF Giants Fan: No.

MagickBulletMan: Robert, I think SF is Danny Lester. I think he's here trying to find out where Henry's parents are so he can harass them like he did right after Las Vegas.

Robert Cramer: OK, just settle down, MBM. SF, are you associated with Danny Lester?

SF Giants Fan: No.

Robert Cramer: Well, you've never been on my site before and you're asking about Thompson's parents. Danny Lester is known to have made a habit of tracking down those poor people to harass them about Thompson's whereabouts.

SF Giants Fan: I am not Danny fucking Lester.

Robert Cramer: I'll take your word for that. But I would prefer
that there were no swearing on this site. And just to be on
the safe side I'm going to declare Thompson's parents as an
off limits topic for the rest of this session.

MagickBulletMan: Good idea, Robert.

USER SF GIANTS FAN HAS LOGGED OFF

And so it goes.

I haven't read Robert Cramer's *The Man Who Came Back* and I
can pretty much guarantee I won't be reading *The Man Who Got
His Due*. I can guarantee these things because I did read his first
book about me, *The Man Who Got Away*. Once around the block
with that shit was more than enough. It was apparently also more
than enough to put him on an equal footing with Sandy Candy
and Danny Lester as an acknowledged Henry Thompson expert. I
guess I was lucky to hit his site on a day when he was doing a live
chat, but it doesn't feel that way.

I look out the window. It's getting dark. I've been sitting in this
place on Twelfth Street for hours, setting up free e-mail accounts
on Hotmail and Yahoo and using them to create screen identities
at various Henry Thompson chat sites. But there's only so much
traffic on the sites. Most of them are devoted to posts, and it
takes far too long to generate responses to my questions. And
the freaks on these sites, my fan base, are cliquey as hell. They
chat, post, and e-mail to each other constantly, but newcomers
aren't made to feel overly welcome. It's not as if I lack for Henry
Thompson trivia knowledge to prove my devotion to the topic at
hand, but just getting anyone to acknowledge you is a challenge.
I spend two hours slowly creeping my way into a chat on www.

therealhenrythompson.com, but when I try to get any actual information about my folks I'm shut down.

I put my fingers on the keyboard. They're shaking. Hours of sitting here, staring at the screen and drinking coffee have fried me out. I need to take a walk.

I log off and go to the counter. The NYU student at the register checks how long I've been on and rings me up. I hand her some money. She looks up as she's handing me my change.

—Nice hat.

I put my hand on my head. I took off the sunglasses and put my jacket on over my wife-beater, but I'm still wearing the I ❤ NY hat.

—You want it?

—No. I was being sarcastic.

—Your loss.

I walk outside and drop the hat in a garbage can.

It really is her loss. A hat like this, worn by Henry Thompson? She could sell it on eBay to one of those assholes for a few hundred easy.

I WALK UP Seventh Avenue.

Adam and Martin won't get on a plane for Oregon right away. They don't know what I'll do. They'll want to find me before I can tell David anything. They'll want to protect their aunt.

I walk out of the West Village and into Chelsea.

David won't do anything right away, either. He'll wait for my next move. He knows the thing I'm most likely to do is come walking in just like he wants. But I know him, too. I know he likes to talk about the bottom line, about the expense of revenge. But I've seen the bodies; men and women killed to send a message. I've broken bones for his spite.

I walk out of Chelsea and into Midtown.

The cops. I can walk into a precinct house and turn myself in. But it will take time. Time before I can get anyone to listen about the danger my parents are in. Time before anyone who can do something about it appears. And then for how long? For how long do the police protect them?

No.

David has to die. Adam has to die. Martin has to die. Branko has to die.

But first I'll take another shot at the Internet. See if I can find someone with a phone number. See if I can talk to them. God, I don't want to talk to them.

I'm standing on the corner of Forty-second and Seventh. The southern edge of Times Square. I look down toward Eighth Ave., the block they used to call the Deuce. When I first came to the City, it was lined with titty bars and porn shops. It had already been cleaned up a lot when I left, but now it looks like a giant mall. Movie theaters, a McDonald's, Chili's, a Hello Kitty store. And a huge Internet café. I stand there staring at it, and a guy in a bright orange poncho forces a piece of cardboard into my hand and walks on. I look at the card.

It's an advertisement for Legz Diamond, one of the old Midtown strip clubs. I look at the guy who gave it to me. He walks down the street, pulling the cards from the kangaroo pocket in his poncho and handing them to the men streaming past on the sidewalk, ignoring the women. Well, at least that hasn't changed. I start down the block headed for the Internet place, flicking the card's edge against my thigh as I walk.

I guess it's a good thing, all this renovation, all this cleanup. But I miss the old city. I miss that feel. The character. I look at the card again. At least they haven't cleaned it up entirely. At least there are still strippers.

Strippers.

At least there are still strippers.

Oh, God, there are still strippers.

PRIVATE EYES IS a strip club. Being a strip club, it is just like all other strip clubs. I pay my twenty-dollar cover, get my hand stamped, pay eight bucks for a soda, and take a seat at the bar. I am the only patron at the bar. Just me, a scantily clad bartender and scantily clad cocktail waitresses picking up drinks. I'm alone at the bar because of Rudy Giuliani.

While he was still mayor, Rudy got a public decency law passed that targeted strip bars and porn shops. The essence of the law is that adult trade can comprise no more than 49% of a business. The strip clubs' answer to this dilemma was to wall off the majority of their physical space, and enclose their stripping in a carefully measured 49% of their total square footage. Inside that 49% they wanted room for patrons and strippers and little else. Thus the bar at Private Eyes features a wide expanse of elbow room because you can sit there all night without seeing a single bare tit. I sit there alone and let the bartender fisheye me.

She's wondering what's wrong with me. She's wondering what a guy is doing coming into a strip club and paying eight bucks for a soda and not going into the next room to look at the naked girls. She's waiting for me to start talking. She's expecting me to turn out to be a talker. I don't talk. I sit and I sip and I don't go into the next room. The minute I go into that room, dancers will start coming to my table and offering me lap dances. I don't want a lap dance. I don't want to look at naked women. I want to sit here and wait. So I wait. And after about half an hour I hear what I've been waiting for. I hear the voice of the DJ, who sounds like every other DJ in every other strip club ever.

—That was Misty. Misty. Misty coming around to your tables right now. A special dance from Misty coming your way. And now we're gonna bring out our special guest dancer. She's here just for the weekend. You've seen her on Howard Stern and Sally Jessy. She had a feature spread in Hustler. The most infamous dancer in the world. Sandy Candy!

The DJ plays her song. Van Halen, "Ice Cream Man."

I go in.

SHE'S GOOD.

I've never actually seen her dance, and she's really very good. Not a lot of titty and ass shaking, more a slow strip with some low-key pole work. Classy, as these things go. And she looks great. Still wearing the Bettie Page cut. Never did get rid of the tattoos, the half circle of stars along her collarbone and the pin-ups on her shoulders. The crowd is thin this early, but the guys like her. She stays up on the main stage for a couple songs, then scoops her discarded dress from the steps, shimmies back into it, and comes off the stage to a nice round of applause.

There are a couple fans with a table up front. She goes straight to them and kisses them on the cheek. They probably follow her from gig to gig. She signs some 8x10s they have and a couple copies of a book that I assume is the one she had ghostwritten last year. Then she starts circulating, working the tables. She'll do lap dances. The rate will probably be double what the regular girls get. I could wait, but she's pretty popular with the clientele, and if she hits a big spender she might just camp out with him all night. Any stripper would just as soon cash in on one guy as dance thirty or forty. I wave down a cocktail waitress.

—What'll ya have, baby?

—Just a seltzer. And could you ask Sandy to come over?

—Baby, she'll get around. You want to talk to her now, all you got to do is go say hi.

I hand her a C-note.

—I'm shy.

She smiles even wider than she already was, takes the bill from my fingers and gives them a little squeeze at the same time.

—Sure thing, baby. You just sit tight.

She walks across the room. Sandy is leaning against the back of a chair, casually letting her breasts rub the head of the man sitting there, talking to him and his friends, laughing at everything they say. The cocktail waitress touches her shoulder and whispers in her ear and points at me. Sandy looks over, squinting into the dark corner of the room where I am seated on a banquet. She smiles, waves, holds up a finger to tell me to wait just a second, blows me a kiss, and turns back to the guys she's been working. I wait a little longer, turn down several dances, thank the cocktail waitress when she brings me my seltzer that she still charges me eight bucks for despite the hundred she has tucked in her pocket. And while I'm watching her walk away, a hand slides onto my shoulder and Sandy smiles at me and pinches my earlobe and I jump and say something like *Hi, hello, uh, hi,* and the blank look and utter lack of recognition leaves her face as soon as she hears my voice, but she doesn't scream and turn and run, she just drops her hand from my shoulder and lifts it to her forehead.

—Fuck. This is gonna cost a fortune in therapy.

WE SIT AT the far end of the bar, away from the bartender and the customers coming in through the front door and making a beeline for the main room. She drinks red wine that comes in little single-serving bottles with screw-off caps. I pay.

—You're handling this pretty well.

She pours her wine into a glass.

—Yeah. That would be the Librium. There's not much I don't take well.

Librium. Antianxiety agent. Narcotic. Addictive. This information reels itself off in my mind, followed immediately by a strong desire to ask if she has any on her. I drink my seltzer instead.

—When did you start on that?

She's sipping her wine. She stops in midsip, puts the glass down and looks at me.

—When? When did I start taking Librium? Shit, Henry, I don't know, maybe about five minutes after I turned myself in to the cops and they started showing me pictures of the shit that happened in my house.

—Right.

—Color.

—Sorry. I.

—They showed me color pictures of those two hicks with their heads beaten in.

—Yeah, I get it. I'm.

—They showed me a picture of Terry.

She takes a big gulp of wine.

—Terry. What that dog did to Terry.

—OK. Stupid question. Just.

—So it was probably right around then, when I saw the picture of Terry with his dick chewed off, that I started taking Librium. After I got done screaming and all.

She finishes off her wine and signals the bartender for another. We don't say anything while she brings it over and takes more money from my pile of bills on the bar.

Sandy cracks the top and pours.

—And you? How have you been? See you got a new look. How's that working out for you?

—Sandy. I need help.

—No shit? Well, there's a shocker. Wanted man shows up at a Manhattan strip club to see me? And he needs help? I would have had a hard time putting that together.

—It won't take much time. I just.

I look over at the bartender, but the music from the main room is loud enough that she's not hearing any of this.

—Sandy. It's my parents.

—Sandy to the stage, please. Sandy to the stage.

She looks up, the DJ calling her for her next performance. She tosses down the rest of her wine, sets the empty glass on the bar, and kneads her neck with her right hand.

—OK. I'm gonna go dance now.

She stands up.

I put a hand on her arm.

—Sandy.

She moves her arm away from my hand.

—I'm gonna dance, and then I'm gonna come back and help your parents, because they probably never did anything to anyone, except for having you. And then you are going to fuck off out of my life. OK?

—Yeah. OK.

She walks back into the main room, and through the door I see her talking to the DJ, asking him for something, and he digs through his CDs and nods, and she goes up on the stage and dances to "Psycho Killer."

USER SCANDY HAS SIGNED ON

God Zilla: Hey sandy.

MagickBulletMan: Hi sandy.

sidomaniac: What's up sandy?

budthecat: Sandy!

scandy: hey, guys!

sidomaniac: Cool of you to drop in.

MagickBulletMan: Thought you were in NY.

scandy: i am! I'm dancing at Private Eyes! It's so great! I just had some time and wanted to say hi to my real fans!

God Zilla: ty, sandy.

scandy: sure, big Z!

sidomaniac: We were talking about the Danny Lester rumor.

budthecat: I love you, Sandy.

scandy: what rumor, sid? ty, kitty! meow!

MagickBulletMan: Lester is saying that henry has been in contact with you.

sidomaniac: It's bs.

scandy: it sure is, sid. If Henry Thompson ever made contact with me the first thing I'd do is call the cops!

MagickBulletMan: That's what I said.

God Zilla: He's dead anyway.

budthecat: Then show me the body, zilla. habeas corpus. When there's a body I'll believe he's dead.

God Zilla: There's no way he could stay hidden this long. They did a Hoffa on him.

sidomaniac: Who's "they," zilla?

scandy: hey, guys! anyone seen henryhunter today?

budthecat: Not today.

God Zilla: Sorry

sidomaniac: Not here.

MagickBulletMan: Did you try therealhenrythompson? he hangs there a lot.

scandy: this is my first stop. anyone know how to get in touch with him?

God Zilla: Nope

SCANDY: You have a private message from BUDTHECAT.

I know his email, sandy. Want to send a message?

MagickBulletMan: Don't know where he is.

Private message for BUDTHECAT.

could you, honey? Just tell him I'm here! TY!

sidomaniac: Havn't seen hh for awhile.

SCANDY: You have a private message from BUDTHECAT.

Sure!

scandy: hey, guys! I have to go do a couple things. I'm gonna stay logged on, so if hh comes by please tell him I'll be right back!

MagickBulletMan: Sure.

Sandy pushes back from the computer in the Internet café on Forty-second.

—Jesus, they freak me out.

I watch as their chat continues to scroll down the screen. They bounce various theories about me, opinions about Cramer's books, quiz each other on the names of my former "associates," talk about my cat, and whatever else. It's all mixed together with personal talk, mostly about a chronic lack of girlfriends.

—Interesting following.

She slides her eye from the screen to my face, and then back to the screen.

—They're not my fans. They're yours. I'm just extra. If it wasn't for you, they'd have latched on to some other piece of ass.

USER HENRYHUNTER HAS SIGNED ON

henryhunter: Hey room.

God Zilla: Hey, hh.

MagickBulletMan: Hi hh

SCANDY: You have a private message from HENRYHUNTER.

You here, Sandy?

sidomaniac: Sandy candy was looking for you, hh.

henryhunter: ty, sid.

Private message for HENRYHUNTER.

hey, hh! Thanks for coming!

sidomaniac: She said she'd be right back.

SCANDY: You have a private message from HENRYHUNTER.

Sure, sandy. What's up?

Private message for HENRYHUNTER.

um, it's kind of personal. Can we do a room!

God Zilla: You back, sandy?

SCANDY: You have a private message from HENRYHUNTER.

You bet! I'll call it hhscandy.

Private message for HENRYHUNTER.

TY, hh!

USER HENRYHUNTER HAS GONE TO A PRIVATE ROOM

USER SCANDY HAS GONE TO A PRIVATE ROOM

sidomaniac: Oh man! A private with sandy! How'd hh score that?

USER SCANDY ENTERING ROOM HHSCANDY

scandy: hh?

henryhunter: Hey sandy. what can I do for you? You OK?

scandy: well, remember when you did one of my chats a couple weeks back?

henryhunter: Yeah! I love your site!

scandy: TY, hh! Anyway. you were talking about closure and I was thinking about that and you said how talking to someone who actually knew henry might help with my therapy and you said something about his parents and I was talking to my therapist and he said he thinks something like that might really help with my nightmares and stuff and I was wondering if you were like just talking or if you might know how to get in touch with them?!?

henryhunter: Wow, sandy, that's pretty heavy.

scandy: i know! Sorry to like unload on you!

henryhunter: No! it's ok!

scandy: ty, hh! You're so sweet! can you help me? It's really important to me!

henryhunter: Well, pretty much all the serious Henry Thompson people (and I mean the ones who want to seem him brought to justice, not the sickos) know by now that his parents moved to a place in Oregon. Some people have managed to get their hands on an address, but that's pretty secret stuff.

scandy: what about a phone number or something?

henryhunter: Someone might have one. But they would have gotten in illegally so they'd be pretty cautious about sharing it or talking about it.

scandy: you know someone like that hh? I bet you do!

henryhunter: I might know something. But this isn't really what I'd call a secure connection. I could maybe help, but I'd need your private email to send it to you.

scandy: ok

henryhunter: And then maybe we could like exchange some emails. I'd like to hear how things are going with your therapy and stuff. We could even sinc up. Chat some more.

scandy: sure thing, hh! I'd love that! But I have to get back to the club! If I give you my address can you send that number right away?!? Then we can make a date to chat! That'd be cool!

henryhunter: Great!

scandy: super! My address is candicestalbot@earthlink.net

henryhunter: I'll send you a message as soon as I sign off.

scandy: TY, HH! You're my hero!

USER SCANDY HAS SIGNED OFF

—Fucking great. Now I'm going to have to change my private e-mail. Do you know how big a pain that is? All my charges go there. My PayPal. My eBay. Shit.

I point at the screen.

—Candice?

—Candice Sandra Talbot. Sandy Candy. Like it was meant to be.

—It's a nice name.

—Whatever.

She logs on to her e-mail account. She hits the check mail button four or five times until a new message pops up. She opens it.

Sandy,

It was cool chatting with you in private. I think you're making the right decision trying to get in touch with Mr. and Mrs. Thompson. Everything I read about them and all the stuff that was on TV made them seem like very good people. It's not their fault their son did the things he did. They've probably suffered from his crimes as much as anyone. Please don't share this number and please delete this email. Like I said, "someone" (wink-wink) probably had to do some illegal hacking to get this. Write me back and let me know your MSMessenger account. We can chat anytime. I live in Ohio, which isn't so far from Pennsylvania, so maybe we could even meet! That would be great. Good luck and I can't wait to hear how it goes. Have fun dancing.

HH

(But my real name is Sam)

Sandy scribbles the number at the bottom of the screen onto a scrap of paper.

—Ol' Sam probably started jerking off to a picture of me as soon as he hit send.

———

SANDY GOES TO the bathroom while I pay for our time on the computer. She comes out and walks past me. I grab my change and run after her. She's walking fast down Forty-second on her way back to Private Eyes.

—Sandy. Wait up.

She keeps walking.

—Hey.

I catch up to her, but she keeps storming along.

—What do you want? You got the number. Go use it.

—Yeah. Well.

—What? You want something else?

—I just.

—What?

—I could use a place. For a couple hours. To make my call and think for a little while.

She nods.

—So, what, you thought maybe my hotel room or something?

—Whatever. I just need someplace quiet to make this call. And I need to sit and—

—I have to get back to the club.

—Sure. I just. I.

—Need more help?

—Yeah. I do.

She stops in the middle of the sidewalk and the Saturday night traffic splits and flows around us.

—Jesus! What have you ever needed from anyone but help?

—Sandy.

—That's your fucking MO.

She cups her hand over her mouth and talks into it like it's a radio.

—Calling all cars, calling all cars. Be on the lookout for a mass murderer that often needs help and who fucks up people's lives.

—They're. They'll kill my mom and dad.

She raises her eyebrows.

—So. Fucking. What.

She puts her face close to mine.

—Your parents. Your fucking mom and dad. Like no one else was ever born. Like no one else *has* a mom and dad. My mom and dad are in Phoenix. They got problems. My mom is a bank teller and she's worried about all the weight she's been putting on since she turned fifty, and my dad just took early retirement from his job with Xerox so they wouldn't lay him off. Their biggest problem is their stripper daughter that they don't understand and can barely talk to. But at least she never did anything to put their lives in danger. And I didn't do anything to put yours in danger, either. It's not my fucking fault. It's yours. So you fucking save them.

She turns to start walking and I grab her arm. She looks at my hand and then back up at my face.

—Let go.

—I can't. I. I just. Sandy, I'm sorry. I don't have anyone else.

—I wonder why that is. Could it be because everyone who helps you gets killed? Let go of my arm.

I don't.

—Let go of my arm or I will scream.

I let go. She jerks her head and leads me away from the middle of the sidewalk.

—Just so we're clear. I don't like you. You fucked up my life. I was already pretty messed up. I mean, stripping at Glitter Gulch, dealing grass and fucking Terry the steroid king wasn't the greatest way to live, but at least I didn't wake up screaming five nights out of ten. I want you to leave me alone.

I look at her. I look at the Lucky jeans and the Michael Kors top she changed into when we left the club. I look at the Louis Vuitton shoes on her feet and the matching bag on her shoulder. She watches my eyes as they inventory these items.

I shrug.

—You seem to be doing pretty well out of the deal.

She nods. Smiles.

—Yeah. Pretty good. Pretty good with the creeps that come out of the woodwork every time I turn around. Pretty good with the guys who like to pretend they're you. Or with Danny Lester when he gets drunk every couple of months and finds my latest unlisted number and calls to accuse me of hiding you and ends up telling me how much he wants to fuck me in the mouth. Or whatever ex-cop bounty hunter who wants to grill me. I do really good with all the assholes at the clubs who want a lap dance so they can tell their friends they rubbed crotches with Sandy Candy. Fuck you! Fuck you, Henry! You think I want this? You think I want to live off your carcass like those freaks on the computer? This is what I have. This is how I can get by. It's totally fucked, but it's what I have. And I didn't do anything. I didn't do anything to deserve this shit. You did. You killed people. That's why your life is fucked. I didn't do anything.

She yanks her bag open, pulls out a pill bottle, tries to open it, but can't stop shaking. I know how frustrating that is. Wanting what's inside the bottle, but not being able to get to it. Hell, I want what's in that bottle as much as she does.

I take the bottle from her hand, open it, take out one of the caps of Librium and hand it to her. She pokes it to the back of her tongue, tilts her face skyward, and swallows. I look at the bottle in my hand. I look at the pills inside. I put the cap back on, twist it into place and hand it to her. She takes it and drops it in her bag.

—Oh, and by the way, you forgot to ask about T.

I lick my lips.

—How's T?

—He's dead. His leg got infected and he wouldn't let me take him to a doctor and he had a fever of like a hundred and fifteen and I was freaking out and didn't know what to do and he died and I put his body in the car and drove it to a lake and filled his pockets with rocks and shoved him in so no one would find him 'cause that's what he told me to do 'cause he didn't want anyone to find him he just wanted to be dead like everyone he loved, like *his* mom and dad. And his fucking dog.

—Sandy.

—Go away, Henry. And don't try to follow me. I called the police when I was in the bathroom and told them a creep with a scar was hassling me and they said they'd send a car to the club. So now I got to get back 'cause I'm gonna have to give the fucking cops free lap dances.

I put a hand on her cheek.

—Sandy.

—Go away! You're going to die. Go do it away from me.

She slaps my hand from her face, turns and walks back to the club.

I lean against the wall of the Yankees Store and watch the pedestrians flicker past. My arms are at my sides, my fists balled tight. In one of them is the piece of paper with my parents' phone number. I guess I should call them. Sandy was so happy to hear from me, why wouldn't they be, too?

I WALK AROUND a little bit, looking for someplace quiet to sit down and make the call. I should find a flop is what I should do. I should find a cheapass motel that will let me pay cash at an hourly rate. I remember some places on Forty-eighth or Forty-ninth and head in that direction.

A cop car stops at a light as I'm waiting on the corner. One of the officers is checking me out. Sandy said she told the cops she was being hassled by a guy with a scar on his face. I should get off the street now. There are two choices on the block, a bar and grill or the inevitable Starbucks. I take the bar.

It's an old dive. Above the door is the neon sign that lights up one letter at a time: S-M-I-T-H'-S. The long bar is lined with old-timers watching the last couple innings of a Mets game. I take a seat at one of the teetery tables. A waitress as old as my mom comes by. I order a deluxe burger medium and a seltzer. She walks away. I take out my phone and smooth the piece of paper with the number on it. I look at the number, breathe in and out a few times, and dial.

It rings.

And rings.

And rings some more.

Then it picks up. And I guess I shouldn't be surprised that it's an answering machine, or that it's one of those robot voices. I'll have to talk into the machine. If they screen all their calls I'll never get them to pick up unless I say something first. But what if it's not them? Worse, what if they're not home? What if they come home and just hear my voice out of the blue on their machine and they have no idea if it's really me or just someone fucking with them? Shit. The machine beeps.

—Uh. Hi. Hello. Is. Is anyone home? Um. This is.

Shit.

—This. Is this the Thompsons'? Because.

Because what, asshole?

—Because, if it is. If it is, I have something. I—

My phone beeps loudly in my ear. I look at it. The lone remaining power-bar is flashing. Fucking. Fucking-fucking-fucking.

—Um. I'm. My phone is gonna die here and. I'm looking for the Thompsons'. So. If.

—Hello. Hello?

Oh.

—Hello. Is? Are you there?

Oh no.

—Hello. We're. Is that? We're here. Is that?

Oh. It's.

—Please. If this is a joke. Please hang up. Is that? You sound.

Oh, Mom.

—You sound like.

Oh, Mom. You sound.

—Is that you?

You sound so old.

—Mom.

—Henry?

My phone beeps again, and dies.

———

THE FIRST CABBIE asks me where I want to go before I get in. When I tell him Brighton Beach, he screeches away. There is no second cab because it's around 10:30 on a Saturday night in Midtown and the shows are all getting out and traffic is stacked up and all the tourists and the couples from New Jersey are fighting over every cab in sight. I walk back into Smith's. The waitress is standing by my table with my food in her hand. She gives me a nasty what-the-hell-do-you-think-you're-doing look, and I point at the food and point at my table and point at myself and point at the pay phone in the back.

I get change and a phone book from one of the bartenders and start making calls. The first three car services tell me it will be at least forty-five minutes before they can get me anything. I offer to pay double, triple, whatever, and they tell me it's the busiest couple hours of the week and they just don't have a car.

I have to get to Brighton Beach.

I have to get there now.

I have to get to Brighton Beach so I can tell David I'm sorry. So I can beg him to leave my parents. So I can beg him to kill me and just leave them alone. And protect them from Adam and Martin. Hearing my mom's voice. I can't. I have to stop this. It has to end. Now.

I start to dial another car service. I stop. I flip a couple pages. I dial.

—Mario's personal car service.

—Yeah, do you have any cars free right now?

—There's about a forty-five minute wait. You want to reserve?

—Uh. Is Mario there?

—Who's calling?

—I'm an old friend and I'm in town and I'm trying to get in touch.

—You got a number he can call?

—No.

—He's busy.

—This is really important. Tell him it's Henry. Tim's friend Henry. He'll know who I am. He'll want to talk to me. Just put me on hold and tell him and if he says he doesn't want to talk you don't even have to tell me, just disconnect and I'll fuck off.

—Look, guy—

—Please, man. Please. I need to talk to him. Please.

—Jesus H. Hang on.

There's a click. The hold music kicks in. Tito Rodriguez doing "Cuando, Cuando, Cuando."

Will Mario want to talk to me? No. Why would he? All we had was a business arrangement; he gave me a couple rides and I gave him a bunch of money six years ago. What does he know about me since then? Just what he's seen on TV. The bodies. If he's smart, he'll tell the guy to hang up on me. If he's really smart, he'll call the cops.

The music stops.

—Where are you?

—Place called Smith's. Corner of—

—I know where it is. Be out front in ten minutes.

He hangs up. I hang up. I walk back to my table and poke my cold burger. I eat a cold french fry. I take a sip of my seltzer. I put a twenty on the table. I think about going out the back door. I look around. There is no back door. I think again that if Mario is really smart he will have called the cops. But if he's really, really smart, he will have found out where I am and then called the cops and then he can collect on the huge reward that is available for information leading to my capture and conviction. The capture has always been the tricky part, conviction on at least a few of the crimes I've been accused of being a foregone conclusion. Which is only right, seeing as I have done some fucked-up shit. I think about what it would mean to get scooped up by the cops right now. As opposed to my other options. Which are?

Suicide by Branko.

Kill everyone.

I eat another cold fry and walk out the front door. It seems about as good an idea as any of the others. And maybe it is, because a brand-new black Lincoln Continental pulls smoothly to a stop just as I hit the curb and the driver side window zips down and there's Mario, with his short Puerto Rican fro and his carefully etched beard, and he takes a look at me and nods and I get in the backseat and close the door.

He turns around.

—I'm gonna show you something, man.

I look out the back window to see if a squad of SWATs is surrounding us. Nope. I look at Mario and nod.

—OK.

He brings his hand above the seatback and shows me the little automatic resting in his palm.

—See?

—Yeah.

He points at the gun with his other hand.

—You try anything, I'll use it. I never shoot anybody, man. But I got kids. You try anything, I'll fucking do it. OK?

—OK.

He shakes his head and bites his lower lip.

—OK. OK then.

He puts the gun back in his pocket, turns to the wheel, drops the car into drive and rolls.

I lean forward and put my arm on the back of his seat.

—I need—

—You just sit the fuck back, man. Sit back.

His right hand has gone to his pocket.

I sit back.

—Right. It's cool.

His eyes flick at me in the rearview mirror and he shakes his head.

—You just chill and I'll take you to your money. Take you to the fucking money and then I'm through with this shit.

IT'S A TWENTY-FOUR-HOUR self-service place on Third Ave., down near the Bowery. I watch from a couple hundred miles away as Mario slips a plastic card into the slot next to the door and enters a code. There's a beep and he pulls the door open and it buzzes loudly. He walks through and looks back at me standing there, watching him.

—Come on, man.

I walk through the door and he lets it go and it swings shut behind me and the buzzing stops. He goes to the elevator, slips his card into another slot, enters his code again, there's the same beep and the elevator doors slide open. He steps in, and again he has to prompt me.

—Son of a bitch. Move!

I get into the elevator. He pushes a button and we go up for a few seconds and the elevator stops and the doors open and he gets out and shakes his head at me standing there not moving and grabs my sleeve and pulls me along with him down the corridor of identical doors.

—You stoned, man? You on something?

I shake my head.

I am not on anything. But I can see where he got the idea. I've been acting like this ever since he said the magic words. Ever since he told me where we were going. I want to snap out of it, but I can't. I know this feeling. I've had it before in my life. It's the feeling you get when you realize nothing is going to be the way you thought it would be. When you realize nothing has been the way you always thought it was.

The first time I had this feeling was when I woke up after the surgery on my leg and saw the rods sticking out of it. The second time was when I plowed my Mustang into the tree and saw my friend smash through the windshield. The third time was in here in the City before I ran, when I found Yvonne's beaten body. The last time I felt it was the first time I killed someone for David. The Kid. And now it's here for one final visit.

Mario stops in front of one of the doors.

He slips the card into its slot.

He enters his code.

Beep.

He pushes the door open and steps back out of the way and I look inside the tiny storage unit and see the large, rectangular black travel box, the kind people use when they have to haul around expensive electronics and whatnot. I walk over to the box. It's standing on end; its top reaches the bottom of my rib cage. I fumble with one of the key-shaped clasps. I fumble with it because my fingers are suddenly sausage-thick and about as useful. Except they're not. Not really. They just feel that way. I manage to pop the clasp down and twist it. I repeat the action with the other three clasps. I wrap my sausage hand around the handle on top of the case and pull. It's fitted tightly and sighs off. A little sand from a Mexican beach is caught in the cracks and rains down onto the concrete floor. I hold the lid in one hand and look inside the box.

It's packed in tight, right up to the top.

Packed and wrapped in plastic.

Just like I left it.

Mario steps close behind me.

—It's all there, man. I never touch the shit. Even this unit, the money came out of my own pocket. I almost dumped it in the river a couple times, but I never took none of it.

I nod.

I'm sure he's telling the truth.

Anyway, it looks like all 4 million is in there. It surely looks like it.

PART FOUR

GAME THREE

—Just before Christmas. Year before last. Tim came to town. He gave me a key for a unit. He said hang on to the key. Said he probably wouldn't be coming for it. Said I might have to send it somewhere. Said you might come for it. Asked me if I remembered you. I said, *Timmy, you think I forget that shit? Think I forget I drove him to the airport? Think I forget I could be up to my ass in aiding and abetting if I ever opened my mouth about him?* But, Timmy, I said, *I got kids now. I got two kids and a wife and a business and employees. I can't be in that kind of shit no more.* He said you needed help. He told me to remember where I got the money. I could start my own business in the first place. He said hang on to the key. He said nobody comes to pick it up, just pay the bills on the unit and hang onto the key. Shit. I saw his body on the TV, I almost threw the key in the garbage. Then I think, *What is it? What's it all about?* Came over here. Looked in the box. That stain on the floor? That's where I threw up when I saw that shit. I saw that money. I just about died. *This shit is trouble. This shit is trouble like no man should have.* I think, *Throw it in the river.* Then I think, *What if he comes for it and I threw it in the river? What a man gonna do then?* Shit. So I hang onto the key. Sweat every day. Say to myself, *Two years. He ain't here in two years, it goes in the water. Two years means he's dead.* After two years I don't want nothing to do with shit like this. This shit. I have an ulcer from this. I yell and my wife, she don't know why. Can I tell her? No.

Got to lie to her about some shit at work. Try to play with my kids, all I think about is this locker and that box. Shit. Now, I'm finished.

I'm still standing there, the lid in my hand, staring at the money. Mario's hand appears from behind me and he snaps the key-card down on top of the cash.

—This is the spare key. You gotta use it to get back out. Code is 4430640. My card, I'm gonna toss it in the sewer as soon as I get out of here. So that's it. I'm leaving.

I don't say anything. And he doesn't move.

—You hear me, man? I'm out. OK? Sweet?

I manage to nod.

—Yeah. Sweet.

I hear him walk out of the unit. I stand there, listening to his footsteps retreating down the corridor. Then I drop the lid, rip the plastic and dig out two fat handfuls of cash. Two chunks of money. I rush out the door.

I turn the corner and there he is, just stepping into the elevator. He hears my footsteps and spins. He sees me and starts jabbing at the buttons. I hurry toward him, my arms held out in front of me, the bills clutched in my hands, the individually rubber-banded packets stacked high between my fingers. His hand is trying to find its way into his pocket, pawing for the gun inside. I stop and show him the money. I take a step closer, offering it to him.

—For you. For your kids. I.

—Keep that shit away from me. I told you, want nothing to do with that poison. That shit, it kills people. Keep it away from me. Keep it away from my family. I ever see you again, long as I live, I'll think it's bad, and I'll kill you.

The doors slide shut on him, and the money squeezed so

tightly between my fingers slips loose and spits onto the floor. I bend over and pick it all up.

IT'S AFTER MIDNIGHT.

I close the door of the unit and haul the case to the elevator. I use the key card. I have to punch in the code three times before I get it right. The elevator takes me down. I walk out of the storage place and look up and down the street. I need someplace safe. Just for a little while. Just till I figure out what to do with this shit. There's a pay phone at the end of the block.

I find the scrap of stationery in my pocket and make the call. Then I tilt the case onto its side, sit on it and wait.

Times like these. Times like these I wish I still smoked. Wish I still drank. Wish I had some pills. Times like these I wish I had all my bad habits to make the time pass more quickly, and to keep me out of my own head. But I don't. So I sit and watch the traffic flow by until an airport shuttle bus jerks to a stop right in front of me and rocks back and forth on its shocks, shades pulled down over the windows.

The door folds open and a huge cloud of tobacco and pot smoke rolls out along with the sound of "Lovin', Touchin', Squeezin'" at full volume.

—Yo, Scarface.

I get up, lift the case, and climb up the steps. Jay moves out of the way and I squeeze past him.

THE PARTY BUS is packed. Cyclones players, girls from wherever, and assorted odds and ends are crammed onto the banquets that wrap around the interior. More bodies heave in the wide center aisle, swaying to the music as a disco light spins above their heads and fog pumps in from below their feet.

Miguel squirts out of the press of bodies, the bartender from last night hanging off his arm. He has to scream over the music.

—My man! Where you been?

—Had some things to do!

—No shit? What's in the box?

I look at the box.

—Something I lost!

Jay grabs me.

—Lost? Yo! You know we don't talk about losing up in here! This is where the winners roll! Missed a game, Scarface! Missed my man's first official pro home run. Missed the Cyclones beating the fucking Yankees!

He shakes the beer he's holding and sprays it in my face.

—Now get your party on, yo! Tonight's the night!

The song hits the *nah-nahs,* and everybody sings along at the top of their lungs.

I DRIVE THE party bus.

I drive the party bus because Jay has been feeding cocktails to Walter, the sixty-year-old chauffeur who's supposed to be driving it. Now Walter is squashed into a corner in the back of the bus, passed out cold and sleeping it off. So I drive the bus with a box of money riding shotgun beside me.

Jay sticks his face through the curtain that separates the driver's compartment from the rest of the bus.

—Yo! We're running low on supplies back here. Need a beer stop.

He disappears back into the maelstrom. I cruise around until I spot a grocery on the corner of Third and Eleventh Ave. I double-park on the avenue, find the button that opens the door, hit it, and a crowd of drunken kids tumbles to the street and charges into the grocery for beer and cigarettes and snacks. I turn on the emergency blinkers, set the parking brake, and go into the back of the bus.

The lights are still spinning, but the fog has slowed to a trickle. Whatever the machine uses for juice must be just about out. I kick through the litter of empties, crushed cigarette butts and discarded clothing. The stereo is still blaring. I find the controls mounted above a cluster of empty decanters and switch it off, silencing "No Sleep Til Brooklyn."

A lone couple has stayed on the bus. They're half naked and twisting around on one of the banquets, oblivious to me. I have to push Walter out of the way to get the bathroom door open. I step inside the tiny cabinet and close the door.

I take off my sweaty, crumpled jacket and hang it on the hook on the back of the door. I flip up one of the levers on the sink and a sluggish trickle of cool water dribbles out. I hold my hands under it until they fill and splash the water onto my face. I look at myself in the mirror.

My hair is twisted and crushed from sweat and the hat I was wearing. There are streaks of dirt down my neck and on the front of my wife-beater. I get some water on a couple paper towels and use them to wipe away the dirt on my skin and blot at my shirt.

The bus rocks as people start to pile back on. I get more water on my hands and rub them over my head, brushing my clipped hair back into something resembling its usual shape. Someone turns the stereo back on. Someone else bangs on the bathroom door.

I look at my face again. Would Mom recognize this face? The way she recognized my voice, would she see me inside this thing?

More banging on the door.

—Yo, Scarface, time to roll.

Yeah, right, time to roll. Not sure to where, but got to keep rolling.

I open the door and edge out into the press of bodies. Jay bugs his eyes at my tats.

—Jesus, yo. Look at you, all inked up and hooded out.

He squeezes into the can and closes the door. I maneuver back to the wheel, the kids around me cracking open fresh sixteen-ounce cans of Coors Light and tearing into bags of Doritos and packages of Chips Ahoy. I part the curtain and drop into the driver's seat.

—Hey, man.

Miguel is sitting in the passenger seat. He's shoved the box aside and has one long leg propped up on it.

—Mind if I ride up here?

—Nope.

He looks me up and down.

—Where'd all the tattoos come from?

—Different places.

—Cool.

—Thanks.

—I've been thinking about getting one. My nickname in college was The Hammer. I've been thinking about getting a sledgehammer hitting a baseball. Cool, right?

—Yeah. Cool.

I close the door, turn off the flashers and the brake and drop the shifter into drive.

—Where to?

—Doesn't matter. Just driving is cool here. Everything is cool here. I fucking love New York.

We catch green lights down the avenue. Miguel has his arm stuck out the window, his hand flattened into a wing riding the wind.

—We missed you today, man. What happened?

—I got a call. Had to do some stuff.

I pull to a stop at Houston.

—Stuff for David?

—Yeah.

He reaches over and tugs the curtain closed all the way.

—What's that like? Working for him?

I watch the signal light up ahead cycle from red to green. Traffic doesn't move.

—It's a job.

—Sure. I get it. You can't say much. But, David. Is he OK? I mean, this deal I have with him. You think that's OK?

The light goes to yellow. We move forward maybe a car length.

—It's a deal. You take what you can get, I guess.

He turns in his seat to face me.

—Yeah, I know you work for the guy and all. I'm not looking to get you in trouble or anything. It's just. You know I think you're all right. So I'm just looking for your opinion if, I don't know, if I'm doing this right.

I look at the box of money right next to him.

—Look, Miguel, here's the thing—

The light goes red.

Jay yanks the curtain open.

—What's up, yo? Where we headed?

Miguel points at the street.

—Cruisin'.

—Yo, man. We need to get out and stretch.

—We just got out.

—No, we need to like really get out. Get some air. This party needs some air before it punks out.

Miguel looks back into the throbbing heart of the bus.

—Man, this party ain't punking anytime tonight.

—Uh-uh. Major punk danger. Must have O_2. Driver, take us to a park or something.

I look at Miguel. He shrugs.

—Sure. A park. That's cool.

The light is green and we move forward this time. I turn west on Houston.

Jay grabs Miguel's sleeve.

—Get on back here, yo.

—Gonna sit up here for awhile.

—No, yo. Party needs you.

He tugs on Miguel. Miguel tries to pull away.

—Chill, Jay.

—Yo. You got guests here.

—They're cool.

—No they ain't. Come on back with the party.

He drags Miguel up out of the seat.

—OK. Chill, chill, chill. I'm coming.

—Then come on, fag. Chicks back here need you.

Miguel pats my shoulder.

—Check you later, man. I want to finish this.

Jay shoves him into the mass of sweaty kids, looks at me, nods, and follows Miguel, pulling the curtain closed behind him. I drive.

I take a left on West Broadway. The money box tilts and clunks against the door. I think about it. It's pretty much impossible to think about anything else.

I reach over and touch the top of the box. I rest my hand on it. And I drive like that all the way down to the Battery.

—Yo! All out. Everybody out. Time to recharge.

There's some bitching, but Jay herds them all toward the door. Through the windshield I see Miguel, the bartender riding on his back. I leave the engine running and go through the curtain. I need to find a pay phone again.

Jay is standing in front of the door, blocking the exit. In one hand he has my jacket. In the other hand he has two pieces of paper. The photocopy of my old ID and the clipping from the *Post*.

—So, yo, Scarface. What's the most fucked-up thing you ever did?

—You were supposed to be the shit, right, yo?

—How's that?

—That was the deal. You were like the all-American boy. That was the way they played it on the TV. You were, like, the shit. Baseball stud. Top prospect.

—Yeah. I guess so.

—Yo. *I* was the shit.

We sit on a bench that faces Hudson Bay. The plaza here is cobbled. Benches surround old trees. The ferry landing for the boats that take you to Ellis and Liberty Islands is quiet. We can see the statue in the middle of the bay. I have my jacket draped over my lap. Jay sits with his elbows on his knees and fiddles with the two pieces of paper.

—*I* was, yo, *I* was *the shit*. Little League. High school. I was the shit.

The gang from the bus is drifting around. A few of the players and their girls flag down a couple cabs on State and take off. Some others are wandering away toward the bar at American Park. Looks like the party is breaking up.

—Shortstop, yo. Started freshman ball, JV *and* varsity. Had all the school records, and a bunch of the district's, too. Stolen bases. Hits. Runs. Fielding percentage. Average. Big numbers. Mad numbers. 'Course there was a problem. I'm five-fucking-six in cleats. That's a fucking problem. Plus, you know, I'm playing with *that* guy.

He points at Miguel. The bartender is perched on the railing by the water, Miguel snugged between her knees as they make out.

—My man Mike was part of the problem. I was setting records, but he was, too. And he had the power. All-time single-season home run champ, California high school baseball. And he pitched. Led the state in strikeouts. And, yo, he had *the body*. Scouts come around to watch us both play, but once they get a look at him, I'd just drop right off the fucking scout-radar. Word got around I was even smaller in person than I was on paper and they stopped even pretending they were interested. Like a bunch of chicks, yo. All over Mike. All about the body.

He drops into a hick accent.

—Seen the body on that A-ray-nuz kid? Six-four, two hundred, and growing. Not a ounce a fat on that boy. Ripped like a NBAer. Kid's got the pro body an he ain't even eighteen. Kid's gonna be a star.

He spits between his feet.

—Shit, yo. All about the fucking body. Mike got picked in the first round. The Brewers. That was a no-brainer. Said no thanks and took the Stanford scholarship. Me? Didn't get picked by no one. Got a couple semipro teams called. Got a partial ship at UCSD. But, yo, my boy was headed up north. He says, *Come up-state. Can't break us up. Hang out. Take some classes. Get you on the team next year. Scouts see what you do in a big-time program, they'll be all over you.* Blew off SD. Went up there. But my grades weren't good enough for that place. And they didn't care I was Mike's boy. Spent all my time hangin' with him, working on his swing. See that flat swing he's got, yo? That shit's mine. Way he plays the field? Always getting the right jump on the ball? My shit. That ain't no college coaching. That's me and him. That's what I did. I worked his ass, yo. He wants to fuck around with chicks, booze. Wants to find a poker game, head up to Reno. I kept his ass working. Junior year he goes back in the draft. First pick. Mets. Big time. My boy is big time.

He takes his elbows from his knees, leans back and looks over at Miguel.

—But I was the shit, yo. I was most definitely the shit.

Cooler air is starting to drift in off the water. I pull on my jacket.

—So, Jay.

—Yo?

I point at the papers in his hands.

—What were you doing in my jacket?

He smiles.

—Shit, yo, thought you might have some more of that x in there.

He holds up the papers.

—Imagine my surprise I find this shit.

—Uh-huh. You got any plans for those?

He dangles the pieces of paper, one in each hand pinched between his thumb and forefinger.

—These? I got a plan for these? Yeah, I got a plan. My plan is to get your ass away from Mike as quickly as fucking possible.

—Seems wise.

—Yo, it does.

I put out my hand.

—So let me have 'em and I'll be on my way.

He pulls the papers back and shakes his head.

—Uh-uh. First there's something you're gonna need to do.

I look at him. Sitting there. Leaning back. I could put my elbow in his throat and grab the papers. But I don't.

—Jay. Can I say something?

—Sure.

—Don't fuck with me.

—Yo?

—Seriously. Don't fuck with me. I'm. You really have no idea how at the end of my rope I am right now.

He sits up straight.

—I'm not fucking with you, yo. I'm not looking for. Shit. I'm not looking for . . . I don't know what. Like money? I don't. Yo. Fucking with you?

He pulls out his cell phone.

—See this? I could have called the cops. Found this shit, I could have dialed 911 right away and had them here. Think I want to fuck with you? I want something from you. I need. Yo. I need your help. This?

He starts folding the papers into a little square.

—Fuck this. Yo.

He points at Miguel.

—I need help with my boy. He's starting to listen to reason. He's here. He's playing pro ball. He likes it. And he's starting to think for a change. He's thinking how shit can get off track. He's looking around at the guys he's playing with and how bad they want the bigs, and how none of them, yo, not one, is gonna make it. But him? All he has to do is keep his eyes on the ball and he's in. He's starting to think about that shit. But he's sick of hearing from me. I can't open my mouth about the gambling or the debt without him tuning me out. Not what he wants, to be lectured. So you. You have a talk with him. You sit his ass down, yo, spell it out. Tell him this ain't shit to be messing with. Tell him to pay off now. He can get his moms that house later. He can dump the Escalade and drive a fucking Olds like you. All that will come later. Tell him about this Russian. An, yo, any doubts I had about that guy not being bad news have been put to rest by the fact he has someone like you working for him. That guy can take a stone-famous psycho off the map and cut his face up and turn him into a driver? That's some fucked up, top-ten-box-office-summer-blockbuster-movie shit. And we don't need any of that, yo. So you tell him that he's dealing with some bad motherfuckers and it's time to get out while he can. You help him out. You back him. *This.*

He holds up the square of folded paper.

—*This* shit, yo?

He tears the square into tiny pieces, tosses them in the air, and they fall to the ground where they are stirred and scattered by the breeze coming off the bay.

—Fuck that. You do this, yo. Help my boy. Do it 'cause it's the right thing to do. How's that for some shit, yo?

THE THIRD TIME was The Bank Manager.

She was a compulsive gambler. Ponies. She had run her losses to over a quarter-million. She'd already taken the second mortgage on the house and refinanced the car. Already taken all that money and blown it on long shots, trying to get even. Messages had been sent. I imagine her showing up at the bank after the first message, explaining away a black eye and a limp as the result of a fall. After the second message things probably got tricky. Maybe one of her friends sitting her down at lunch to ask if there were problems at home. That kind of thing.

Someone doesn't find a way to generate more income after the second message, they get offered suggestions. She's a bank manager? Maybe she can approve some loans.

She declined.

We got her after work. She stopped at a bar on the way home, had the three drinks she'd been having every night since things started getting bad, put a couple dollars in the progressive slot machine, hoping for a jackpot. All the usual things losers do. She came out, just a little drunk, walked to her car. As she was putting her hand on the door I came walking up and called her name. She looked up, squinted against the darkness, and Branko appeared behind her and hit her on the back of the head. She fell down. I walked over.

I was working the pills pretty hard by then. Hard. I was stoned out of my gourd. I reached in my pocket for whatever kind of gun I was carrying, but couldn't find it. Branko had to show me that it was already in my hand. The safety was off, a round was chambered. The woman moved and Branko bent and hit her again with his sap.

She was wearing bank clothes; a conservative skirt suit in a dark color, flesh-tone hose, low heels. She was nearly fifty, plump, and had fat ankles. I emptied the gun into the back of her head and kept pulling the trigger until Branko took it from me, wiped it, and dropped it. Then he towed me to the car he'd bought for the job and drove us away.

He came by the Suites the next day and found me with the newspaper, looking at the photo of the dead woman when she was still alive: a family portrait with her husband and two daughters. He crumpled the paper and stuffed it in the trash. *These things,* he said, *are better forgotten.*

Good tip. Wish someone'd told me sooner.

I LOOK AT the scraps of paper being spread across the pavement. One of them flips over and I see a tiny photocopied image of my face from my old driver's license.

I think about The Bank Manager. I think about killing mothers. I think about killing Mickey's mother. I don't want to do that.

I think about doing the right thing.

Jay is watching me.

I find my phone in one of my jacket pockets. I remember the battery is dead. I look at Jay.

—Can I borrow yours?

He tilts his head.

—Yo.

He pulls his out and passes it to me.

I stand up.

—Give me just a minute here.

He shakes his head and laughs.

—Sure. Whatever.

I walk a little ways away in the direction of the war monuments. I dial a number. I get an answering machine like I knew I would.

—Hey, it's me. Call me back at this number.

I say the number and hang up. Less than a minute later Jay's phone rings. I answer it.

—Hello, Henry.

—Hey, David.

—Have you decided to come in?

—Well, yeah.

He sighs deeply, letting the air slowly drain away like tension. *It is sad, but it will be for the best.*

—Good.

—Yeah. The thing is.

—Yes?

—The thing is, and this is kind of funny, the thing is I found something. And I think you're gonna want it.

IT'S NOT EASY. You don't just tell someone, *Hey, remember all that money we thought was lost forever. Well you won't believe this, but it just walked up to me and turned itself in.* But he listens. And he asks questions. And in the end, he believes.

We work out a deal. It's pretty much the kind of deal I've come to expect in these circumstances. David gets the money. I get my mom and dad. I get protection for Mom and Dad.

I'll go to David's office in the morning. He'll be alone. I'll show him the money. He'll shake my hand and embrace me and congratulate me on fulfilling my contract. And then he'll turn me around.

And Branko will be standing there.

And before I can say or do anything, Branko will do something to me, and I will die.

And I can live with that. So to speak.

Because 4 million dollars is not enough to buy my life at this point. But it is certainly enough for David to stick on a scale against the hassle of killing my folks after I am already dead. It's enough to count on as a guarantee that he'll take care of Adam and Martin.

At least it seems that way to me.

Having no other choice and all.

I HANG UP and walk back over to Jay. Miguel is by the curb with the bartender. She's climbing into a cab. I hand Jay his phone. And with nothing to lose, I can afford to do the right thing for a change.

—Sure. I can talk to Miguel. I can tell him to stay away from David. Want me to do that now?

Jay takes his phone and stands up. He looks over at Miguel trying to get in the cab with the bartender. She pushes him out, the door slams, and the cab drives away.

—Better wait, yo. Hit him when he's sober. Tomorrow after the game maybe.

I think about my plans for the next morning.

—That might not work out.

—Nice one, Jay.

Miguel is walking toward us.

—Good plan, taking a break and all. Way to keep the party going.

Jay waves him off and turns back to me.

His eyes open wide.

They're looking over my shoulder.

—What the fuck, yo?

I drop.

The sap ruffles my hair.

Jay leaps over me.

I hear the sound of two bodies colliding. Stumbling feet. Flesh hitting stone. I flip onto my back. I can see Jay tangled up with Martin on the cobbles. Martin rolling on top of Jay. I start to get up. Adam kicks me in the ribs.

Martin is hurting Jay.

I start to get up.

Adam kicks me in the ribs.

Pain spears my left side. I gasp. I try to get up. The pain shoots deeper. Martin is sitting on Jay's chest, pinning him to the ground, whipping the sap back and forth, shattering his young face.

Adam grabs me by the collar and starts dragging me toward the bus.

Miguel smashes into his back and they slam down to the pavement.

Martin is standing up. Jay isn't moving.

Miguel doesn't know how to fight. I can see from here that he doesn't know how to fight at all. But he's just so strong he's crushing Adam into the concrete. Martin is walking toward them, sap raised. Adam has stopped resisting Miguel. I'm on my hands and knees. I see Adam's hand slipping into the pocket where he carries his knife. I start to crawl.

—Miguel! Mike! Mike!

His head comes up. The knife comes out of the pocket. I fling myself forward and catch Adam's wrist as the blade flicks open. Martin's sap smashes down on the back of Miguel's neck and he sprawls on top of Adam, jarring his arm, and I twist the knife free.

Martin grabs my hair and jerks my head back and forth.

—Tetka Anna! Tetka Anna! Tetka Anna!

Adam is heaving Miguel's bulk off of him.

—Martin!

I aim for the center of Martin's foot, miss, and jam the blade down into his toes. Blood squirts out of the cut in his Pumas. He brings his foot up, yanking it free and tearing the knife from my hands. It flips through the air and clatters back down. Martin hops a couple times and stumbles over Miguel, falling on top of him just as Adam squirms free.

I look for the knife. It's lost in the darkness. But Adam is crawling after something. I crawl after him. I grab his ankle and pull. Pain worms through my rib cage. I yank Adam's right leg out from underneath him and he balances on his left leg and his arms and looks back at me, kicking and jerking, trying to rip free. I clutch his leg with both hands. He gives up on the knife and tries to turn himself around, coming back at me.

Martin is getting up. He stands, his right foot planted, his left raised gingerly, blood leaking from his shoe. He looks at the ground, bends, picks up his sap, and looks at me.

Adam flips himself onto his back and kicks me in the forehead with his left foot. I let go with one hand and feel at the cobbles, my fingers dig in around a loose stone and pull it free.

Martin is hopping toward me.

Adam's left foot tags me on the ear. I heave my weight on top of his right leg and pin it. I raise the cobblestone and smash it down on his ankle. He screams and stops kicking me. I bring the stone down again and feel the bone give beneath it. He screams again. I hammer him once more. He doesn't scream this time.

I let go of the leg and roll onto my back, the stone in my hand. I feint a throw at Martin's leaking foot. The memory of the balls I fired into him at Coney pops up in his eyes. He flinches. I throw the cobblestone at his good knee. He's back on the ground.

I take off my shoe.

I stand up.

Hunched over the pain in my ribs, I walk to where Martin is trying to figure out the best way to stand up on his mutilated foot and his cracked kneecap. He looks up at me. I hit his face with the shoe. I keep hitting him until I'm sure he gets the point. He collapses, blood and snot leaking from his nose.

Adam has pulled his leg up close to his body, his foot dangling from the pancaked ankle. One of his hands is scampering over the ground, feeling for his lost knife. I take a couple steps, bend, and pick up the knife.

I point at the ankle.

—Can you walk on that?

—No.

I put out my hand. He takes it. I pull, wincing at the pain in my ribs.

—Come on.

He leans on me, hopping on his good leg as I lead him over to the railing.

—Wait here.

He slumps against the rail, digs a cigarette out of his pocket and lights up.

I walk over to Martin. He's out. I look at Jay. His face is cracked and swelling. Bubbles of blood inflate and pop between his lips. Miguel shifts. He groans and puts a hand to the back of his neck. His eyes open.

—What the. What the fuck, man?

—Jay's hurt.

—Huh?

—Jay's hurt.

—Where? What?

He sits up too fast and his eyes spin. He starts to go back down. I kneel. A new and different pain in my ribs. I hold him up until he stops spinning.

—OK?

—Yeah. Yeah. OK.

I point his face toward Jay.

—You see.

—Oh fuck. Oh shit.

—Can you stand now?

He stands.

—Get Jay in the bus.

—Oh fuck. Oh shit. Oh, Jay.

He walks over to his friend, squats, slips his arms under him, and easily lifts him off the ground. He carries him toward the bus.

I look at Martin. I still have the shoe in my hand. I tuck it into my armpit, bend over and grab Martin under his arms and drag him toward his brother. Miguel sticks his head out of the bus.

—He's in. Should I call 911?

—Just wait in there. Put a towel on his face or something.

He disappears back inside the shuttered bus.

I get Martin to the rail. Adam reaches out and helps me pull him up and lean him there. His hands open and close a couple times and his puffed eyes open to slits. He grabs at the rail and holds himself up, but there's nobody home yet.

I move my arm. The shoe drops out of my armpit to the ground. I push my white-socked foot back inside, not taking my eyes from Adam, his knife still in my hand.

—You been following them since you lost me?

Adam chains a fresh smoke, blood from his fingers smears the filter.

—No. We went home. Tetka Anna. There were things broken in the house. She was gone.

—Uh-huh.

—David.

—Uh-huh.

—Martin wanted to go there. To get her.

—Uh-huh.

—But they would have killed us. I thought you. David will want you. You tried to kill him.

—Yeah. He does.

—We followed your friends.

—You followed these guys, came looking for me?

—Yes.

—That wasn't a bad idea.

—No.

—No, it wasn't.

He takes a drag.

I blink. Wait to change my mind. But I don't.

—A bad idea, was when you threatened to torture my parents.

The knife is very sharp. It pokes through his windpipe with great ease. I pull it out and blood sputters from the hole on a stream of cigarette smoke. His mouth opens and closes. The cigarette falls from his fingers. I bend over, grab his good leg, haul upward, and he tips over the rail into the bay. Martin turns his glazed, slitted eyes to me, but I am already pushing him back over the rail. He grabs at me, barely conscious of what is happening. His back is bent over the rail. He is held balanced only by the grip he has on my forearm. I rake the blade of the knife across his knuckles, and he falls.

I don't bother to look. Adam with his slit throat, Martin with his lamed foot and knee and addled head, they will both drown. I turn and walk toward the bus, collecting Martin's sap from the ground as I go.

Having made David's end of the deal that much easier.

I climb into the bus. I close the door. I look at Miguel sitting on the floor next to Jay, holding a dirty T-shirt over his face.

—How is he?

Jay's hand comes up and pushes the towel off.

—Fucking fine, Scarface. Fucking fine for a guy who's gonna look worse than you.

And he passes out.

———

—You were fighting.

—What?

—You were fighting. You were drunk and you got into a fight with each other and you beat the crap out of him.

—Oh no. No, man. I don't want to say that.

—Listen. If it's a fight between friends, no matter how bad it is, the cops won't fuck around if neither of you presses charges.

—Oh, man. That sucks. That just. It sucks. I don't want people to think. Fuck! Who were those guys?

—They were. They're like business rivals. Like people who have a problem with David.

—Shit! Oh, shit. Are they? What if they—

—Look. Don't worry about those guys. I ran those guys off. They won't be a problem.

I take a left on Maiden Lane, drive another couple blocks, and pull over on Gold Street.

—Come here.

Miguel gets up. I push the button that opens the door and get out of the driver's seat. I try to lift the box, but it hurts my ribs too much.

—Pass me that thing.

I go down the steps. Miguel hands the box down. I set it on the curb.

—Thanks. There's a hospital just up the street here. Beekman, I think, at the university. Just drive straight up and start honking.

—Right, OK.

—And, Miguel, it was a fight. You beat him up.

—Man.

—Do it. Handle it that way. Cops go poking into tonight and shit will hit the fan.

—OK. OK. Got it. What about. Wait. What about you?

—I took off when everybody else did.

—No. Where are you? What are you?

I put my hand on the box.

—I have to take care of this thing.

—OK, yeah, but you'll be back. Here. You'll.

—Just call your agent, OK. Him you can tell anything you want. He won't be letting your ass get in any trouble.

—OK. But what?

—Tomorrow. I'll see you tomorrow, OK? At the game.

—Yeah. Yeah. OK, man. I. This is fucked up, man.

—Take Jay to the hospital.

—Yeah. Yeah, man.

He gets behind the wheel, looks at me, nods, and pushes the button that closes the door. I watch the party bus lurch down the street. Then I drag the box back to Water Street where I can find a cab.

It's heavy.

The fucking box is heavy.

And it hurts me.

THERE WAS THIS bar Yvonne liked to go drinking at in Brooklyn. Nights when neither of us had to work at Paul's, we'd sometimes take the A train over to the Heights. We'd walk up Henry Street to Clark, to this place. It was a dive, all our favorite places were dives. I'm not sure how she found it. We'd drink. I'd suck down bottles of Bud with a few Turkeys neat thrown in to keep me going. She'd have Corona and shots of tequila. Tequila made her crazy in bed. We'd play pool and darts, get good and drunk, and on summer nights we'd walk back to Manhattan across the Brooklyn Bridge, stopping a couple times along the way to make out. Those were good dates.

The owner of the place was nuts. He was a bit of a hood. Yvonne told me he was the local loan shark or something. Whatever else he was, he was crazy. He had this big dog, a huge mongrel. The dog would wander around the bar, sniffing the floor, looking for a peanut or a piece of beef jerky that might have been dropped. The owner left the dog in the bar overnight as protection for the place. There was a big old hotel across the street, a transient hotel that was chock-full of crackheads. He worried about them breaking into the bar. He had a training program for the dog, a program designed to make it hate crackheads. He'd do it a few times a week, whenever one of the crackheads got hard up enough to need the cash.

One of them would come across from the hotel and knock on the window until he got the owner's attention. The owner would ignore him for awhile, then finally look over and nod. The crackhead would start banging on the glass, and the dog would run over, barking. The crackhead would walk back and forth in front of the place, banging on the window and the door as the dog barked and the owner knelt down next to it and whispered in its ear.
—Kill. Kill the nigger. Kill.

The dog would be utterly spazzed out and the owner would nod at the crackhead again. The crackhead would come over to the door, edge it open, and stick his arm inside with a jacket or an old sweatshirt wrapped around it. The dog would latch on and jerk the arm back and forth as the crackhead struggled to keep from being pulled inside, and the owner laughed his ass off. After about a minute he'd stop laughing, drag the dog off, and pass the crackhead five bucks. The crackhead would wander off looking for his man, unwrapping his arm to check out the massive bruises that would be there for weeks.

After the show was over, anyone in the place who hadn't seen it before would tend to put their drinks down and take off. It wasn't the kind of joint most people felt comfortable in. But if you stuck it out, saw the scene go down a few times and kept coming back, the owner figured you must be his kind of people. We'd go in a couple times a month. Saw the whole thing three or four times. But I don't think either of us ever considered ourselves the owner's kind of people.

Anyway, if it wasn't for that bar, I wouldn't know about the hotel. So there's that.

THE BAR IS gone. There's something there in its place, some kind of café or diner. But the hotel is still across the street, right on the corner. I give the cabbie a couple extra bucks and he carries the box inside for me. The place is cleaned up. I see a kind of plaque above the check-in that tells me they're using it as housing for the Brooklyn campus of Long Island City College, but the desk clerk is still housed behind a couple inches of Plexiglas, and there are still crackheads in evidence.

—I need a room.

She doesn't say anything, just slips a registration card under the window. I find a pen on the end of a chain and fill in the information. I don't have the energy to make up anything new so I just use the vitals from my Las Vegas identity.

—Can I pay cash?

She looks at me this time, takes in the dirty jacket and undershirt. I wiped my hands clean of blood in the party bus, but they're still filthy.

—Yeah. Gotta leave a deposit.

—Sure.

I ask for a room next to the elevator and she gives it to me. I pay for the night, plus an extra night as the deposit, plus extra to have the TV switched on, plus another deposit to have the phone. I give her the cash. She gives me a receipt and a key and buzzes me into the lobby. I drag the box in, wait for the elevator, go up two floors, drag the box across the hall and into my room, close the door and do all the locks, collapse on the bed and close my eyes.

Immediately I see Adam and Martin.

I open my eyes.

Jesus. Jesus.

Who are they? Where do they all come from? All of these orphans I collect. All of these brothers I've killed.

THERE ARE SOME take-out menus in the night table. I call the twenty-four-hour deli down the street, a place called Pickles & Peas. I can remember stopping there with Yvonne on the nights we walked home across the bridge. We'd buy cans of beer and tuck them into brown paper bags so we could sip them as we went. I call and get a woman with a heavy Korean accent. She's fine taking my order for a sandwich and bottles of water, but we run into problems when I ask if they have any first aid stuff. Finally I work out that they don't have anything but Band-Aids. I ask if she has duct tape.

—Duck tape?

—Duct tape.

—No duck. Deli. No grocery.

—Duct. Tape. Silver tape. Sticky.

—Silver tape! Yes! Silver tape. Yes.

—One roll, please.

—Yes. Yes. Where?

—The hotel. Room 214.

—Yes, yes. Ten minute.

—Thanks. Wait!

—Yes?

—Bleach? Do you have bleach? Clorox?

—Yes. Bleach, yes.

—Send a bottle of bleach.

—Yes. Yes. Ten minute.

I hang up. Exactly ten minutes pass before the desk clerk calls and tells me I have a delivery. I tell her to send it up.

The delivery guy smiles when I open the door. He hands me the receipt. I give him some money and tell him to keep the change. He smiles again and bobs his head. I take the bag, close and relock the door.

I turn the bag upside down and empty it on the bed. Everything tumbles out. I crack one of the bottles of water and drink. I tried the water from the taps before I called the deli; it tasted like rust. I drink half the bottle in one go, my ribs bursting with pain every time I swallow. I take the half-empty bottle and the bleach and go into the bathroom.

I pull up the plug in the sink and start to fill it, then turn on the shower. I take off all my clothes and toss my wife-beater, underwear and socks into the shower. When the sink is full, I turn it off and pour a cup of bleach into it. I climb into the hot shower and stand under the water. I unwrap a tiny bar of soap, bend over and pick up my underwear and start scrubbing at the urine stains from when Mickey's mother had her gun stuck in my neck and I almost completely pissed myself. I give the wife-beater and the socks a good wash, too. Then I scrub the sweat and dirt and blood from my skin and hair.

The bruise on my ribs is huge. It's darkest about eight inches under my armpit, and then spreads in various shades of purple, black, blue and red down my side and around to my sternum. I have to wash that side very carefully. Even the jets of water hurt.

I get out and dry myself, blotting the bruise softly. I wring out my whites and drop them in the sink with the water and bleach. My mouth tastes funky. I should have bought a toothbrush and some toothpaste. Oh well.

I go back into the room with the towel wrapped around my waist, get my sandwich and another bottle of water, and ease my-self onto the bed, propped up at the headboard by the two flat pil-lows. I unwrap the sandwich and take a bite. They put mayonnaise on it, even though I asked them not to. Shit, I hate mayonnaise. I take off the top piece of bread, scrape off as much mayo as I can, put the sandwich back together and eat.

There's a remote chained to the nightstand. Students must be as bad as crackheads. I turn on the TV and start flipping. I flip and chew. There's not much, just very-basic-cable stuff. I roll around the same dozen or so channels while I eat. When the sandwich is done I get up and go into the bathroom. I drain the sink, rinse the bleach from my things, and hang them on the shower rod. I look at my jacket and jeans. I take a damp cloth and rub at the worst of the stains, then give up. I go back into the room where I've left the TV tuned to the Madison Square Garden Network. I get back on the bed, pick up the remote, but before I can change the channel I see Miguel's face. He's on the TV.

I panic for a second. Then I realize that they are not breaking a story about the Mets' top prospect and two bodies that are floating in the Hudson Bay. It's just a rebroadcast of the day's Cyclones game. I watch it. I watch how well Miguel plays. I watch the homer Jay told me about. I watch.

I watch a baseball game.

It's not a great game. Hell, it'd barely be a good game if I didn't know one of the players. But that doesn't matter. I watch the game. Somewhere in the eighth inning I can't keep my eyes open any longer. The chatter of the announcers, the hum of the crowd, the crack of the bat; all the sounds of who I once was, they lull me finally to sleep. And that's really the best part.

I SIT ON the couch with the controller in my hands, trying to make the players on the screen do what I want them to. We've been playing for hours now.

—This is boring.

I hit a button and the pitch flies at The Kid's hitter. He slams it, the ball shoots down the right field line and he clears the bases, scoring two more runs.

—Shit! That was foul.

The Kid laughs.

—Argue the call. Get kicked out of the game. I love that.

—This sucks.

—For you. I'm having a great time.

I look at the score, 63–1, top of the sixth.

We play. He leans forward, his elbows on his knees. I look at the huge hole in the back of his head.

—When you gonna get that fixed?

He fouls off a pitch.

—Huh?

—When you gonna get that hole fixed?

—What are you talking about?

—Your hole, when are you gonna get that taken care of?

—You're high. You can't fix that. I'm stuck with it. Don't be a dick.

—You're the dick. This game. Let's just declare mercy rule and go outside and play for real.

The Kid shakes his head and the strings of spaghetti in his hair waggle.

—No mercy.

—But I'm sick of playing. And these guys want to do something, too.

I point at Adam and Martin, sitting by the open window, both of them dripping water.

Adam shakes his head.

—I do not need to play. I will smoke.

He brings a cigarette to his mouth, takes a drag, and blows rings out of the hole in his throat.

The Kid points at him.

—Hey! Blow that outside. My folks will shit if they smell it.

Adam waves a hand at him and blows a stream of smoke out the window.

I slap the controller against my thigh.

—OK, but I want to go do something else and so does Martin.

—No he doesn't.

—Yes he does.

The Kid looks at Martin.

—Marty, you want to go outside?

Martin slaps his sap into the palm of his hand.

—Tetka Anna! Tetka Anna! Tetka Anna!

—See. He's fine.

—But I want to go.

—Don't whine. Tell you what. Get this next hitter out, and we'll go outside.

I point at the TV.

—That's Jackie Robinson. I can't get Jackie out.

—You can try.

The door opens. The Bank Manager and The Culinary Rep walk in.

The Kid looks over at them.

—Hey, Mom. Hey, Dad.

The Rep waves.

—Hey, Kid.

The Manager comes over and kisses him on the cheek. I see the huge hole in the back of her head.

—Hello, baby.

She looks around.

—Do I smell cigarette smoke?

Adam flicks his butt out the window.

The Kid sniffs.

—Not from us, Mom.

—Hmm.

The Rep walks over. He turns around, sniffing the air. I see the huge hole in the back of his head.

—Smells like smoke.

—Naw, I don't think so.

The Rep gives him a hard look.

—Don't lie to me, Son.

—Dad, you're in the way of the game!

I throw a pitch.

—Don't yell at me. I smell cigarette smoke in my house.

The Kid hits a button, Jackie swings and pops up the ball and it drops into my catcher's glove. He throws his controller at the floor.

—Shit! Shit! Shit!

The Manager covers her mouth with her hand.

—What did you say?

The Culinary Rep walks to the TV, unplugs the game console and starts to wrap the cables around it.

—OK, that's it. Everybody out.

I stand.

—Yeah, let's go play.

The Kid stands.

—OK. Jeez, I was going for the single-game scoring record. Would have had it, too. You suck.

The Rep puts a hand on his shoulder.

—Uh-uh, not you. You aren't going anywhere. Not after using language like that.

—Daaad!

—No! Game over. Everybody out. And I'm calling all of your parents and telling them one of you was smoking.

Adam and Martin don't say anything, they just help each other stand and start hobbling to the door, Adam pulling a fresh smoke from his pack.

I follow them out. The door closes behind us.

—C'mon, guys, let's go play pickle.

Adam looks at me, blows more smoke out of his neck.

—No. I must smoke.

—C'mooooon.

Martin points at his ruined knee and foot.

—Tetka Anna! Tetka Anna! Tetka Anna!

—OK, OK. Be spoilsports.

I watch them as they weave and lurch down the street, leaning on one another for support.

—Yo!

I turn around. Jay and Miguel are in the middle of the street. Miguel has a ball. He's throwing it up in the air as far as he can, positioning himself underneath it and practicing basket catches.

I point.

—That's bad fundamentals. You want to get under the ball, get the glove up and catch it with both hands. Showboat like that and it'll cost you a run someday.

Jay looks at Miguel.

—Check out Sparky Anderson, yo.

Miguel makes another easy catch.

—Whatever. Let's play three flies.

I watch the ball go up in the air again.

—I don't got my glove.

Miguel tosses me his.

—Use mine.

The ball drops and slaps down into his bare hand.

—Take the field.

Me and Jay walk down the street. Miguel walks in the opposite direction. When we're far enough away he tells us to stop. We take spots in the middle of the street. Miguel tosses the ball up and swats it with his bat, popping it toward us. We jockey for position, lightly elbowing one another, trying to create space as the ball drops at our faces. It veers slightly at the last second and I leap and twist and flop over the hood of a car, snowconing it before it can hit and leave a dent.

Jay slaps me on the ass as I walk over with the ball.

—Nice one, yo.

I throw the ball back to Miguel. He catches it and points up the street behind us.

—Car!

We take a couple steps out of the way and let the car go by. Then we play some more.

I WAKE UP.

I look at the clock.

It's after 10:00 a.m. Late.

I get up, grab the duct tape and go into the bathroom. I splash water on my face and rub it over my head. I rinse my mouth. I look at the bruise on my ribs. It's bigger. My whole side is stiff and aches. I peel off a long strip of duct tape and plaster it to my side. I peel off another strip and do the same.

I use the whole roll, taping up my side, fixing the cracked ribs in place. When I'm done it looks like I have a plate of lead covering my left side, bands of it wrapped around my middle and arcing up over my shoulder. It pulls at my skin and makes it hard to breathe, but the ribs don't move as much.

I put on my wife-beater and underwear and socks. Everything smells of bleach. I pull on my jeans and my jacket and go back into the room and get my shoes. There's blood on the heel of the right one. I leave it there and put them on. I fill my pockets with my cash and my wallet and the keys to my shitty apartment in Las Vegas. I pick up Adam's flick-knife and Martin's sap and the last full bottle of water.

Anything else?

Before I die, anything else?

I take a last look around the room.

No, not really. Nothing else.

So I take the box to the elevator and go downstairs and drag it through the lobby to the curb and hail a cab and the driver puts it in the trunk and I tell him to take me to Brighton Beach.

Wasn't much of a last night. But at least I got to see some of that game. That was nice. That was OK.

THE CABBIE DROPS me off right in front of the building, but he doesn't want to help me with the box no matter how much cash I offer him. He does lift it out of the trunk for me, and then I stand at the bottom of the steps looking up. There are only about eight of them, but it's gonna hurt like hell getting the box up there. I force my water bottle into the right side-pocket of my jacket and lift the box up on the first step. Sure enough, it hurts like hell. There are a couple middle-aged Latinos sitting at the top of the steps playing cards on a little crate between their knees. They watch me struggle to get the box up another step, and then one of them calls into the lobby of the building.

—Chiqui!

A skinny twelve-year-old kid wearing shorts and nothing else comes running out. The man points at me and my box. The kid scampers down the steps, wraps his arms around the box, and muscles it up to the top. I climb up after him. He starts to run back inside.

—Hang on.

He stops.

I get a five out of my pocket and hand it to him.

—To the elevator, OK?

The kid looks at the five and then at the man playing cards. The man nods and says something in Spanish. The kid smiles, grabs the bill and hauls the box over to the elevator.

I nod at the man.

—*Gracias.*

—*De nada.*

I walk across the tiles that spell out El Marisol and into the cool lobby. The kid smiles again, pushes the elevator button for me and runs outside. I look around the lobby. I figured David would have someone down here, waiting for me. Nope. The elevator dings and the doors open. I scoot the box in. Standing inside the elevator, looking through the lobby and out the front door, I can see the ocean beyond the two small brown men playing cards. I hear them mumbling to each other in Spanish and, faintly, the crash of a wave. It feels like Mexico for that one second. And then the doors close and the elevator takes me up.

—Henry.

—Hey, David. Can you help me with this?

He comes into the corridor and we carry the box down the hall

and into his office. I wait for a moment while he goes back down
the hall, closes and locks the door and returns.

—A drink?

He walks toward the sideboard that holds the bottles, going
around the box, treating it like just another piece of furniture in
the overcrowded room.

I work the water bottle free of my pocket.

—No thanks.

He nods.

—It is early for me. And you do not drink. But still.

He picks up two glasses and brandishes them at me. *Today of
all days.*

—No. Thanks, but no.

He puts down one of the glasses in surrender.

—Well, it is good to be true to one's convictions. Bravo, Henry.
But I will drink. You do not mind?

—No.

He pours himself a brandy, sniffs it.

—I need a drink. After this last day, I need a drink.

He takes a drink.

—Yes, I need a drink.

He stands there, staring down into the glass. I stand there, staring at him.

—So, David.

—Yes?

I put my hand on top of the box.

—You want to check this out?

He looks at the box, lifts his glass and waves it back and forth a
little. *If that will make you happy.*

I flip and twist the clasps, pull off the top and set it on the arm of the couch.

David takes a couple steps closer and looks at the money. He smiles. A tiny breath of laughter escapes from his nose.

—To be honest, Henry? To be honest, I half expected you would have a weapon or an ally hidden within.

—Someone with a tommy gun waiting to pop out?

—Just so.

—Yeah, that would have been good. Nope, just the money.

He comes closer, reaches out, takes one of the packs of bills from the torn plastic, fingers it, and drops it back inside.

—And it was waiting here?

—Yeah.

—Your friend left it here for you?

—Yeah.

—I have said before.

—What?

—He was a good friend.

—Yeah, he was.

—A loss for you.

I don't say anything.

—Think of all that could have been avoided if he had lived just long enough to tell you what he had done. Imagine.

He looks up at the ceiling, shaking his head in wonder. *The waste, the waste.*

I unscrew the top of my water bottle, take a sip and screw it back on.

—What I imagine is that if I had known where the money was that day, you would have killed me there and then.

He raises a hand in objection, lowers it.

—I would like to say, I would like very much to say that you are wrong, Henry, but it is not a day to tell lies. Yes, that would have been the case. But. But it has not all been a tragedy. There have been benefits. Some of the work you have done for me has been good. And for you? Some extra time. Who, if asked, would not do what you have done to extend their life for a year? More than a year. And it has not been your life alone that you have spared. Yes? This is the point, yes? This is the why and the wherefore of it all, yes? This is why you are here now with this money rather than on a plane. I tell you, it has not been all bad. You have done well in this, Henry. You are a good son. No one can question that. Ever.

He lifts his glass to me, brings it to his lips, drains it. *And I salute you.*

He sets the glass on his desktop.

—Are you carrying any weapons, Henry?

I nod.

—Yeah.

He points at the box.

—Put them there, right on top. When the time comes, instinct sometimes takes over. It is best if you are not armed.

I take the knife from my pocket and put it on top of the money.

David looks at it. He sees the blood. He raises an eyebrow. *You have been busy?*

I nod.

—The nephews.

—Yes?

—They found me.

—And?

—I killed them, David.

—Yes. What else could have happened? Always you are under-estimated, Henry. Always.

—Except by you.

He shakes his head and holds up a hand. *Do not flatter me.*

—No. Even by me. On some occasions, even by me. Do you have any other weapons?

I take out the sap and put it with the knife.

He smiles.

—You will have to turn around and raise your arms.

I do it.

He comes close behind me and runs his hands down my arms and sides. I flinch when he touches the ribs.

—An injury?

He lifts my shirt and looks at the tape.

—The nephews?

—Yeah.

He drops my shirt and finishes patting me down.

—Yes. That is good.

I turn around.

—What now?

—Branko.

I jerk my head around, expecting to find him behind me. But he's not.

David pats my shoulder.

—No, Henry. There is time. He will not sneak up on you.

—Where is he?

—Here. In the bedroom. I am not a fool. I would not have you here and be alone. No matter, no matter how much I trust that you love your parents, I would not do that.

—So?

—So we will go in. You will see him. We will talk for another moment or two. And he will take you away somewhere. Yes?

—Yeah. Sure. That was the deal.

—Yes. That was the deal.

He gestures to the hall, to the doors that open off the hall. Two of them are open: one the kitchen, the other the bathroom. The closed door will be the bedroom.

The deliberateness of the exercise has kept it at a distance, but now, walking up the hall, my heart starts to bang. It bangs, and each beat seems to knock against my ribs and pump up the pressure in my face.

My feet stop. Just short of the door, my feet stop.

—Henry?

I try to tell him I'm OK, try to tell him I just need a second, but I can't get the words to fit together in my mouth. He steps around me, looks at my face.

—Yes. It is hard.

I can't even nod.

—Here.

He tugs the water bottle from my frozen hand, opens it, holds it to my mouth. He tilts the bottle, water dribbles off my lips, I start to swallow. I reach up and take the bottle, drink a tiny bit more, and lower it from my mouth.

—Thanks.

—Of course.

He hands me the cap and I put it back on.

—That is better?

—Yeah, better.

—Good, good.

He puts his hand on the doorknob.

—Because, Henry, there is, I am afraid, one more thing you will have to do.

He opens the door.

It's a small room. There is a bed for taking naps on, a TV, a comfortable chair, and a matching footstool. And there is Mickey's mother, bound and gagged in the chair. And there is Branko, sitting on the edge of the bed.

Branko looks from the woman to the door as it opens. David is standing with one hand on the knob, holding the door open, waiting for me to walk past him into the room. He is watching my face, waiting to see the surprise there when I register his final twist of the knife, when I realize he wants me to kill Anna before he'll send me away with Branko, before he will ensure my parents' safety. The smile on his face says it all. *Now you see? Now you see what you fucking get when you fuck with me?*

And I do see.

I see what I get.

But I don't want it.

And I'm not going to take it.

Too late, Branko sees what I have in my hand.

—David!

But David is enjoying the moment so thoroughly, he doesn't see the water bottle coming until I smash it across the side of his head.

The shock of the blow sends the bottle spinning from my hand and David toward the floor. I grab him before he can go down and jerk him up in front of me, my arm around his neck. Branko comes off the bed, the .22 Magnum in his hand.

We freeze.

David is slack in my arms, blood is leaking from his left ear.

Branko stands by the bed, the gun out, but not yet raised.

I look at Mickey's mother and back at Branko.

—That's pretty fucked up, Branko.

He brings his empty left hand slowly to his face and adjusts his glasses.

—David will have things his way. Always.

—Still.

He lowers his hand.

—Yes. Still. It is not how I would have wanted this.

—You're a pro, Branko.

He tilts his head.

—My mother would not be proud.

—Neither would mine, man.

He gives his little laugh-grunt.

David stirs in my arms.

I charge Branko, shoving David ahead of me.

The gun comes up. Branko wastes a moment trying to get some exposed part of me in his sights, then he shoots at our legs. He gets off two rounds. One bullet snaps into the floor, raising a cloud of tiny splinters. I feel the other one, or at least the shock of it as it enters David's thigh. And then we are plowing into Branko.

He drops his shoulder to take the blow, but the mass of two bodies striking him sends him backward onto the bed. David is sandwiched between us, howling, his wounded thigh being knocked about.

Branko still has the gun. It is in his right hand, pinned between his body and David's. He tries to writhe away from the bulk on top of him, tries to free his gun hand. I grab at David's hair, but it's too short to get a grip. I latch onto his ears instead, one in either hand. I pull his head back and slam it forward, smashing his face into Branko's. Things crunch, and I do it again.

David is jerking and twisting, trying to free himself. All his thrashing batters Branko.

Branko moves his head to the side. His nose is a bloody mess. His eyes meet mine.

The gun goes off.

David tenses.

And goes limp.

The gun goes off again. I feel the bullet shiver through David's corpse. I pull his head back and bash it again into Branko's face.

The gun goes off again.

This bullet finds a path through David's ribs, slicing his soft tissues, punching out his back and into my chest.

I yelp.

I heave on David's ears, slam his head forward again.

And again.

And again.

The gun doesn't go off anymore. But I keep pounding David's face into Branko's, hitting him over and over with something other than my fist.

When David's ears are too slick with blood for me to keep my grip, I roll off of the two corpses, slide to the floor, and sit with my back to the bed. I pull up my shirt and pick the small, spent slug from the duct tape layered over my ribs. I look at it, and then look up. And see Mickey's mother as she stares at me.

The maddog who killed her son, in all his glory.

———

WHEN THE PAIN in my ribs has subsided, when I can breathe again, I go to the living room/office, collect Adam's knife, and go back to the bedroom. Mickey's mother is still in the chair. I walk toward her. She sees the knife.

—It's OK. I'm not. Look, it's OK.

I kneel in front of her and cut the cords around her legs. She draws them up, away from my touch.

—Your hands.

She doesn't move.

—Give me your hands.

She doesn't.

I set the knife down, take hold of her hands and pull them out so I can see the bindings. She leaves them there as I pick up the knife and cut her free.

—You can do the gag.

But she just sits there, knees pulled up, hands sticking out.

—This will hurt.

She closes her eyes. I tease up a corner of the tape on her face, then yank. It rips free. She coughs once and spits the racquetball from her mouth. I look at the floor, find the water bottle, bring it over and offer it to her. She just stares at it. I look. Some blood from David's ear is on the side. I bend and wipe it on the carpet. She takes it from me this time, fills her mouth, swishes the water around, and spits, trying to rinse out the taste of rubber. Then she drinks.

I go to the bed. I pull David off of Branko. He falls to the floor. There are wounds in his right thigh and three in the right side of his chest. I look at Branko, but not at what I've done to his face. I take the gun and go through his pockets. There are no more bullets, but I find his phone and some car keys.

I turn around. Mickey's mother is watching me. She's still clutching the half-empty water bottle. I point at it.

—Done?

She nods. I put out my hand and she gives it to me. I drink. When it's empty I drop it on the floor.

—Let's go.

She looks at me.

—We have to go now.

She stands up.

—Come on.

I walk to the living room. She follows. I put the lid back on the box.

—I'll need help.

She doesn't move.

—Anna, I'll need your help with this.

THERE ARE HANDLES on either side. We carry the box between us, like two pallbearers carrying a child's coffin.

THE MEN ARE still playing cards. They look up as we come out, and then look right back down at their game. I look up the street and see what I want.

I point with my chin.

—There, that one.

We walk over and set the box down. I fish the car keys from my pocket and push the trunk release and it pops open, the only rental car on the street: a Camry. We lift the box into the trunk, close it, and I lead her to the passenger side. I hold the door open.

She gets in. I go around and see her through the windshield as she reaches across and unlocks my door. I get in.

—Put on your seat belt.

She does.

I start the engine and turn us around.

—I have to make a stop. A quick stop. And then we can go.

IT'S STILL A couple hours before game time. I find a spot by the player's entrance, right next to Miguel's Escalade. I pull in and turn off the engine.

Anna hasn't moved. She sits up in her seat, legs together, hands flat on top of her thighs, looking straight ahead.

—I have to do something inside.

She doesn't move.

—I'm gonna go in for a couple minutes. I want you to stay here. OK?

Nothing.

I look at the dash clock. Time is passing. I need to move.

—Anna.

She looks at me.

—Don't go anywhere. OK?

—OK.

I open the door and get out. The sun is bright and hot. I turn my face to it. It feels good on my face, makes my bones hurt less. I take off my jacket so I can feel the sun on as much of my skin as possible. I bend over and drop the jacket on my seat. I look at Anna.

—Stay right here.

—OK.

—OK.

I close the door, go around to the trunk and pop it. I work the top off the box and start scooping money out into the trunk. I scoop what looks to be half of the money. Then I put the top back on the box, hoist it out and close the trunk.

The box is much easier to handle now. I walk around the car toward the player's entrance. Through the windows of the Camry I can see Anna, still and quiet. Somewhere inside, her brain is churning, trying to find someplace to settle, but nothing gives her peace.

I think about helping her with that. I think about not just getting her away from David's place and the cops who will be showing up. I think about whoever is going to come along and take over where David left off. Will they know about his crazy sister-in-law? Will they think she had a hand in his murder? Possibly. They won't know about me. I'm David's ghost. No one knows about me except David and Branko, and the people I've hurt. I'm clear now. Clear and rich. And alone.

I think about showing Anna how to run. Protecting her. It's a silly idea, childish. But I guess it's to be expected. I thought I'd be dead by now, and I'm having to make up the rest of my life as I go along.

THERE'S A SECURITY guard just inside the entrance. I tell him I'm Miguel Arenas's bodyguard. He checks out my bruises and tattoos. I guess he decides I fit the bill because he picks up a phone and makes a call and then waves me on down the corridor.

There's a buzz in the air, the slow anticipation of the game that will start in a little less than two hours. A groundskeeper passes me, bases stacked in his arms. The door to the promotions room is open. It's packed with giveaways: mini-bats, key chains, stuffed seagulls, hats, batting gloves. There's a guy going through a pile of what look like hot dog costumes. Around the corner, Miguel is waiting for me outside the home clubhouse.

—Hey, man.

—Hey.

He looks me over.

—You're a mess, man. Did you look that bad last night?

—Yeah. Pretty much.

—I was loaded.

—Yeah.

—Yeah.

He kicks at the concrete floor. He's half dressed for the game: pants and cleats, but he's wearing a Stanford T-shirt.

—How's Jay?

He rubs the top of his head.

—They had to wire his jaw shut. It was broken. And his nose. And his cheekbone was cracked. They said he was lucky his eye didn't pop out.

—You talk to him?

—A little. They got him totally stoned.

—He say anything?

—No, not really. Can't talk with the jaw shut.

—How's he gonna deal with that?

He grins.

—Gonna drive him nuts.

—Yo.

He laughs.

I point at the bruise on his neck.

—How're you?

—OK. It's sore. And I got some scrapes on my hands and stuff. No biggie.

—Uh-huh.

—Yeah. But. Someone in the emergency room recognized me. And they, I guess they know someone, so they called that Page Six deal and a photographer showed up.

—Oh, shit.

—No, it's cool. My agent and a lawyer for the club made some calls. They promised those guys a better story later if they killed this one. Said publicity like that two days in a row would hurt my career. Whatever.

—That's cool.

—Yeah, but. The club is sending me back down. After the game. Sending me back for rookie ball. Said I can play, but I'm not ready to handle life in the City. So. Shit.

—Sorry.

—Yeah.

Another player ducks out the clubhouse door. He nods at Miguel and heads for the tunnel to the field. Miguel watches him, and then turns back to me.

—So look. I'm thinking.

—Yeah?

—I'm thinking this is maybe not gonna work out with, you know, with your boss and all. I'm thinking. Man, you said those guys last night were hooked up with him?

—That's right.

—Well. I mean, that's not cool. Those guys hurt my best friend. That's not. I can't live like that, man.

—Uh-huh.

—So. I'm thinking you can talk to him. And tell him I want to make an arrangement. Start maybe making some payments. Work something out. And. I mean. I can't.

He gestures, taking in the stadium above us.

—This, all this. The game. This chance. I don't want to lose this. Jay. I can't have that kind of thing happen. Ever. I can always play. That I can do. I can play this game wherever. But I can't have my friends being hurt. So. Will you talk to him? Tell him. I don't know what.

A guy comes around the corner. He's carrying the hot dog costumes. I wait till he's gone.

—Here's the thing, Miguel. I talked to David this morning. And things are gonna change a little. Someone, I don't know who, but someone else is going to have your paper. My guess is they won't be interested in the kind of deal you had, that whole letting-the-debt-float thing. Payments won't really cut it.

—Oh, shit.

—No. Now. Look. Don't worry about it. It's gonna be OK. I'm gonna help. And it will work out.

—I don't know, man. This is. I need out.

—We're gonna get you out. I. Hey. I'm gonna get you out. I am. I really. I am. So do something for me.

I put my hand on the box.

—This is for you. I mean, really, it's for whoever comes to collect on your paper. What you do is, you put this someplace safe. When they come around, when they call, you give them this.

He looks sideways at the box.

—Man, do you know what I owe?

—Yeah.

—And you got something there that will cover it?

—Yeah. This will do it.

—And. Is that drugs?

—No.

—'Cause I want nothing to do. No more trouble, OK. So no drugs.

—Miguel. Take the box. I want you to have this. Get out, man. Get out of trouble. This will do that. Take it, man. Take it and use it. Trust me.

He doesn't say anything. Then he reaches out and puts his hand on the box.

—OK. OK, man. Thanks.

—Sure. OK. I. I got to go.

—What?

—I got to.

—The game!

—Yeah, I know.

—Maaan.

—Sorry.

—So when?

—Later. Later sometime.

—That bites, man.

—Yeah.

I put out my hand. He grabs me and crushes me, slapping my back hard a couple times. It feels like he's breaking more of my ribs.

Miguel goes back into the clubhouse to get ready. He has to play the rubber game of the first series of the season. Must be nice. I walk back out the tunnel.

Outside, the sun is still hot and it still feels good. Cops may be at David's right now, but they won't know who they're looking for for awhile. I can figure out what to do with Anna, how to help her best, and be on my way. I may not get a full thirteen thousand mornings out of the deal, but I'm going to get something. I open the car door.

BANG!

The shock wave vibrates out of the car, ruffling my shirt, and dissipates over the parking lot. I bend over and look inside. Anna has my jacket on her lap, the pocket the gun was in is flipped inside out. Her hands are over her ears. The .22 is in her left hand, smoke oozing from the barrel. Her eyes are fixed on something. I look down to see what it is. There's a hole in my shirt and, under that, a hole in my stomach. It's about five inches to the left of my belly button. I get in the car. Anna is still staring at the hole she put in me. I have the tail of my shirt pulled up. I'm staring at it, too.

She says something.

I look at her.

—What?

She shakes her head.

—No.

I nod.

—It's OK.

—No. I'm sorry. I.

—It's OK.

I reach for the gun.

—Here, let me have that.

She lowers the gun.

BANG!

This one is up higher. The tape slows it down, but it gets through and buries itself between two ribs. I inhale and feel it grinding against the bone.

It hurts.

I black out.

I come to.

Anna still has the gun in her left hand. She's crying. She shouldn't cry.

I point at the gun.

—I didn't know you were left-handed.

She nods.

—Here. I've got it now. I'll take it.

She nods, and pulls the trigger again, but the gun is empty. I take it from her hand and drop it on the backseat.

—OK. That's over, that's. Oh. Oh, man. Wow. This hurts. This really. OK. Here's what. Can I have my jacket please?

She hiccups a couple times, covers her mouth with her hand, holds it there, then moves it away when she doesn't vomit.

—My jacket, Anna. Please.

She picks up the jacket. I lean forward.

—Just, just wrap it around me, around my middle.

She leans over and wraps the sleeves around me.

—Good. Thanks.

I lean back, adjust the sleeves so that they cross the wound in my belly, and tie them in a tight double knot.

—OK. That's better. That's. And see.

I show her the hole in the tape where her second bullet entered. There is only the slightest dribble of blood leaking out.

—That one's not bad at all. So now. Now all we have to. All we have to do is.

My head spins. I grip the steering wheel. It stops spinning.

—I'm gonna sit still for a sec, OK?

I lean back.

—Why did you kill my son?

I turn my head to face her.

—What did he do to you?

—I.

—He must have done something.

I remember Mickey. How smug he was when he figured out who I was and he demanded money from me. I remember how he threatened to tell David where I was, how he threatened Mom and Dad. I think about Mom and Dad, what it must feel like knowing some of the terrible things I've done. How much worse it would be if they knew them all.

—He didn't do anything to me.

—No. He must have.

—Anna. Nothing. He did nothing. All he did. He. He just stumbled across me and recognized me. I got scared. I couldn't take a chance he'd tell. That's why. I killed him. He did nothing. He was a good kid. I. I liked him.

She closes her eyes. Tears leak out.

—Yes. Yes. He was a good boy.

I've started. I've started, and I find I can't stop.

—And. I. I dream about him sometimes, too. Like you. I. I dream about all of them sometimes. And. If I could. Anna, if I could change. I was. When I was young, when I was a kid. I was driving and I, I hit this, this tree. And if. My friend was in the car and he died, you know. It was. And I thought, sometimes I thought I wished it had been me. But I really didn't. When I was honest, honest to myself, I was thanking God that it was him and not me. But. Now. Now I wish, God, every day I wish it had been me. All the lives, Anna. You have no idea. All the lives that could have been saved. Oh, shit.

I spin again. Stop spinning.

Anna reaches over and presses her hand over the wound in my chest.

—I'll get someone. An ambulance.

I look past her, through the window, and see the water beyond the boardwalk.

—That's OK. That's. Here's what. OK, I'm gonna go and. I'm gonna go. I'm. I think I'm gonna just go down to the beach, OK? I think that's what. Jesus. Jesus. I'm gonna go to the beach.

She still has her hand pressed against my chest. I put mine over hers.

—What you. There will be people. David has other people. They'll want to know what happened. So the best thing. What you should do is. There's money in the trunk. There's a lot of money in the trunk. You need to take it. Take the car and go somewhere. Take the money and go somewhere. Back to Russia. Somewhere. Go away.

She's staring at the blood seeping between her fingers.

—Don't look at that. Don't.

I put a finger under her chin and tilt her face up to mine.

—Don't worry about that. I can. I know how to fix that. You just need to go. Just go. OK?

Her upper lip is glazed with snot.

—OK. OK.

—Good. Good for you. OK. So.

I open the door. I swing my feet out. I stand up. My head swirls. The parking lot swirls with it. I lean over and puke. It hurts. I look into the car. Anna is still in the passenger seat. I reach in and pat the driver's seat.

—Here. Scoot over here.

She looks down at the seat. Some of my blood is pooled there. I brush at it, smearing it over the material.

—Don't worry about that. That comes out. Just come on over here.

She lifts her legs over the gearshift and scoots her bottom into the seat.

—Good. That's good. You can? Can you drive?

She nods.

—OK. Great. So start 'er up.

She turns the key and the engine starts.

—Good. OK. So. So. So. Out of town. That's where you want to go. Drive. Boston. Maybe Philly. One of those places. Get a bag on the way. For. You'll need it for the money. And go to an airport. And buy a ticket. And go away. Go away. It's OK. You can go away. And. You just don't come back. And. Oh, hey, and Anna?

—Yes?

—Don't worry about this.

I point at the hole in my stomach.

—This is. I'll be fine. This is nothing. OK?

—OK.

—Good. So. OK. Bye-bye then. Bye-bye.

I push the door closed. She sits there, staring at me through the window. I wave bye-bye to her. Bye-bye. She puts the car in reverse and pulls out. I wave again. Bye-bye. She looks at me, raises her hand. Her lips move. *Bye-bye.* And she drives away.

I look up, over at the beach. Wow, that's a long way away. If I want to get there I better start now. So I do. I start walking to the beach.

And close my eyes long before I get there.

EPILOGUE

OPEN MY EYES.

I'm sitting on a beach.

I'm sitting in the sand watching a dog trailing its own leash as it runs through the surf. It barks madly, running from the waves as they crash in, chasing them as they roll out. The dog bites the waves, swallowing seawater, crazed by the ocean. It runs around in little circles, jumps into a pile of rotting seaweed and rolls around on its back. It jumps up, chases and bites another wave, then sprints up the beach toward the dry sand, squats and starts spraying diarrhea.

—Don't shit on your leash!

I look back over my shoulder and see a middle-aged couple holding hands and walking toward the dog. The man is yelling at the dog.

—Don't shit on your leash, for Christ sake.

The dog ignores him and shits seawater on its leash.

—Ah, Jesus, that's gonna be a pain in the ass.

The couple is next to me now. I look up at them.

—That's good advice.

They look at me. The man smiles.

—What's that?

—Don't shit on your leash.

The woman laughs.

—Oh, she's a good dog. She just goes crazy at the beach.

The man nods.

—Goes maddog on us.

I look at the dog. It has returned to harassing the waves.

—Yeah, I know the type.

The man and woman sit down a couple yards away. The man picks up a piece of driftwood and starts sketching something in the sand.

—You a dog person?

I nod.

—Yeah, mostly. But I had a cat once.

He shakes his head.

—Could never stand cats.

—Well, this was one hell of a cat.

The woman looks at me.

—Are you local?

I shake my head.

—No. Not really. Just moved here.

The North Pacific wind gusts and she pulls her jacket tighter around her shoulders.

—We moved here a few years back.

I feel at my pockets and take out a pack of cigarettes.

—My folks used to bring me here every year. That's how I know the place.

—We used to come here. With our son.

She looks at the sun dipping into the ocean.

I shake a cigarette loose.

The man passes the piece of driftwood to the woman and she takes over the sketch. He points at the pack of Benson & Hedges in my hand.

—Bad habit.

—I know. I quit for awhile, but something about the weather up here, it makes me want to smoke. You mind?

He shrugs.

—We all got bad habits.

I light up.

—Yes we do.

The dog is slowing down, wandering after the waves now rather than chasing them, a stream of thin, green fluid leaking from its backside.

—Dog looks sick.

The man nods as he gets up.

—Yeah. She's a good dog, but she has to learn the same lesson every time we bring her here. Don't drink the water.

I take a drag on my smoke.

—And don't shit on your leash.

He smiles, helping his wife to her feet.

—Yep, that one, too.

The woman plants the stick of driftwood in the sand next to their sketch.

—Nice to meet you.

I wave.

—Nice to meet you, too. Take care.

She smiles, waves back, and they walk together, calling to the dog as it wanders toward them, tired and sick, but still lolling its tongue and barking happily at the ocean.

Stupid maddog.

I smoke and watch them walk back up to the road where their car is parked. When my cigarette is done I grind the cherry out in the sand and tuck the butt back in the box. The sun is almost gone now, sliced in half by the horizon. I close my eyes and try to feel what little heat it gives.

The sun is down.

The wind cuts deeper. I stand up and tuck my hands in the pockets of my jeans. I take a step over to where the couple was sitting and look at their sketch.

A heart with an arrow piercing it.

In the middle, a word.

Henry.

Funny they didn't recognize me. I touch my carved face. But I guess not. Not really. I think about going after them. But that would be a bad idea. They already have one maddog to deal with. I think about smoking another cigarette. But I don't. I think about going home. But I don't. I stand here and watch the stars come out.

And then I close my eyes.

I OPEN MY eyes.

I'm sitting on a beach.

The sun shines. I can feel it baking my face, the heat occasionally relieved as clouds sweep across the bright blue sky. A wave crashes and the surf washes up over smooth dark sand, stopping just short of my toes. "Easy" is playing somewhere behind me.

I look at the people on the beach.

There are kids, mostly Latino, playing in the surf. Off to my left is a woman in a lime green bathing suit and pink headscarf, knitting something orange. A man with skin tanned like an old, brown penny jogs past. A tiny, round Mexican woman is pushing a shopping cart filled with mangoes through the sand.

I raise my hand to her. She pushes the cart over. The mangoes are on sticks that are stuck into a giant Styrofoam block. She plucks one out and offers it to me.

I wave my hand up and down.

—*No bolsa. Por favor.*

She undoes the twisty at the top to the stick and pulls the mango free of its plastic bag. Thank God. It would have taken me an hour to get that thing off. I take the mango and offer her a dollar. She takes it. She looks at it, then at me, then she grips her cart and shoves it away. I look at the rest of the money in my hand. It's bloody.

I look down. Blood is soaking through the knotted sleeves of my jacket, dripping slowly to be sucked up by the sand between my legs. That's not good. You only have so much of that.

I crane my head around. There is a trail of tiny red spots on the sand leading back to the boardwalk. They might be the drippings from a child's Popsicle, but they're not.

The boardwalk is very far away, the music is coming from Rudy's. How'd I get all the way here? Lucky, I guess. I look down again. The sand had absorbed too much of my blood; it has begun to pool at my crotch.

So, not that lucky.

I look at the mango in my hand. It's been peeled, slit in rings around and around. It looks like a giant, pale orange artichoke dusted with chili powder. I bring it to my mouth. It's sweet and peppery on my lips, but I'm no longer strong enough to bite into the soft fruit. It feels heavy. I want to put it down. I try to jam the stick in the sand, but I can't get it in deep enough to stand upright. It lists slowly to one side until it falls and is crusted in sand.

What now?

Shoes.

Gonna take my shoes off.

It's not easy, but I manage. Then I tug my socks off. Then I get to push my bare feet deep in the sand. And you know what? It was worth it. My eyes try to close. I open them. My eyes closing now would be a bad thing.

My eyes start to close.

I stop them.

Look for something to look at.

Some teenage girls sit in a circle to my right, all of them talking into their cell phones.

Cell phones.

I shift, and tug at my jacket. It pulls at my wound and I gasp. I feel in the jacket pockets and find Branko's phone. I go through my pants pockets and find the number.

I dial.

It rings just once.

—Hello!

—Hey, hey, Mom.

—Oh, God. Oh, God. Oh. Oh.

—Hey. Hey. Sorry I. Last night. I didn't mean to scare you. My phone. The battery.

—I knew. I knew. Henry. Oh. Henry. Henry, Henry.

—I love you, Mom.

—Henry. I love you. I love you so much. I.

—Is Dad there?

—He's here. He's.

—Henry? I'm here. Where? Are you OK? Where are you? Are you? What can we?

—Dad. Hey, Dad. Wow. You guys sound.

—What is it, Henry? We. How do we?

—Hey. Hey. I just. I can't talk. Just. I wanted to tell you. I really love you guys. And.

Mom clucks her tongue.

—Are you drunk, Henry?

—No, Mom.

—You sound drunk.

—No, Mom.

—Well. I. Oh, God.

—It's OK, Mom. Dad?

—Yeah?

—I love you guys. And. I know. Nothing I did. You guys were great to me. No matter what people say. Nothing that happened. It was all me. And I love you. And.

Mom is crying now. Of course. Making Mom cry is the easiest thing in the world.

—Don't cry, Mom.

—Don't be stupid. How can I not cry?

—Dad, tell Mom not to cry.

—Your mom cries at TV commercials.

—Right.

Mom cries for awhile. Nobody says anything. She stops.

—I'm better. Sorry.

—That's OK.

More of nobody talking. The beach spins a couple times. My eyes try to close some more.

—OK. I. I need to go, guys.

Mom starts crying again.

—Will you call again? Are you OK? Do you need anything? I can send something. What do you need?

—No, Mom, I'm fine. I just. I love you both. And I miss you. Every day.

My eyelids dip. I force them to stay open.

Mom talks.

—We love you, Henry.

Dad coughs.

—Love you, Hank.

—Love you guys. Bye. Love you.

I hang up.

I start to close my eyes.

Stop myself.

If I close my eyes now, I'll never open them.

I'm tired. My body is too heavy to keep upright. I lean back and let myself drop into the sand. I look up into the bright blue sky. It feels good on my face, but it hurts my eyes. I start to close my eyes. Open them.

If I close my eyes now, I will never open them.

If I close my eyes.

I will never open them.

I close my eyes.

ACKNOWLEDGMENTS

Not a word of the Henry Thompson trilogy would have seen print were I not the beneficiary of amazing good luck, remarkable friendships, and love.

My thanks to Johnny Lancaster, friend. You changed my life.

To Robyn Starr and Simone Elliot, benefactors.

To Cindy Murray, Ingrid Powell, Paul Taunton, Daniel Lazar and Michael Mejias, all of whom have done me great services, and shared a drink or two.

To Maura Teitelbaum, Simon Lipskar and Mark Tavani, co-workers and friends, the ones who showed belief. My debt is great.

Thanks to my readers, those who feel the money was well spent, and those who want it back. It's nice to know you're all out there. I am grateful.

I was given special technical assistance in the writing of this book by Anna Isaacson of the Brooklyn Cyclones. She took me around the ballpark and, among other things, showed me where they keep the hot dog costumes. Alas, my suspicions were correct, the race is rigged. Thank you, Anna.

I have been taken in by the Smiths, Farmers and Kressmans.

My east coast family. Thank you for the love, and for the young woman in question.

My mom and dad have given me what every child should have, faith, hope and love. All without bounds. If only I had more to give back.

Virginia.

My wife.

My greatest piece of luck.

Stay with me. Make me a better man.

I'll try to deserve you.

New York City
February 3, 2006

ABOUT THE AUTHOR

CHARLIE HUSTON is the author of The Henry Thompson Trilogy, which includes the Edgar Award–nominated *Six Bad Things,* as well as The Joe Pitt Casebooks. He is also the writer of the recently relaunched *Moon Knight* comic book. He lives in Los Angeles with his wife, the actress Virginia Louise Smith. Visit him at www.pulpnoir.com.

ABOUT THE TYPE

This book was set in Fairfield, the first typeface from the hand of the distinguished American artist and engraver Rudolph Ruzicka (1883–1978). Ruzicka was born in Bohemia and came to America in 1894. He set up his own shop, devoted to wood engraving and printing, in New York in 1913 after a varied career working as a wood engraver, in photoengraving and banknote printing plants, and as an art director and freelance artist. He designed and illustrated many books, and was the creator of a considerable list of individual prints—wood engravings, line engravings on copper, and aquatints.

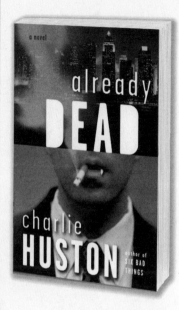

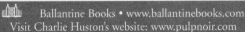